Tainted Water

Dan Farrell

Acknowledgements

This novel most likely wouldn't have been possible without the initial support I received from my good friend James Hughes. He was the first person I told about the project and he saw the birth of it all the way back in 2014. Thank you for reading the terrible first draft chapters and offering guidance in how to improve the story.

This would also not have been something I could have done without the help of my family. Thank you to every member who encouraged me in this endeavour – and to those who read it in its early stages.

I owe a lot of gratitude to all my friends who read through my drafts during multiple points in its development: Holly Trevena, Rebecca Curran, Michael Bartlett, Emily Coxon, Amanda Moore and Jordan Lloyd Beck. I thank you all for your honest opinions and suggestions – as well as for being there for me in my personal life, of course.

I would like to thank my online family for all their support, too. The last few years would have been tougher on me if not for the community I found myself a part of via Twitter. My followers always show me reassurance in my darker moments and have cheered me on whenever I've been for job interviews or when I've started at a new workplace. It means the world to me.

And lastly, to Tom Suddes – the man who has been my anchor in the months leading up to this book's release. I really don't know where I'd be right now without you.

The cover of this novel was designed Mark Anthony Grieves back in 2015, and I couldn't have asked for more beautiful artwork. I am very grateful to have my readers see it as their first impression.

Table of Contents

Prologue

The street was completely empty as I limped towards my house. I could see a few lights on in the neighbouring homes, but there was a definitive stillness in the air.

Or maybe my mind had just blocked everything out.

Thankfully, my dad wasn't awake when I entered through the back door. He didn't have the best sleeping pattern, so I had been worried that he would be up and there's no way I could have hid the fact that there was something wrong.

Our bathroom was downstairs and part of an extension, so I knew starting a shower wouldn't wake him up. My hands were shaking uncontrollably, and I could feel a twitch in my jaw, though I still managed to lock the door and start unbuckling my belt. There was blood on my jeans and underwear that had also run down my leg. I quickly dumped them on the floor. I would get rid of them as soon as possible – burn them.

I glimpsed my reflection briefly in the mirror. My eyes were watery and my face blotchy. I couldn't bear to look at myself properly at that moment.

Once I was fully undressed, I stepped into the shower and began to scrub myself furiously, determined to make every inch of my body as clean as possible. As I did so, I kept repeating the same five words in my head.

Nobody must know about this.

Part 1

Chapter 1

I tried to pretend as though I was content with my life, but I knew that no matter what I longed to believe, the truth was that I was becoming more disillusioned with every day that passed.

When my alarm went off one Sunday morning in early March, I wanted nothing more than to smash my phone to pieces and go back to sleep. I could see from the small gap in the curtains that it was raining outside, something which did nothing to improve my frame of mind. This wasn't helped when the silence was suddenly broken by a loud knock, followed by my sister's shrill voice calling up the stairs.

'Come on, if you're not up in five minutes then I'll drag you downstairs myself!'

'I'm coming now,' I managed to croak. My mouth was extremely dry, and I was in no mood to try and say anything else back – though there were a few choice words I'd have said to her if it were possible.

Using all the energy I could muster, I hauled myself out of bed and stumbled across the hallway and towards the bathroom. Both my sister and her husband had well-paying jobs, so their house was filled with expensive décor and it was always immaculate, which no doubt made the sight of me drowsily ambling through look extremely out of place.

I left the toilet seat up once I'd finished for no other reason than I knew it would drive my sister crazy. I then walked over to the medicine cabinet, doing my best to ignore my bloodshot eyes that were burning into me from the glass. My head was throbbing, and I was having constant flashbacks to how much I'd drank the previous night, so I swallowed a few pills in the hope that they would at least ease the tenderness.

When I entered the kitchen a few minutes later, I was greeted by a cold stare. Amber had never been much of a people person and she had a knack for making you feel like you'd done something wrong even if you hadn't. She didn't bear any resemblance to me. I shared similarities with our dad, inheriting his brown eyes and dark hair, whereas she favoured our mam – complete with her blue eyes and dirty blonde hair. There was a ten-year age gap between us, which may account for why she considered herself the more mature one, even though I didn't think she had changed much from when she was a teenager. Growing up, her poisonous attitude had often left a bad taste in people's mouths and earned her several enemies. I ignored her glare that morning as usual and sat down at the table where there was a cup of tea waiting for me.

'I'd appreciate it if you were dressed more appropriately when sitting at my table,' she commented, eyeing me reproachfully.

Having gone to bed late the night before, I'd left most of my clothes on the bedroom floor and was now only wearing a pair of boxer-shorts. I shrugged and took a swig of the tea. She was just lucky I wasn't giving her an eyeful of something else; back home, I was prone to sleeping completely naked – now that would certainly have given her something to squawk about.

'Honestly,' she continued, laying down two slices of buttered toast in front of me, 'you really need to think about getting your act together, Luke. You're twenty-three, for Christ sake. Start acting like it.'

'*I am,*' I said, stubbornly. The toast she'd given me was burnt, so I merely picked at it, figuring that I could just as easily pick up something more edible on the way home.

My response merely caused her to sigh. It was moments like this that reminded me why we didn't spend more time together. The only reason I'd seen her the night before was because we always did the week before the anniversary of our mam's death. I was so inebriated by the end that it was easier for me to sleep over. Ordinarily, my brother and I would've shared taxi, but his girlfriend had gotten in touch and so he left early.

Before Amber could say another word, the patio doors opened. Her husband, Noel, walked in with their golden retriever, Tobey. They were both completely drenched.

'It's really coming down out there,' he declared, though this was wholly unnecessary given that the thundering drops falling against the windows were very much visible.

The dog gave an almighty shake, which I was sure would give my sister a heart attack. Her precious kitchen was now thoroughly soaked.

'Noel, get him into the utility room!' she cried. When he merely gave her a questioning look, she groaned and made a grab for the leash. 'Oh, give him here, you prat.'

She dragged Tobey out of the room, muttering under her breath.

Noel merely sighed and took his coat off, before putting it on the back of a chair and sitting down next to me. Compared to my frosty relationship with Amber, I got on surprisingly well with him. In fact, the two of us were probably more akin to siblings than was the case with my actual blood relations. If I had to describe Noel, I would say he was one of life's rare good guys. Goodness knows what he was doing with my sister.

'God, I'm starving,' he said.

I pushed my plate towards him. 'Here, have this.' There was a full slice of toast left and the other was still good apart from the pieces I'd torn off.

He accepted it and asked, 'Are you not eating?'

'I'll get something when I'm out,' I told him. 'I don't think it's best to start the day with burnt bread.'

This made him chuckle. 'Well, beggars can't be choosers.'

As he began to crunch his way through breakfast, I finished my drink then went back upstairs to get dressed. As much as I would've liked to have stayed and chatted with him, I needed to get out of there as soon as possible before Amber got onto me further about all the ways in which I was apparently failing at existence.

*

I was starting to feel the full effects of my hangover by the time I was on the bus home and the bacon roll I'd purchased beforehand wasn't exactly settling my stomach. Perhaps I shouldn't have set an alarm and tried to sleep-in, though I can't imagine my sister would've been too please about that. Luckily, the town her house was in was near to where I lived, so I wasn't travelling for long.

Blackhall Colliery is a village on the North Sea coast of County Durham in the north eastern area of England. It was once built around an extensive mining industry, but this had been discarded for many years. This was where I had grown up and spent most of my youth. It was a pretty obscure place and most people I spoke to outside the area had no idea of its existence, which summed up my life.

I lived with my friend Matthew Forrester, who wasn't exactly the best influence. As much as I hated to admit that my sister had a point, the fact of the matter was that I was ready to start growing up a bit – but Matt seemed determined to remain a perpetual adolescent and I looked to be going the same way.

'You look like shit,' he observed as I entered the house.

'Cheers,' I grumbled.

I stepped over the crumpled clothes and empty pizza boxes that littered the floor and made my way into the kitchen, where I immediately began rummaging through the refrigerator. Taking out two cans of lager, I opened one for myself and passed the other to Matt. I knew that it was too early to start drinking, but I pushed this thought to the back of my head and tried to enjoy the sparkling taste in my mouth, which had again gone dry.

It's five o'clock somewhere, as they say.

'Are you alright, mate?' Matt asked, surveying me with concern.

I took another swig and placed the cold can against my forehead, which was throbbing. 'Yeah, I just hit it pretty hard last night, you know.'

He nodded. Most people would probably take this opportunity to lecture me about the fact that I'd been consuming a hell of a lot of alcohol recently and that the answer wasn't to continue doing so, but I knew he wasn't one of them and for that I was grateful.

As I stood finishing the drink in my hand, I watched myself in the door of the microwave. There was no denying it: I looked terrible. I was very visibly someone with major problems. Even my facial hair, which I normally kept neatly trimmed, was beginning to look unruly. I couldn't blame the bags under my eyes as just being a product of the night before, either, since my lack of proper sleep was a problem which had been plaguing me for years.

Matt signalled towards the living room. 'The match is on soon if you fancy it.'

'Nah, I'm going to have a look out.'

'But it's soaking.'

I threw the empty can into the bin. 'I know, but I need some air.'

*

Living on the coast might sound exotic, but this certainly wasn't the case for where I lived. The beach was nothing special, it was covered in rocks mainly, though I found it ideal for clearing my mind. I often found myself drawn to the ocean in my darker moments.

And so, I made my way to the shore and spent my time looking out at the waves for no reason other than it felt right. I lit a cigarette too, despite my constant promises to myself that I was going to quit. I must have been making the same vow to give up smoking at least twice a week for a year. It was hard to believe that I was once a strong advocate for healthy living.

After a few drags, I threw the cigarette on the floor and put it out with my foot. I'd have loved to have said it was going to be my last one, but I knew that would be a lie.

It had turned into a surprisingly calm day with the tide out just enough so that I could walk around the cliff edge and into a cave. I exited through an opening on the other side and came out in a small cove where the water had become very shallow amongst the rocks and seaweed, with rock-pools formed at the shore. A bit further out, just near where the tide was gently meeting the beach, someone was sat in the water.

She was positioned so that her left arm was covering her breasts and was holding her sodden blonde hair in place as she combed it with a serrated shell. From below the waist, she had no legs. Instead, she had a long glistening fish tail. The scales were flesh-coloured, starting dark and getting lighter as they faded when reaching her stomach, which lacked a naval. Despite the extreme paleness of it, her skin looked soft and her face delicate, accommodating a small nose, pallid lips and golden eyes with large black pupils.

I checked to see if there was anybody else in the vicinity who was also a witness to this incredible sight. As I expected, I was the only person there with no one else in sight.

'Hello?' I called out, cautiously.

She immediately turned to face me and let out an audible gasp, revealing a set of sharp teeth. I managed to slip out of my trainers and socks, and then bent down to roll up my jeans – all without taking my eyes off her. The water was extremely cold, so I took my time in approaching. Her eyes were as wide as mine with shock.

'It's okay,' I said. 'I won't hurt you, I promise.'

It then occurred to me that she may not speak English, so as I began to get closer, I held up my hands to visually convey that I meant no harm. This didn't seem to register with her, though, as she immediately began to back off into the water.

'No, please don't be scared,' I begged. 'There's really no need to worry.'

She had now retreated enough so that she was past the rocks and deeper into the water. However, after a few moments, she steadily began to make her way back towards me.

'Hello,' she whispered. Her voice so gentle it took me by surprise.

'You speak the same language as me?' I asked.

She nodded. 'Yes. My name is Osiris.'

'Hello,' I said, with a reassuring smile. 'I'm Luke.'

Chapter 2

The mermaid was analysing me as she got closer, her eyes darting across every inch of my body. I wanted to say something else to her, but my mouth was suddenly refusing to speak. It seemed ludicrous that this was happening, and I kept waiting for myself to wake up. I would have considered the possibility that this whole thing was a joke had it not been for her undeniably real tail.

'I'm not supposed to get this close to the human world,' she said.

I cleared my throat and croaked, 'Why not?'

'It's our most important rule. For centuries, our elders have warned us about the dangers of humanity and have forbidden us from ever going even close enough for anybody to see. We live in depths too far for you to get to and thankfully you have never been able to reach us, but still we are prohibited from swimming where they deem unsafe.'

Her story was absurd, though so was the entire notion that I was stood having this conversation with a mythical creature that supposedly didn't exist.

My friendliness had evidently relaxed her as she was noticeably less tense and it looked like she was becoming more engaged with the conversation. This made me more comfortable in questioning her further. 'Why did you come to the surface if you're not allowed?'

She sighed, her eyes filled with torment. 'I wanted to experience something new. I don't feel like I belong down there. For as long as I can remember I have felt that way, but I never realised to what extent until I would hear others talking about humans and it fascinated me. Even though I knew there were risks involved, I decided to take the chance.'

I admired her for this and took this time to fully appreciate what was happening. I took in how she moved and looked – so human, and yet so alien.

'You're not the first to break the rule,' I told her.

She squinted in confusion. 'What do you mean?'

'Well, there have been stories about mermaids for centuries. From sailors and other people who are around the sea for long periods of time. I never thought they were actually true, and I don't think many people do nowadays.' This also made me realise how many questions I had about her and others of her kind. After careful consideration, I settled on asking, 'How can you live under water but breathe air, too?'

Osiris immediately pulled back her hair and leaned to the side, displaying a set of gills on her neck. 'These are what are used for me to breathe underwater,' she clarified, 'but I have lungs that allow me to breathe air.'

I couldn't think of anything to say in response other than to grin like an idiot. Who cared what the science of it all was? Another person, like someone who based their lives rooted firmly in fact, may have questioned her further, demanded tests to be done – I just stood and took in the wonder. It was like being a child again, when you would accept anything to be fact, no matter how outlandish.

She seemed to be as equally intrigued by me. 'May… may I?' she asked, signalling to her webbed hand, which she was raising close to me.

I guessed what she wanted and beamed, crouching down so that I was level with her. 'Go for it.'

The palm of her hand touched my cheek and she tenderly moved it across my chin, allowing her soft flesh to contrast against the bristles. Osiris was taking in everything about my appearance with as much awe as I had given her.

She then stopped, her elation turning to a frown.

'What's the matter?' I enquired, noting her deflated expression.

'I wish I had more time to talk to you. I would love to know everything about your world and I think you want to know more about mine.'

I smiled widely. 'I would. Maybe we could meet up again?' My heart was beginning to palpitate from the idea that I may have regular contact with such an extraordinary individual.

She looked deep in thought for a few moments, but then exhaled a heavy moan and replied, 'I can't. I think I've been lucky this time, but can we really be sure that we could get away with this again?'

I must have looked crestfallen, but I knew she was right. Had any other person discovered Osiris, there was a very high chance that they'd have tried to capture her. And even though the beach was currently empty, we couldn't guarantee that this would be the case during any future meeting. I wouldn't want her to get caught.

'You're right,' I admitted. 'And you should probably stay away from the shore altogether. It could be dangerous if you're spotted by the wrong person.

This clearly wasn't something she wanted to hear and yet she nodded in agreement. 'I'll try to keep as far away as possible.'

It was with deepest regret that I would have to say goodbye to Osiris since there really was so much I wanted to ask her about. However, I knew that it was for the best and so watched without protest as she began to swim back out to sea. As I did so, a small fleck of water landed on my nose. Before I knew it, a drizzle of rain was showering down upon me.

'It was nice meeting you, Luke,' she called.

'You too,' I replied.

Then with a final solemn wave of farewell, Osiris disappeared.

Even when she was gone, I continued to stand in the same place. The cool breeze was whipping my face and tiny speckles of rain were running down my cheeks.

It took a while to sink in: I had just spoken to a mermaid.

*

The first thing I did upon my return home was go straight to my bedroom. Matt had tried to convince me to join him on the sofa since our football team was winning and he wanted to celebrate, but I had to pass on this. My head was swimming with questions, so I took a bottle of beer with me and I got started on some investigation into mermaids.

Without even replacing my sodden clothes for drier ones, I sat down on my bed and pulled out my laptop. It was old, and I barely used it anymore, but it would do for what I needed. The page loaded and I immediately typed "mermaid" into the search engine. Over one hundred million results showed up within a second and I scrolled down until I could find a link that would be of help. There was a lot that was useless, like ones that would take me to websites dedicated to random people's artwork or those by fans discussing a film or book featuring them. There were also some for videos that were clearly not real.

I went through a few pages of the search results before deciding to refine my original topic, replacing it with "mermaid evidence".

This time, just fewer than seven thousand results matched, and I groaned when I saw most of the links dedicated to some phoney documentary claiming to have proof about the existence of mermaids, but which was in fact proved to be faked.

Despite these setbacks, I persevered and ultimately came across a scientific website that went through the entire history of the mermaid legend. It started with the stories of a Syrian goddess who jumped into a lake in order to be turned into a fish, though only her lower half ended up as one. After this, more stories of such creatures persisted, and even famous explorer Christopher Columbus claimed to have seen them near Haiti in the fifteenth century. This site was logical, though, and attributed this to him (along with other sailors who told similar tales) having seen marine mammals like manatees and mistaking them for mermaids.

In the end, I gave up and turned off my laptop. I felt annoyed, but then something suddenly occurred to me and I began to furiously hunt through the stack of old books I had piled up in the bottom of my wardrobe.

Eventually, I found what I was looking for in a thin, hardback book. The front cover displayed the title *The World's Greatest Mysteries* with the latter two words printed in bold red text. Underneath this were two images: one was a black and white picture displaying numerous flying sauces, and the other a photo of the sun shining down upon Stonehenge. This was something I had owned for a lot of years; it was slightly frayed and a few of the pages were torn with use.

The contents page listed the different mysteries by categories: *The Power of the Mind, Human Mysteries, Unsolved Crimes, Strange Creatures, Mysteries of the Universe* and *The Spirit World.* I flicked to page eighty-nine for the *Strange Creatures* chapter where I turned over a page on the Loch Ness Monster to find the section *Merfolk: Wild Creatures of the Sea.* The entire middle of the two pages was taken up by a black and white drawing of a rather malicious mermaid crushing a man with her tail. Around the edges was text about the beings, as well as reports of people claiming to have encountered them.

One story took place in the Shetland Islands; the legend went that in 1833, six fishermen caught a mermaid in their net – they hauled her aboard and kept her there for three hours, but let her go when they took pity on her miserable moans. This had supposedly happened near the island of Yell. I was unsure on whether I believed this, simply due to the details they gave of the mermaid. The description, according to the book, was that she was a metre long, with bristles on her head that went to her shoulders – her tail was like a fish but without scales and she had a slight resemblance to a monkey. This did not fit with what Osiris looked like and I doubted others of her kind would differ in appearance so drastically, so I was a little sceptical about this report.

Another story involved a ship called the Leonidas, which in 1917 was sailing from New York to Le Havre. Whilst doing so, the crew reported seeing a creature which they described as resembling a human from above the neck, with black hair and white skin, but like a fish below the arms. It swam beside the ship for a few hours, with moments of raising itself out of the water to gaze at the spectators. They all, including the captain, believed it to be a mermaid. This again did not fit what I had seen as the descriptions seemed to suggest that the mermaid they saw had no human upper body, which Osiris definitely did.

I almost gave up hope, until I read one that sounded like it could be trustworthy – one that had eerie similarities to my own account.

This story was the most recent, coming from 1947, involving an eighty-year-old fisherman who claimed to have seen a mermaid combing her hair on a herring box off the Hebridean island of Muck. Upon realising that she had been seen, she dived back into the sea. Nothing could change the old man's story and he remained adamant that he had seen a mermaid that day, despite having no proof to back up his claims.

This was certainly plausible given that Osiris and I had deduced that others must have come to land years before her, and there was no description of the mermaid given to contradict what I knew to be true. If this man was telling the truth, then I admired him for coming forward so openly with his story. He must surely have faced ridicule from many.

There were no more stories, so I sat for a few minutes mulling everything over. I heard a knock from the front door and I could hear Matt get up to answer it. Then I heard him talking to someone, the conversation muffled. Finding out who it was would have to wait, though, because an idea had just come to me: I would find someone local that believed and go from there.

I returned to my laptop and started to look up groups dedicated to the area of unsolved mysteries. There were hundreds. Many of them included members from all over the world, though, and I was hoping to talk to someone a little closer to home. I wasn't necessarily going to tell them specifically that I had communicated with a mermaid – that could put Osiris and her kind in trouble – but I wanted to converse with someone who wouldn't think I was crazy for discussing such a polarising topic.

The conversation downstairs had moved from the doorway to the living room, leading me to guess that whoever had knocked was here to stay. This naturally piqued my interest, so I tore myself away from the screen and headed down to see who our visitor was.

As soon as I could hear their voices more clearly, I had an idea as to who Matt was talking to. Sure enough, I walked in to see him with our good friend who lived across the street from us.

Valerie McRae was unique in her appearance. Her dyed black hair was matted and enclosed her pale pointed face, which was also home to a silver nose ring. She often wore clothes that were deliberately chaotic; today sporting a puffy purple coat, a short denim skirt with black tights and green trainers. She also had her old jacket slung over her shoulder. Together, these would normally look unflattering, but they matched her personality perfectly, so she was able to pull it off.

She immediately ran forward and kissed me on the cheek before pulling me into a tight embrace. What I appreciated was that she didn't have to say a word; she knew that this time of year was tough for me and that I would need my friends more than usual.

'Hi, Val,' I said, returning the hug.

'You want a drink?' Matt asked her.

'Just the one, thanks,' she replied. 'I can't stay long – told Alice I was just nipping out to talk to my manager about something. I suppose she won't mind waiting a short while for me.'

'Why did you lie?'

Val groaned and took a seat on the arm of the nearest chair. 'Because she's really irritating me at the moment. I get that she wants to spend time together, but I swear there's only so much I can take. She's practically suffocating me.' She took the can from Matt and cracked it open at once. 'This is bliss. Alice has got me on some new healthy diet – she reckons we could both do with cleansing ourselves or some crap.'

'Oh, so… it's off then?' Matt sighed.

I looked from one to the other. 'What are you talking about?'

Val shook her head. 'No, it's still on,' she said, a determined tone in her voice. 'I've told her I'm not cancelling it no matter what she says.'

'What are you talking about?' I repeated.

'She's meant to be throwing a party for your birthday,' Matt said. 'So, it's still going ahead, Val?'

'Of course it is. Alice can preach her hippy politics later. You are up for it, aren't you, Luke? I was thinking it could be on your actual birthday. So, it'd be next Friday night.'

It took me a few seconds before I answered. 'Sure,' I said, eventually. It wasn't that I didn't think it would be fun, it was just that I was so preoccupied with thoughts about Osiris. I knew I couldn't let Val down, though. She always made sure to make a fuss about me on my birthday to make me feel better.

'Great,' she beamed. 'I promise there won't be many people there. It'll just be a nice, relaxing evening. And I apologise in advance if Alice is in a mood... but once we're all drunk, we won't care, will we?'

Matt laughed and the two began to discuss plans for the night, including drinking games and whether she was inviting any girls he could possibly hook up with. I tried my best to join in, but my heart just wasn't in it.

I excused myself and returned upstairs. I liked spending time with them very much – they were my closest friends – but I just couldn't spend time going over trivial aspects on life when there were such possibilities as mermaids in existence. Heck, for all I knew, the other unexplained phenomena in my *World's Greatest Mysteries* book were real. Perhaps aliens do visit Earth to probe humans and maybe vampires do look for fresh victims in the dead of night. And, all the while, I was stuck in a mundane life when I could be experiencing so much more than that.

I thought about Osiris and what she could be doing at this very moment. What exactly do merfolk do in their spare time? Dance with crustaceans and collect human artefacts was what I was led to believe from films, though I guessed the truth would be vastly different.

The poster hung up directly opposite my bed suddenly caught my eye. It showed a cat clinging desperately to a washing line, alongside the caption "Hang in there, baby!" I'd put it up a while back, when I needed inspiration to keep getting up even when life continued to throw obstacles at me. Without further ado, I reopened my web browser and vowed not to stop until I found contact details for another believer who was reasonably close by.

Chapter 3

Jodie Grayson was nothing like I had pictured. When I had looked her up on social media, there were no images. Her profile photos were always something aquatic-themed. Therefore, I'd only had my imagination with which to envision her. Since she was someone who spent a lot of time discussing conspiracy theories online, I had thought of her a squat, older woman with greying hair and more cats than she could handle. Instead, I was stood looking at a rather tall, middle-aged woman with brown hair almost as dark as my own, which she had tied back in a strict ponytail. The grey suit she was wearing meant she wouldn't have looked out of place in a business firm – certainly more manager than internet nut.

'Luke Holden?' she asked. I got the feeling she was someone who liked to mask their feelings as much as possible, though I sensed there was underlining enthusiasm as she greeted me.

'Yes,' I confirmed, holding out my hand for her to shake.

'Wonderful, please come in.'

She stepped aside and I was led through to the living room. It was quite small and decorated sparsely. Most of the ornaments consisted of small porcelain ships and other examples of ocean life. The only personal item she appeared to have was a framed photo of her and a man of a similar age. I'd have thought it was her husband had she not made it explicit online that she was single. Perhaps she was a widow.

As she directed me to the couch, I became suddenly conscious of my appearance given the more formal attire she was dressed in. I began flattening my hair, which I knew was sticking up at the back. Thankfully, I had taken time that morning to make sure my stubble didn't look too scruffy.

Clearly noticing how nervous I was, Jodie said, 'There's no need to look so worried, Luke. Rest assured, I'm not going to murder you.' We both chuckled and then she continued, 'Now, why don't I get us both something to drink – would you like a cup of tea?'

'That would be great, cheers.'

'How do you take it?'

'Just milk, no sugar. Thanks.'

She bustled off, leaving me alone.

I had chosen to email this woman instead of the various other people I found during my search for a few reasons.

Firstly, most of the others hid behind a username and restricted information that meant I couldn't get a clear idea of who they were, where they lived and whether they could provide me with enough information. I sifted through numerous pages until I found a link leading me to a forum called *Belief in the Impossible*. The owner was listed as Jodie Grayson, with quite a lot of information provided about her. Although her social media accounts were all set to private, the biography she provided on the forum was more than enough to convince me that she was worth talking with about mermaids.

Another major plus was the proximity at which Jodie lived in relation to me. She lived in a city not far away, which meant I was able to get from my house to hers within half an hour.

That morning, I'd nearly convinced myself to call the whole thing off since I had started to have second thoughts. However, I needed to unload to somebody, even if it was a complete stranger.

A short while had passed when Jodie re-entered the room, holding two porcelain cups that were decorated with starfish and crab patterns. She handed me one and then took a seat on a large armchair opposite me.

'Don't worry, I haven't poisoned it,' she laughed.

I smirked and took a sip. I appreciated the playful nature she was employing to the situation because I had mentioned in our correspondence the fact that I wasn't used to meeting up with strangers online to discuss conspiracy theories. I had watched way too many shows where enthusiastic introverts ended up killing people they'd lured to their homes.

Even though she seemed quite reclusive in terms of her social media presence, Jodie had been remarkably candid over the forum, explaining to those reading it how she had often been mocked for her vocal belief in aspects of life that others believed to be a myth.

'I'm still a bit nervous,' I admitted to her.

In our brief communication, we hadn't spoken a lot about what we were meeting up to discuss. I told Jodie how I was interested in learning more about mythical ocean creatures and, since she was so close by, she responded swiftly asking for me to come over to her house so we could talk about her findings without fear of it being intercepted. I wasn't anticipating this reaction, but I wasn't too shocked since she gave off a distinct vibe of paranoia in her messages. I was half-expecting her to answer the door wearing a tin foil hat.

'It's understandable,' she said. 'After all, it's not every day you meet up with someone you don't know to discuss such things. But please, Luke, don't worry. I've invited you over because you seemed very enthusiastic about what I dedicate my life to. Did you happen to ready many of the threads on the forum?'

'Just a few,' I said. 'There seems to be a little... I don't know, *community*, on your site. I noticed a lot of the same users posting quite a bit. It was nice to read everyone's take on different stuff.'

She nodded and said, 'That's why I set it up. Back when I first began to do research into the unknown, I often felt like an outsider. The internet had made it so simple to communicate with likeminded individuals. Though of course it means we must be more careful. I'm not saying that the government or anything are watching us, but you can never be too careful.'

I nodded, even though I thought she was being a little over the top. I drank a bit more of the tea to be polite and then asked, 'So, on your site, you say that you're still in hope of actually exploring the ocean for yourself – do you really think you could find something like, I don't know, a mermaid? Would it really be so easy?'

Jodie finished her drink and replied, 'I'm not sure about easy, but I certainly think it's possible. Have you ever heard about the Zuiyo-maru carcass?'

I shook my head. 'Never. What is it?'

'Well, in 1979, a Japanese fishing trawler caught the rotting body of an unknown creature and took photos that show its resemblance to a plesiosaur – that's what a lot of people speculate the Loch Ness Monster to be. Scientists soon refuted this notion and instead theorised that it was probably nothing more than a decomposed basking shark. I know this might very well be the case, and perhaps I shouldn't assume otherwise, but what fascinates me is the idea that it was never proven conclusively. Therein lays the proof that there could be many unseen wonders below the surface.'

'How come it was never proven?' I asked. 'What happened to the carcass?'

She snorted with derision. 'The captain made the moronic decision to dump it back into the sea so as not to ruin the fish they'd caught. What an idiot, can you imagine how famous he could have been had it turned out to be something more than a mere dead shark? I've discussed the case with people many times on *Belief in the Impossible* – you'll probably find the thread on it if you look back far enough. It's usually the case we all point to as the main evidence that regular folk can find extraordinary things out there.'

'And that's what you want?'

'All I've ever wanted from a young age is to explore the ocean. It's my dream to find things out there that have yet to be discovered. I've tried many times over the years to convince people to help me, to assist in a mission of deep-water exploration, but it's difficult when you don't have someone to help you financially. My family and I have never seen eye to eye and so it's been an uphill struggle for me.'

Jodie stood up and walked towards the window, staring out wistfully. I noticed the cheery nature she had been presenting until that moment was threatened by the obvious resentment emitting from her story.

'Did you know that over ninety percent of the oceans remain unexplored?'

This fact genuinely intrigued me. 'Over ninety percent, seriously?'

'I know. Almost unbelievable, isn't it?'

'It definitely makes finding something more of a plausible goal,' I said, though I felt a mild apprehension about encouraging her. I knew for a fact that there were at least some secrets in the ocean, such as mermaids, and I didn't know exactly what Jodie would do if she were to find one. I decided to alter the topic slightly to see if she had any goals she wished to pursue through her site. 'So, what are your thoughts on other stuff? Like, do you believe in werewolves or witches? On your site, you focus on the ocean, but where do you draw the line? Do you go, like, monster hunting or something? Have you been to Scotland to search for Nessie?'

She gave a small laugh, though it didn't quite reach her eyes. 'I'm very open-minded towards all manner of paranormal phenomena, but I find myself drawn towards the ocean. I just have an intuition that there are things beneath the surface.'

I wasn't sure I liked the certainty with which she spoke because it was hitting a bit too close to home. I was also now open to other possibilities in the world, but only had evidence of mermaids so was more focused on that – was it possible that Jodie, too, had encountered one before and that's why she was so dedicated to exploring the sea?

'So, tell me,' she said, 'how exactly did you develop such an interest in the unknown? You seem to be new to this, a little unsure. Have you perhaps seen something?'

I debated with myself on whether to tell her or not. On the one hand, it would be a relief to admit the truth to someone. However, there was something about her that I just didn't trust. I couldn't explain what it was. In the end, I firmly responded, 'No. I haven't actually seen anything with my own eyes. I've just been really fascinated by the prospect of it lately.'

With a look of distinct annoyance, Jodie heaved a heavy sigh and said, 'That's a shame. It's so very rare to hear of a sighting from someone normal. I was ecstatic when you got in touch, Luke. You're not like the usual lot I get messages from on a weekly basis.'

I thought it rather hypocritical of her to be calling anyone out for being somewhat eccentric considering the way she spoke. I also found it strange that she'd complain about people regularly getting in touch with her about alleged sightings since her whole website was dedicated to doing just that.

'Bur what suddenly brought this on?' she continued, clearly determined not to let the subject go. 'You must have had a reason to find my site.'

'I just...' I tried to get more words out, but I stooped myself.

I wasn't exactly sure what I'd expected by arranging this meeting, but every instinct in my body was telling me to make up an excuse to leave. I could see her icy glare cutting into my skin and knew that I'd have to answer her question, even if it was with a lie.

'Bigfoot,' I eventually spluttered out, much to her obvious shock. 'That's what got me interested.' She raised an eyebrow, so I went on. 'I saw a documentary about the Sasquatch, and it made me curious about other things that people debate the existence of. That led me to the ocean – you know, because I live right next to it.'

It wasn't entirely false. I had indeed seen something about Bigfoot sightings in the Pacific Northwest – it was a few years back, during my repeated bouts of insomnia after leaving secondary school. It had barely made an impact on me, though, and only came into my head now because Matt and I had watched a low-budget found footage horror film on the subject a few nights before.

'Oh,' Jodie said, nodding politely. 'I've heard from a few Americans who've visited my page about possible Bigfoot sightings. One was actually from the Lost Coast in California and was adamant that it was more than a legend.'

'Did you believe them?'

She gave a nonchalant shrug. 'I didn't disbelieve them.'

It appeared Jodie wasn't as interested in myths and legends as she was with ones in the sea. I could hardly judge her for this, though, since I didn't know if they were real either.

'I'm sorry, but I really should get going,' I said suddenly, taking a swift glance at the time as if I was in fact paying attention to what it read.

Jodie looked a little taken aback. 'So soon?'

I stood up and rustled my hair nervously. 'Yeah, well – err – I've got a footy match I need to be at shortly. And I've got a few things I need to get done before then.'

Again, this wasn't a total lie. I was indeed meeting up with a few of the guys later – it just wasn't going to be for another few hours.

Jodie looked up at me. I may just have been paranoid, but I could've sworn there was a slightly suspicious look in her eyes. 'And you're absolutely sure there's nothing else you want to get off your chest?'

'No,' I said, determinedly. 'There isn't anything.'

'Very well,' Jodie replied, sipping the remainder of her tea through pursed lips. Her gaze never left me as she did so.

I gave a civil nod and made a quick exit.

I was walking across the road to my car when I registered someone watching me. I looked over to see a middle-aged man with a flannel shirt on and a satchel slung over his shoulder staring intently in my direction. I was shocked by how blatant he was being about it as he made no effort to hide what he was doing as I got closer.

'Can I help you, mate?' I asked.

He stared for a few more seconds and then said, 'You've just come out of that house, haven't you?'

'Yeah, why?'

He didn't reply, but instead took a few cautious steps closer. 'Were you talking to Jodie Grayson? Did she arrange for you to meet her?'

'Again, yeah. Why?'

'Just wondering,' he said, vaguely.

'I'm sorry, who are you?'

He looked at me and there was something in his expression that told me he wasn't just trying to make idle conversation. 'Sam,' he said. 'And you?'

'Luke.'

'Do you know her well, Luke?'

'Not really.' I had no idea who this man could possibly be or why he was so interested in my business. 'I just came over to discuss something with her and now I'm going home.'

'Well, take care. There are bad people in this world, you know.'

'Are you saying Jodie is a bad person?'

'I'm just saying that even the cleverest people can be tricked by the big bad wolf in disguise. Watch your back, yeah?'

His ramblings didn't make a lick of sense and I was thankful when he turned and started to walk away. I got in my car quickly before he could change his mind and come back for more inane conversation. I watched him disappear into an alleyway, then put my keys into the ignition and began to drive.

Looking out, I saw Jodie watching me through an upstairs window. For some reason, I felt a prickle of fear creep up my spine.

Chapter 4

I hated my job. There was no use pretending any different.

On the one hand, I was very grateful to have gotten it when I did. I'd been made redundant the year previously and was terrified as to how I was going to contribute to the household bills. That's when my friend put a good word for me at our local petrol station. Within days, I had the job without an interview or need of references. However, it soon became clear that this wasn't a pleasant place to spend most of my time.

There was no doubt in my mind that the place was, for lack of a better word, *dodgy*. For starters, I had to do my month's training for free. I had agreed because I was in need of a job and couldn't afford to lose out on it, but looking back it was the first sign that things weren't totally legitimate. Then there was the fact that we had to do whole shifts on our own and were responsible for everything that went wrong – which, in a rundown place like that, happened a lot. We had money deducted from our wages for every little thing, as well as big things like someone driving off without paying for petrol. Worst of all, there was no official contract in place and the rota was constantly subject to change. I found myself spending way too much time there due to my co-workers constantly dropping out of shifts. I was hoping to leave soon enough and couldn't wait to see the back of it. I was certain the manager was avoiding taxes and I didn't want anything to do with such an untrustworthy establishment.

Nevertheless, I entered the garage on Monday morning determined to keep a positive attitude. The co-worker currently behind the till was my friend, Emmie Walker, who was looking down at something on the desk and pouting. Closing the shift was never any fun, especially when the print-out informed you that you were down in cash. You had to then pray that the next shift would make it up.

'Morning,' I said, joining her behind the counter.

She gave a small laugh. 'Morning, what have you been smoking then?'

'Nothing,' I replied, mockingly holding my hands up.

'Yeah, right,' she said.

'Nah, honest, I'm just… feeling good.'

She smiled. 'I'm really happy to hear that. You've been a bit distant lately and I was starting to worry about you.'

'Well, there's honestly no need to,' I assured her.

'That's good, because your friend Val's invited me to a party for you on Friday. I thought after the last few weeks that maybe you wouldn't be up for it – but you are, aren't you?'

'Yeah, of course I am. I was talking to her about it the other day.'

'Great, it should be a good night.'

Most people would probably be excited about the prospect of spending their birthday with friends having a few drinks, but I could barely concentrate on anything other than what I had spoken about to Jodie. I faked a casual smile on my face for the sake of those around me – yet all I could think about was everything she had said about believing in mermaids and how unwavering she seemed to be in her quest to prove her theories correct. I also couldn't shake the feeling that she suspected I knew more than I was letting on.

'I'm just going to quickly finish stacking the crisps and then I'll be off,' Emmie said.

I positioned myself behind the till, prepared for the inevitable onslaught of early morning drivers. It was always rather hectic on a morning with people either going to work or on the school run. Hopefully it would distract me.

I watched as the owner of the only car currently on the forecourt entered the shop. She was a tall, thin woman with scraggly dark hair. I greeted her with a smile and a friendly greeting as I did with every customer and sorted out her payment transaction.

Just as she was about to turn away, she suddenly squinted and stared at me like I'd done something extremely interesting. 'Your eyes…' she whispered, leaning forward.

I glanced over at Emmie, who looked as surprised as I must have done. I was hoping she would cause some sort of distraction, but she seemed to be enjoying my discomfort and so I was forced to deal with the old woman on my own.

I chuckled slightly. 'What about them?'

She continued to squint, as though she couldn't quite be sure if what she was seeing was really there. 'They… they've seen things…'

'Well, yeah – they're eyes.'

Emmie snorted loudly and tried to disguise it by rustling the crisp packets.

I may have been trying valiantly to remain calm, but in actual fact my heart had begun to palpitate faster. This woman couldn't be referring to my encounter with Osiris could she? Surely not – that would mean she would legitimately have some sort of psychic powers and I highly doubted that could be the case. Then again, who was I to dismiss such a thing now? Perhaps Jodie was right when she spoke about there being a lot more to the world than most humans chose to comprehend.

'Young man,' the woman said, taking her hand away from me at last, 'have you ever had a reading before?'

Now it was my turn to squint. 'A reading?'

'From a medium,' she clarified. 'Your life examined, future foretold.'

'You mean like having my palms analysed and stuff?'

She gave a curt nod. 'That's one method.'

'No,' I said. 'I've never really believed in that sort of thing.'

'I see.' Evidently undeterred, she began rummaging in her coat pocket and pulled out a small business card that she handed to me. 'My name is Natasha Malini, known professionally as Madame Malini. I have a shop not far from here. I have no appointments this afternoon should you wish to come and see me for a reading. If not, then you can give me a call and we can arrange one for whenever you are available. The address and number are on the card.'

I was quite taken aback, though I shouldn't have been too surprised that she was desperate to drum up business considering that she had just admitted to having nobody scheduled for an appointment with her. Perhaps she spent most of her time attempting to convince retail staff to visit her shop.

'Look,' I said, 'I appreciate the offer, but I really don't think I can afford to spend my wages on something I'm not entirely sure about. We don't exactly earn a lot here.'

Far from looking somewhat deflated by my dismissal, she reacted with a smile. 'Actually, I see that when you laugh you have dimples.' I subconsciously found myself touching my cheek. 'The reading is free for you.'

'Right,' I said, unsure of exactly what to say. 'I guess I'll think about it.'

'Please do. I have a feeling you'd be a fascinating subject, Luke.'

'Hang on, how do you know my name?'

She winked. 'Your nametag.'

As soon as she had gone, Emmie rushed over. 'What the hell was all that about?'

In response, I handed her the card that the woman had given me.

'*With Madame Malini, find out what the future holds*,' she read aloud. 'Oh, Luke, please don't tell me you're actually going to pay this nutcase to make up a bunch of rubbish?'

'Of course I'm not,' I said, quickly.

She breathed a sigh of relief. 'Good, because you know she'll just tell you what you want to hear. And I bet it isn't cheap, either. People like that just like to manipulate you.'

'So, I take it you don't believe in any of that stuff, then?'

Emmie rolled her eyes. 'Luke, if she was actually clairvoyant then why on earth would she have a business round here? And be driving such a cheap car? She'd be rich and swindling big earners down south. Plus, she'd have been able to tell that there was bird crap on the back of her coat.'

I laughed and returned to my duties. However, I couldn't stop myself going back to the business card. After all, it would make sense to be more open-minded given what I had witnessed on the beach. And she had said that my visit would be free. Then again, that could have just been a ploy to lure me there and then she would possibly start hinting towards payment the further along we got. Was I willing to potentially waste money? And would it really be a waste if it could signpost me towards another meeting with Osiris?

I pocketed the card and decided to mull it over.

*

Even once my shift was finished, I hadn't decided for certain as to whether I would take Madame Malina up on her offer. I kept going over the pros and cons, but just couldn't decide if it would be a good idea.

I wasn't completely unfamiliar to the concept of a psychic reading. I had gone to school with a girl who strongly believed in that sort of thing, along with astrology and the like. I had listened to what she had to say on the matter, but never found myself taking it seriously. That was long before I had spoken to a mermaid – I was a lot more conflicted now on whether I should take it seriously.

And so, I found myself stood outside the shop, debating on if I should take the plunge and go inside. It looked fairly small and the window was completely covered with a display showing ornaments like crystals, beads and stones. Ordinarily, I would've walked straight past it without so much as a second glance.

With a deep breath, I marched forward and walked in.

I was immediately met with almost too much furniture to handle. The window display was nothing compared to the amount of elaborate decoration she had scattered about the floor, walls and ceilings inside. It was a good job I wasn't claustrophobic, otherwise I may have had to consider leaving there and then.

Almost on cue, a curtain at the far side of the room drew back and Madame Malina stepped out. 'Luke!' She cried. 'You came!'

I managed a smile as she bustled forward.

She grabbed my hand and started leading me towards the curtain. 'Please come through to the back room. I'll make you comfortable.'

I tried to ignore any sordid connotation from this and obediently followed her. She led me into an even smaller room that was taken up mainly by a large round table. There were no windows, but dozens of lit candles lined the walls to give an eerie glow. I was prompted to take a seat on a rickety old wooden chair, whilst she sat on a much grander and seemingly much sturdier one opposite me.

'We will begin momentarily,' she assured me.

As she fiddled with a deck of cards and rearranged a small crystal ball in the centre of the table, I took off my jacket in an attempt to cool down and began to scan the room. There wasn't a lot of space, but a small desk had been shoved in one corner and I noticed an Ouija board placed on top of it. Was I expected to use it? I really didn't think I could stomach the thought of contacting any dead relative, even if I did have a slight morbid curiosity.

'Right then,' Madame Malina said, and I snapped to attention, 'let's begin, shall we?'

'Okay…' I said, both cautious and excited.

'Your left hand first, please.'

I offered my hand, which she gently took in her own. With her free hand, she began to use her fingers to caress the lines in my palm. I felt rather stupid having to sit there whilst she stared intently at what I considered to be nothing of any importance.

'And now the right,' she gestured.

She did the same for my other hand, taking a little more time on this one. When she was finished, she looked up at me as though she was examining every aspect of my face.

'I was right,' she declared. 'You make for a most fascinating read.'

I shifted slightly. 'How so?'

'You were born with an innate sadness. I see an absence that affected you greatly.' I tried not to make any facial expressions that she could analyse; I knew that was how con artists worked and I wanted to see if she was authentic. 'There's loneliness, but from not a lack of friendship. In fact, that's one aspect of your life where you excel. No, you're more... lost.'

Some of what she said resonated with me, but it sounded awfully vague and it wouldn't be too out of the question to imagine they were things she'd say to anyone.

'You doubt me?' She questioned.

I stammered and then replied, 'You just haven't said anything specific.'

This did not seem to faze her. She merely nodded. 'Then we shall move on to the crystal ball. That should provide you more with what you desire from a reading.'

'Okay then,' I muttered, rather doubtfully.

She smiled and looked down at the small glass orb on the table. I wondered what was going to happen when she suddenly picked it up and held it in front of her, whilst closing her eyes and breathing softly. It appeared like she was meditating. After a few minutes, she opened her eyes and carefully put the ball back on the table.

'Images are coming through,' she told me.

I nervously gripped either side of the chair, feeling irrational for doing so. Surely this wasn't for real... I couldn't really believe that she was about to predict my future, could I?

Madame Malina narrowed her eyes and looked deep in thought for several minutes, then she looked up at me. 'You are in for an incredible journey,' she said, staring directly into my eyes. 'Yes... you certainly have a unique path ahead of you.'

'Okay,' I said, releasing my hands and placing them on the table. 'Can you a be a bit clearer about what you mean?'

'Certainly. I see great challenges ahead for you, Luke, but I also see a lot of rewards. There is someone destined to join you on your journey, someone you may already have met.'

I felt my mouth twitch. 'Can you see who it is?'

She smiled. 'I do not see a face, but I do see... the ocean.'

It felt as though my stomach had dropped. I tried to recover, but it was clear that she had registered my immediate reaction.

'Does this mean something to you?' she asked.

'Maybe,' I answered, trying not to give too much away. 'Are you sure you can't make out a face, or... anything else about this person?'

She returned her gaze to the ball as I waited in bated breath.

'I'm afraid not,' she said, though I wasn't sure if she was being entirely truthful. 'There is a lot of black cloud. It's as though there's a certain aura of darkness to everything, though this doesn't have to be permanent.'

'I don't understand.'

'From what I can see, Luke, you have a difficult road ahead of you. There's a sinister aspect present, but this can go away if correctly handled.'

I didn't like how unclear she was being. 'Can't you tell me if it'll go away or not?'

She sighed. 'The future isn't set in stone; it all depends on what choices you make. If you are lucky, you'll find yourself on the right path. Perhaps fate will give you a helping hand.'

'Right,' I said. There wasn't a lot I could gauge from what she said. Only the part about the ocean had given me a certain shiver, but even that was inconclusive. I saw her reach for a pack of tarot cards and immediately stood up. 'Thanks a lot, but I think that's enough for one day.'

She didn't look surprised. 'Alright. But please, at least pick one card.'

I slowly leaned forward and took one from the pile she signalled to and handed it back to her. It seemed to be one that she had anticipated.

'I thought so,' she said, flipping it round so I could see the illustration of a naked man and woman with a short caption at the bottom. '*The Lovers* – very curious indeed.'

Maybe I was meant to ask her exactly why it was curious, or else why she had been expecting me to pick out that one specifically. However, I didn't want to encourage her any further and so instead thanked her again and made for the exit.

'Luke,' she called, and I turned back. She was now on her feet. 'Please bear in mind that your past does not define you. I know you might not think so, but I see a great strength in you. If you can learn to get over the past, then maybe you can handle the future.'

I could feel myself trembling. There was no way she could know about what I thought she was hinting at. 'And how exactly do I get over the past?'

Madame Malina had an undeniable look of pity on her face. 'By sharing it with someone. You shouldn't keep something like that to yourself. Buried pain is an open catalyst if you leave it to rot.'

'I don't know what you mean,' I said, but my voice audibly cracked.

'Just consider the fact that the past always has a way of coming back to haunt us, even if we try to hide it. Or numb the pain with alcohol.'

'I don't have to consider anything,' I retorted through clenched teeth. 'Thank you for the free reading, but don't ever bother me again.'

Although I knew my behaviour was rather aggressive, there was nothing I could do to stop myself and I quickly left the shop before either I said something else to her or she made another comment about my life. I just needed to get home as soon as possible.
*

On the way back, I found myself stuck in traffic. Of all the days for it to happen then of course it was time when all I wanted to do was hole up in my bedroom and work my way through the twelve-pack of lager I'd picked up out of absolute necessity.

My hands were gripped so tightly to the steering wheel that I was almost afraid that I'd snap it. The radio was blaring out various song, but I couldn't focus on them since my mind was still racing with the cryptic hints that Madame Malina had given. I tried to convince myself that it was complete rubbish, that there was no way she could know about any of that and her comment on the ocean was debatable at best. I made a mental note to not forget going to the gym as soon as possible – I needed to stay fixed on my fitness regime; I couldn't let myself get weak.

At least I still had my birthday night to look forward to.

Chapter 5

On Friday night, Matt and I were greeted at the front door by Val's partner, Alice Curran.

'Happy Birthday,' she said, in the least enthusiastic way possible. If ever there was an extreme opposite to the quirky and eccentric Val, then it was Alice. Even for an occasion such as this, she was dressed as formally as possible – with black trousers, a matching turtle-neck jumper and heels. Her sandy hair was tied behind her head with a small satin pow and, as always, her thick-rimmed spectacles sat on the edge of her nose.

'Cheers,' I replied, giving her a small smile that wasn't returned.

'Party's through here,' she continued, leading us into the house.

We followed her through to the kitchen, where a small gathering of people was already assembled. Val was sat at the table and she immediately jumped to her feet upon our arrival and skipped over to greet us. 'Happy Birthday,' she squealed, giving me a tight hug.

As she did, I saw Emmie stood with a girl whom I did not know. She had long hair, dyed the colour of honey, with about an inch of dark roots. Emmie leant over to her and began whispering something, which caused them both to smirk and the girl to blush.

'I'll get some beers,' Val said when she finally released me. She dashed towards the refrigerator and pulled out two bottles. 'We were just discussing our partners. I was saying Alice should mind her own business as to what I eat because it doesn't concern her.'

Alice shot her a dirty look. 'And I was saying that I only make suggestions because I care for her health,' she snapped. 'Smoking, drinking and eating complete crap is a sure way to find yourself in an early grave.'

'But if I do those things then that's *my* choice!'

'Well maybe you should sort out what you're doing with your life then!'

'Okay, ladies, let's give this a rest.' Jack, a friend of mine from the gym, stepped forward and looked ready to hold one of them back if it got physical. 'This is a party, so let's just have a fun time. Luke deserves a peaceful night.'

The two stopped arguing and instead resorted to glaring at one another. The atmosphere became slightly uncomfortable for a short while afterwards, until the silence was broken.

'You two should be thankful.' Warren, who we knew from school, was stood against the counter with his arms folded. 'At least you've got each other. My last girlfriend dumped me as soon as I lost my job. So much for true love, eh?'

'At least you were together recently,' I said. 'I haven't really had a relationship for about four years now. Consider that.'

Jack let out a low whistle. '*Four years*? I don't think I could last that long.'

A small chuckle came from Matt. 'Yeah, he might not have had a girlfriend in four years, but he's been no stranger to the odd one-night stand. Best way though, isn't it? All of the pleasure and none of the drama.'

Val rolled her eyes. 'Luke deserves a lasting relationship, Matt. Not every man is afraid of commitment like you.'

'Suddenly an expert on men are you, Val?' he replied with a smirk.

'I might not date men, but that doesn't mean I don't hang around with them and I know they're not all worthless. Luke just needs to find the right one, that's all. In the meantime, there's nothing wrong with… letting out a little steam now and again. It's perfectly natural.'

'Ruby's single!' Emmie suddenly announced.

This caused her friend's cheeks to flush furiously. She caught my eye and quickly looked away, smacking Emmie who was in a fit of giggles.

Matt nudged me then winked. '*Go for it*,' he mouthed.

I could feel my face heating up, so made my way towards the door without making eye contact with the others. 'I need to use the toilet,' I mumbled.

I walked upstairs and into the bathroom, locking the door behind me. I stood for a while and thought things over, unwilling to go back down and re-join the discussion. It was true that I had had my fair share of hook-ups since my last relationship ended, but, unlike Matt, I did not find this something to talk openly about – especially not with a group of people. It had always been a touchy subject with me.

When several minutes had passed, I decided that enough time had elapsed that I could return to the party and hopefully the subject matter would have changed.

I exited the bathroom and took notice of several framed photos that were hung on the wall. The one that stood out featured me and Val at our prom. I was wearing a rather dapper grey suit, whereas she had opted for a gothic, blood-red dress with a small black top hat and veil. We're both giving the camera a ridiculously cheesy smile, presumably because we were relieved to finally be leaving school.

A tight knot suddenly appeared in my stomach.

I just want it to stop – why won't they stop?

I could still feel the hands pinning me down, the immense weight on top of me, the heavy breathing in my ear. I was experiencing it as thought it had happened yesterday.

Nobody must know about this.

I ran back into the bathroom and made it in time to violently vomit into the toilet. I then flushed the chain and tried to pretend that all the bad memories were disappearing with it. I had too much on my mind to start reliving that. It needed to be buried forever.

When I returned to the landing, I saw that a bedroom door was open and Val was stood in the doorway. It was clear by her eyes that she had been crying.

'What's the matter?' I asked, stepping forward.

She motioned me to come into the room and I did, closing the door then joining her on the large double bed that took up most of the space.

'What's up?'

'I'm scared,' she admitted, sniffling.

'Why?' I was completely thrown as to what would make her feel that way. The argument earlier had not seemed that serious.

'I'm getting really annoyed with Alice lately,' she said. 'But I love her and I'm scared that we're going to break up. I don't want to be alone.'

I put my arm around her and said, 'Don't worry about it. I'm sure things won't go that far. Every couple goes through hard times, but if you're really in love then you'll come out the other end just fine. You and Alice need to let things cool down and then talk about your problems. You two have been through rougher hardships than healthy eating.'

Val smiled and wiped away the remaining tears from her eyes. 'Thanks,' she said. 'You're a good friend, Luke. And I meant what I said downstairs, about you deserving a long-term relationship. You're going to make some girl really happy one day.'

'Sometimes I doubt that,' I said, bitterly.

'How come?' she asked. 'You've been really... detached, lately. I know you don't like your birthday and you always think about your mam, but you've been a bit off this past week. A lot more than usual, I mean.'

I thought things over as I wondered whether to admit the truth. Val had been my good friend for years and was someone I trusted with most of my secrets, so it made sense to tell her about Osiris. And I really wanted to confide in someone because the fact that I had discovered a mermaid was eating away at me. Talking with Jodie hadn't been enough since I longed to specifically mention Osiris and how much I wanted to see her again.

'There's a reason for my detachment,' I said, finally.

She raised her eyebrows. 'What is it?'

'It was something that happened last Saturday. Just before you came over.'

'Well?' She said, looking at me with expectant eyes.

I composed myself and replied, 'Well, I'd been drinking heavily the night before – you know, because we'd been discussing my mam a lot. Anyway, I needed to clear my head, so I went to the beach. And, well, there was... someone there. This is going to sound completely nuts, but I found a mermaid. We talked for a while... her name was Osiris.'

I stopped for breath and looked at her for a reaction.

Val's mouth was open slightly and she looked bewildered. 'O...kay,' she said, slowly. 'That wasn't what I was expecting you to say, but okay.'

'It sounds crazy, I know, but it's true. Please believe me.'

She stroked my cheek with her hand, whispering, 'I do.'

It was incredible that she did not immediately dismiss what I was saying, making it a lot easier for me to calm down enough to keep talking. 'Good,' I said. 'I could really do with your help. I can't stop thinking about her and I feel like I may never see her again. Out of everyone in the whole world, I spoke to a mermaid and now I have no idea where she is or even if I'll be able to see her again. I had so many questions to ask her.'

'Have you told anyone else about this?'

'No. Well, I nearly did. I found this woman called Jodie Grayson online and she runs a group online where they discuss mermaids and other stuff like that. I was going to tell her.'

'Why didn't you then?'

'It's complicated,' I explained. 'I went to her house and she was talking about finding things out there that have never been discovered. She used this dead corpse of something unknown that a Japanese trawler picked up as an example. I was worried that if I actually told her about Osiris then she would set up some sort of, I don't know, *expedition* to find her and other mermaids.'

Val frowned. 'I don't want to be dismissive or anything, but is there a chance this Osiris girl was in a costume?'

I laughed at this response but shook my head. 'No, seriously, if you'd seen her than you'd know she was real. I'm talking a proper fish tail, webbed hands, sharp teeth – *the lot*.'

'Right, then I guess it's true.'

'You really believe me?'

'We've been friends long enough for me to know that you aren't a liar, Luke,' she said. 'If you say you met a mermaid, then you met a mermaid.'

We sat together in silence for a while after this.

*

Val and I eventually returned to the party downstairs. In our absence, many bottles and cans had been consumed and there was now a significant collection of them stacked up on the kitchen counter.

They were all sat round talking, apart from Ruby, who was by herself and who gave me a small wave when I entered. Alice stood up upon seeing Val and the two walked into the living room.

'You were gone a while,' Ruby said, as I helped myself to a bottle. 'Here, let me,' she added, removing the cap.

'Thanks,' I said. 'I was talking to Val.'

'I thought so. She seemed a bit upset when she went upstairs.'

'Well, she's better now,' I assured her. 'Just needed a shoulder to cry on, I reckon.'

'Yeah, I think Alice was the same,' said Ruby, now pouring herself a glass of wine. 'She was talking to us about their money troubles and how she doesn't think Val is taking them seriously. I guess there are two sides to every story and they both needed to vent.'

The news of a financial dispute between the two took me by surprise because Val had not mentioned anything about that to me, but I wasn't offended because she obviously did not wish to discuss the topic and I respected that. However, I was rather irritated at Alice for openly talking about such a sensitive subject to a group of people at a party – most of whom she wasn't even particularly close with.

'So anyway,' I said, trying to change the subject, 'how do you know Emmie?'

'When I moved up here last year, she was the first person I met and we just hit it off really. Her and Val invited me tonight and I figured it would be a good opportunity to meet people since I'm still kind of new to the northeast area.'

'I'm glad you came,' I said.

Ruby bit her bottom lip. 'Thanks.' She looked away, bashfully. 'Your friend seems to be getting on well with Emmie. She had her sights set on him as soon as the two of you walked in, you know.'

I now realised that Matt was stood with Emmie. They were in a deep conversation and he couldn't stop grinning. 'I don't think he's complaining,' I said. 'He's always worried that every girl at one of Val's parties will be gay.'

'Well, that's definitely not the case.'

I could already feel the alcohol starting to take affect and couldn't help noticing how pretty Ruby was. In fact, there was a slight resemblance to Osiris in her face, if only in a very general way.

After we helped ourselves to more drinks, she looked at me and commented, 'You seem down.'

I sighed. 'I've just got a few things on my mind.'

Giving me a look of sympathy, she reached across and began to play with my hair. Her touch felt good, so when she gently took hold of my hand and led me into the hallway, I did not protest. Before I knew what was happening, our lips were touching. I knew that it wasn't what I really wanted to be doing, but we kept on kissing – my hands finding themselves on the back of her head, feeling through her long, luscious strands of hair.

'I like you, Luke,' she said, pulling her head away from mine.

'I like you, too.' I grinned mischievously, and then added, 'You know, I think there's a spare bedroom upstairs. Maybe we should go check it out.'

'Yeah, maybe we should.'

Smirking despite myself, I followed Ruby upstairs and into the spare bedroom, my heart beating fast with each passing second.

She began to make herself comfortable on the bed as I took of my shirt and closed the door.

Chapter 6

It took me a few seconds to remember why I felt so guilty the next morning, before I looked over and saw Ruby lying asleep next to me in bed.

Cursing profusely under my breath, I slowly made my way out from under the covers and attempted to retrieve my clothes from the floor. The curtains were closed, so only a sliver of sunlight made it into the room and my head was throbbing badly, which didn't help as I tried to coordinate myself into my underwear.

Once I was dressed, I took one last look to make sure Ruby hadn't woken up then left the room, leaving the door open slightly so that I wouldn't make a noise by closing it.

There were voices coming from downstairs and I entered the kitchen to find Val and Alice sat at the table talking and clutching mugs of tea. They both looked up as I approached, though not with the same response. Val smiled and stood up, whereas Alice scowled at me and remained seated.

'Do want a cuppa?' Val asked.

'Aye, cheers,' I replied, sitting down.

Alice swigged her drink quickly, then slammed her mug down on the table. 'Are you out of your mind?' she screeched at me. 'Are you really that desperate that you needed to have sex in my house with someone you only met yesterday?'

'*Alice!*' Val hissed, as she added milk to the tea.

Alice ignored her. 'It's disgusting! We were all trying to have a chat last night when all we could hear was Ruby screaming the bloody house down!'

I could feel my face going red. 'I'm sorry,' I muttered.

'Don't apologise, she's exaggerating,' Val said, passing me the cup of tea and returning to her seat.

'No, I'm not!' Alice cried. 'It was something he could have done in his own house! You better not have stained the bed, Luke. That's for guests.'

'Of course I haven't,' I said, fiercely. I had begun to get weary of her accusations.

At that moment, she got up. 'Then I hope for your sake you weren't too drunk and had the sense to use protection.'

With a reproachful glare, she walked off. I could hear her footsteps going upstairs and the door to her bedroom snapping shut.

Val reached over and squeezed my shoulder. 'Don't listen to her, Luke. She's just in a bad mood like always.'

I buried my head in my hands and said, 'She's right, though. I don't know why I even did it.'

'You obviously needed it,' Val said. 'Honestly, you got laid, don't analyse it too much. As long as you were safe, then I don't see what the problem is. You're both adults, and you just had a little fun at a party. You did use protection, right?'

I had to think hard, but eventually answered, 'Yeah, I did.'

'Then no harm done,' Val continued, taking a sip of tea.

'I suppose not, but I don't even know her. I mean, she's a nice girl and everything, but I don't want her to get the wrong idea and think that I want to start dating her or anything.'

Val laughed and replied, 'I'm sure she won't think that.' After a few seconds passed, she asked, 'Are you still thinking about the mermaid you met?'

I had almost forgotten that I had told Val about my encounter with Osiris and half-expected her to have at least passed it off as drunken ramblings.

'Yeah,' I said, barely disguising the misery in my voice.

'Don't give up hope, Luke,' she said. 'You got lucky once by meeting her, who's to say it won't happen again?'

Her words brought comfort to me. 'That's true,' I said. 'I'll just have to wait and see.'

'Now just the problem at hand,' she said, raising her eyebrows. 'Ruby,' she added, seeing my quizzical look.

'Oh.' A stab of guilt shot through me. 'I haven't got a clue what to do about her. Do you reckon she'll expect me to, I don't know, go on a date or something?'

Val considered my question. 'I'm not sure because I really don't know her that well. I'm sure if you just explain that you don't want anything long-lasting then she'll...'

'Hate me,' I finished for her. 'I shouldn't have encouraged her.'

'Well, it's too late now,' she said, getting up and walking over to the sink. 'You're just going to have to grit your teeth and get on with it. And unless Alice has decided to re-join us, that's Ruby coming down the stairs now.'

Sure enough, Ruby walked in mere seconds later, her hair slightly dishevelled. I walked up to her at once.

'Hi,' was all I could say.

'Hi,' she responded.

Val patted me on the arm and whispered, 'I'll leave you two alone,' then bustled off.

'Do you want a cup of tea?' I asked, feebly motioning towards the kettle.

'No thanks,' she said. 'I better go now actually, I have loads of stuff to do today. And I really should apologise to Emmie for leaving her last night. That's if she didn't end up leaving with your friend. She probably did if she noticed that me and you had gone off together.'

'Right,' I said, my cheeks burning. 'Last night was good.'

'Yeah it was,' she nodded. 'And Luke, before you freak out, I don't expect anything from it. I promise you that it was purely a one-time thing for me, too.

Her bluntness shocked me. I breathed a sigh of relief and admitted, 'I was worried you would, you know...' then trailed off awkwardly.

'You're cute,' she said, kissing me on the cheek. 'I really need to leave now. I'll catch you later, Luke – I hope everything works out for you.'

I watched Ruby leave and then a few minutes later, Val re-entered the room.

'How'd it go?' she asked, tentatively.

'Quite well, surprisingly,' I said.

'You see, I told you it would!'

'I'm going to head off home now,' I announced. As much as it would have been nice to stay with Val for a while and talk, I suspected Alice would eventually make any possible stay uncomfortable for me. 'I'll see you later.

'Alright,' she said, raising her head as she poured a bowl of cereal. 'I'll probably call in to see you and Matt sometime tonight. I'll bring pizza.'

I grinned. 'Sounds good.'

*

Matt would no doubt consider it some sort of miracle that a girl I had sex with did not wish to pursue a relationship. After all, he was regularly complaining about women he took to be bed not getting the message that he wanted nothing else from them.

When I got home that morning, he had his feet up on the couch and was watching the local weather report on the television. I didn't need to even watch it to know what would be forecast – thick grey clouds hung heavy in the sky and there had been a persistent wind as I made my way across the road, so I assumed that rain would be inevitable.

'How was last night then?' Matt demanded. There was a playful twinkle in his eye. 'It sounded like you were really going at it. Can't say I blame you – that Ruby is gorgeous.'

'Yeah, well, she's a nice girl,' I said, quite tactfully I thought.

He laughed. 'Damn right she's nice.'

I was different from him in that I'd never particularly liked having one-night stands and always tried to form some sort of connection to those I considered myself close enough to sleep with. This time, however, I had to regrettably admit that my fling was just that, which made me feel terrible – even though she had felt the same way.

'Anyway, what about you?' I asked. 'You seemed to be getting awfully close to Emmie. She's not upstairs, is she?'

'Nah, I only had my right hand for company when I got back last night.'

'Charming,' I muttered, joining him on the couch. Predictably, the weatherman was discussing expectant showers later in the day. 'Was there anything interesting on the local news, then?'

'Not really,' he shrugged, now flicking through the channels. 'There was something about a woman found naked on our beach this morning. They suspect she was drugged, so they took her to hospital. Didn't give a name. Bit weird, eh?'

'She was probably just drinking with some mates. Remember the beach party we had last year when Val ended up passed out the next morning?'

Matt laughed. 'I thought Alice was going to murder her!'

'With good reason,' I said, fairly. 'She could have drowned.'

'I suppose,' he said, indifferently. 'But you never think of that at the time. The girl from this morning was taken to the hospital so it must have been serious.'

He finally settled on a programme to watch and I sat with him for a while before saying, 'I'm going to hop in the shower, I need a wash.'

He mumbled an 'Uh-huh', not taking his eyes away from the screen.

*

I left the bathroom half an hour later with my headache subdued a lot. I often found that the best time for me to reflect on my problems was during a shower. Usually, as the warm drops of water hit my skin and steam formed around me, everything would become a lot clearer. Therefore, I made sure to stand there for a lot longer than I normally would have, thinking about Osiris and the overwhelming guilt I was still feeling regarding my liaison with Ruby. However, I at least felt more awake as I stepped out of the shower.

Drying my hair off with a towel, I was about to walk through to my bedroom when my phone started ringing. I usually only received text messages, so I felt some apprehension as I picked it up and looked at the name of the caller. It was my brother.

'Phillip, what's up?' I said. There was no way he was calling me just to chat.

'Dad's in hospital, Luke,' he said, followed almost immediately with, 'There's no need to panic – he's alright.' I breathed a sigh of relief. 'He's had a fall this morning and they think he might have broken his leg.'

'So, what happens now? I want to come down.'

'Visiting hours aren't until this afternoon. Once I know more, I'll give you a ring back and let you know what's happening.'

I could hear Matt coming up the stairs, but was concentrating too hard on my phone conversation to even register it. 'Well, cheers for calling. I'll get ready and come down whatever time.'

'Alright. Speak later, bud.'

As I put the phone down, Matt appeared on the landing and immediately averted his eyes. 'Jesus, mate, you're not leaving anything to the imagination.'

I quickly wrapped the towel around my waist and said, 'That was Phillip. My dad's been taken into hospital.'

'Damn, is he going to be alright?'

'Yeah, he's had a fall, that's all.' I nervously ran my hands through my sodden hair. 'Phillip says he's going to call me back as soon as he has more details, so it looks like I'll be going down to see him this afternoon. God, I nearly had a heart attack when he rang.'

'It'll be fine, mate. It's just a little accident, that's all.'

'I know,' I said, trying to get my heart to calm down. The thought of anything happening to my dad filled me with dread, since I honestly didn't know what I'd do without him. 'Anyway, I won't be leaving for a few hours, but I need to get ready.'

Without further distraction, I made my way into my room and started rummaging around my drawers. I don't know why I felt so impatient about seeing him when I knew he was perfectly fine. He'd broken bones a few times in recent months given his advancing age, yet I felt compelled to get to the hospital as soon as possible on this occasion.

I kept telling myself to relax. Everything was going to be fine.

Chapter 7

By the time I arrived at the hospital that afternoon, it had begun to rain heavily. I tried not to see this as a bleak prediction towards how the rest of my day was going to turn out, but this was hard to do as I walked down the corridor with clothes completely soaked.

I wasn't averse to hospitals, there was just something about them that didn't sit right with me. I remember someone back at school once suggesting that I should consider becoming a doctor or a nurse and I couldn't think of anything worse. I'd stick to dealing with rude customers at my current job over dealing with injured people and death on a regular basis, thank you very much.

My dad was sat up in his bed when I walked into the room. I had always been told that I resembled him a great deal, but I never saw the similarities until I'd gotten older. Looking at him, now in his late fifties, it was as though I had aged rapidly; even characteristics such as his nose and his ears were identical to mine. He was clean-shaven, however, and his hair was now grey. Upon seeing me enter, his expression went from a slight frown to breaking out into a huge grin.

'Luke!'

I leaned down and gave him a tight hug. 'Hi dad, where is everyone?'

'Phillip's just left, and Amber's gone to get a coffee,' he said. 'Sit down, son. I want to hear about how your night out went.' There were two chairs next to the bed and I took a seat on the one closest to him. 'You look about ready to throw up.'

'Well, I guess I'm still recovering. I'm not as bad as I usually am after one of Val's parties.'

Suddenly, a female voice interrupted. 'That Val sounds like she needs a good wash.'

I looked over to see Amber standing with a steaming cup of coffee in her hands, appearing as humourless as ever.

'What do you mean by that?' I snarled.

She put her drink down on the bedside table then began to readjust my dad's pillows. 'Well, from the way you describe her she sounds downright grubby,' she said, with a look of disdain. 'I'm surprised she's managed to hang on to that girlfriend of hers for as long as she has.

I glared at my sister and replied, 'I'd rather be in Val's company than Alice's any day of the week. And do you really think it's fair to judge people you've never met purely by their appearance?'

She ignored me and took the empty seat.

'I saw Phillip before he left and he said he was going to come back later this afternoon with Daisy,' she said to my dad, before turning to me. 'He asked her to marry him yesterday and they're having an engagement party in a few weeks' time.'

I was shocked and a little hurt by how I was told about this in such an offhand manner. 'Nice to be told these things as though I wasn't part of the family.' I knew I must have sounded childish, but it struck me that I was always the one left out of the loop. And it also made me uncomfortable to think he'd proposed on such a significant date. 'Someone could have mentioned it to me sooner. How come no-one did?'

Once again, Amber didn't reply. This was her usual tactic when dealing with anything remotely important to me.

'Right,' I said, getting to my feet. 'I need to get going. I'll come visit you when you get out, dad. Sorry I have to go so soon.'

He nodded in response and I could tell he was disappointed to see me leaving as quickly as I'd arrived. I felt bad, though I knew I needed to get out before I said something to Amber that I would later regret. After giving a tight embrace to my dad, and a more subdued one to my sister, I walked out and began to make my way back down the corridor.

I reached the staircase when I noticed a coffee machine. My mouth was very dry, so I took a detour and shoved a few spare coins into it.

There were two nurses stood nearby. As I waited for my drink to come out, I heard one of them say, 'That girl up on the seventh floor, still no name or anything, you know. She can talk, but she's refusing to say anything – won't even eat. Bit weird, don't you think?'

Her friend agreed and said, 'It's suspicious. Maybe she was attacked or something, that would explain why she was naked. Beautiful girl, though, so it would be a shame if something bad has happened to her.'

In the time that had passed from talking to Matt that morning and arriving at the hospital, I had completely forgotten the news about the girl who had washed up on the beach a few hours previously. Now that I had been reminded, I was intrigued enough to go and have a look about. After all, I figured it would be good to get some information which I could relay back to Matt and then tell Val when she came over. It seemed like a stretch and I knew that I probably wouldn't be able to gather much, but I could innocently question some hapless person on the same ward and maybe I'd recognise the girl, which would mean I could help the nurses identify her.

I managed to find my way to where they said she would be. There were no members of staff about, only a few people there to see family. My eyes were immediately drawn to a bed that had no visitors. The occupant was a young woman with long, thick platinum hair which was striking against her pale skin. My jaw dropped when I recognised her.

It was Osiris.

'What the hell are you doing here?' I asked, running over to her. 'And *how*?'

She looked up and gasped when she saw me. '*Luke*? Thank goodness! Please help me, they keep asking a lot of questions! Can you take me away with you?'

I looked round to check that no staff had come into the room since my arrival. 'I can try and sneak you out,' I said. 'You've caused quite a stir though. You were on television this morning apparently; they were reporting on a woman washing up on the beach.'

'I don't know what a television is,' she said, and I immediately realised my mistake. 'It sounds bad though. Can't they just leave me alone?'

'It doesn't work like that.'

'What do you mean?'

I took a deep breath and sat down next to her on the bed so that I wouldn't attract too much unwanted attention. 'Look,' I said, 'you've just been brought here after turning up naked on the coast. That's not normal and it's even more suspicious to people that you won't give a name. You don't have identification which means you don't exist.'

Osiris bit her lip. 'I didn't think about any of that.'

'I don't understand,' I said, staring down at the outline of her legs under the covers. 'How come you're not a mermaid anymore?'

'It's a long story, but I can explain everything if we can get out of this place. Can you get me out of here?'

'Sure.' I decided it would be better to get her home and out of the way of the authorities. 'It might be tricky, though. Can you walk?'

Osiris shook her head. 'I can move them slightly, but when they tried to get me to stand I just couldn't. Is there another way I could get out? You could carry me.'

'That would draw too much attention. Hang on, I have an idea.'

Back in the corridor, I glanced around and saw an empty wheelchair by the wall. I had seen that there were a lot of them unoccupied around the hospital so I knew it wouldn't be too noticeable if I were to take one.

'Right,' I said, wheeling it next to Osiris's bed, 'I need to put you into this. Then I'll hopefully be able to get you all the way downstairs and take you past reception without being noticed. Then, we'll get into my car and I'll take you home with me. Are you okay with that?'

'Yes, of course.'

'Good. Come on, then.'

I pulled the covers off her then lifted her into my arms. She wasn't as heavy as I had expected, and I could see her slender human legs sticking out from her hospital gown. Once she was in the wheelchair, she smiled and I noticed how her pointed teeth were now perfectly normal ones, as well as her hands, which were no longer webbed.

Given that she was so weightless, I was able to push her in the chair with ease. It still hadn't registered exactly what was happening and was fuelled by adrenaline and the rush of seeing her again.

Getting her outside being noticed turned out to be surprisingly easy. I was able to reach the lift on the seventh floor without any interference and it did not stop to let anyone else in until we had reached the lobby, where I pushed her in the chair through the reception area with such confidence that nobody stopped to question me.

The rain wasn't as heavy as before and was now more of a light drizzle. Osiris caught a droplet in her hand and beamed. 'It's just like the day we met,' she said, looking up at me with a look of wonder emulating from her golden eyes.

I smiled back. 'Yeah, you're right. I guess it might not be such a bad sign after all.'

Fortunately, I was parked very near to the entrance, so I made my way to the car swiftly and opened the passenger seat door.

'What is this thing?' Osiris asked me, as I lifted her into my arms again.

'A car,' I said, placing her on the seat and strapping her in. 'It'll get us home fast. Don't panic at the noises or speed. It's safe, I promise.'

I got into the car and started the engine. My pulse was racing as I began to drive without stopping to think anything through. We had been extremely lucky not to have been caught leaving the hospital and I wasn't about to push it by waiting around.

Whilst I drove, I couldn't help but think over everything. Against all odds, I had been the one to find Osiris and was bringing her home. That was a good thing. Despite this, there was a small worry pushing its way forward from the back of my head and it was what Madame Malina had predicted during my reading. Sure, I chose to ignore the comments she made about my past, but I couldn't just dismiss the foretelling of a person coming into my life who had some connection to the ocean. That couldn't possible just be a coincidence, could it? And she had said that there would be a certain darkness to overcome...

'Is everything okay?' Osiris asked, tearing her eyes away from the views outside. 'You look a little distracted.'

'It's nothing,' I said hurriedly, flashing her a reassuring grin. 'I was just thinking over some stuff, but it's nothing to worry about.'

She smiled naively and returned her attention back to the streets we were zooming past. I tried to push my concerns to the back of my head – her appearance was a good omen, and nothing could convince me otherwise.

Chapter 8

'Is this where you live?'

I had pulled up to the pavement next to my house and Osiris was surveying everything out of the window with the same look of awe that she'd had all the way there. Her eyes had been practically bulging at all the sights she was taking in and I couldn't help but laugh at the excitement she was having towards it all.

'Yeah,' I answered. 'You want to go inside?'

She almost squealed. 'Yes, please!'

Chuckling to myself, I got out of the car and took from the back seat the wheelchair which I had folded up and put there. I then brought it round to her side and lifted her into it. Presumably because of the rain, there wasn't anyone in sight – not even somebody rushing into the shop parallel to my house. I considered this a blessing as I didn't know how I would explain the random girl in a hospital gown who I was wheeling into my home.

We were almost at the door when Matt stepped out, wearing a raincoat with the hood up. His expression turned to curiosity when he looked from me to Osiris.

'What's going on?' he asked.

'This is my... friend,' I said, trying to fabricate a lie quickly. 'She's been in hospital and I said she could stay for a few days... you know, until she recovers. I hope that's okay by you.'

Osiris smiled at him. 'Hi, I'm Osiris.'

'Nice to meet you, I'm Matt,' he said, before looking back at me. 'It's no problem with me if she stays. I'm going to the match then I'll be staying out to have a few pints so, err, you'll have the house to yourself for a few hours.'

He winked then strolled off.

I knew what he must have been thinking. I would try to clarify everything to him later, though I didn't know exactly what I'd say. Until then, my main priority was getting Osiris into the warmth of the house and hearing her story on becoming human.

I succeeded in steering her inside and she let out an audible gasp at the living room.

'This is incredible,' she said, before reaching out for an ornament on one of the tables. It was a souvenir I'd picked up during a trip to Spain with my family years ago; a glass orb with two dolphins inside encased with a liquid giving the effect of them swimming in the sea. 'How did you make this?'

'I didn't. I just bought it.'

'It's beautiful.'

Suddenly, Osiris's stomach began to growl and her eyes narrowed in suspicion, then studied me with terror.

'You must be hungry,' I said. 'When humans need food, our bodies tell us by making noises like that and they stop when you eat something. It's no wonder it's happening for you, I heard one of the nurses at the hospital say that you were refusing to eat.'

'I didn't want to accept anything they gave me,' she admitted. 'I've never eaten food from land before and I was unsure as to how to approach it.'

'I'll sort something out in a minute. Until then, I'll get you onto the couch so we can talk some more.' I again lifted her up, noting to myself that it was a good job I went to the gym regularly. 'I want to make you comfortable. It must be hard to have changed... well, *species*.'

Osiris settled onto the couch and I lifted her feet onto a pillow. She looked down at them then back at me. 'I suppose so. It was frightening at first, and I very nearly came close to regretting it with the pain. But it feels right. I've never felt like that before.'

At that point, my phone began ringing and Osiris stared as I pulled it out of my pocket and grimaced at the sight of Amber's name flashing up on the screen.

'What is that?' she asked.

'It's something that allows me to talk to other people. I don't know what she wants but I better answer it or she'll get annoyed.' I tapped the screen and put the phone to my ear. 'Hello?'

'Why did you leave so suddenly?' Amber demanded, with no hint of any standard greeting. This was something that I'd grown to expect from her. 'Our dad's injured and in hospital, for Christ's sake.'

'Yeah, and I came to visit him. Sorry I didn't stay longer, maybe if another of my siblings gets engaged then I'll be told about it straight away. You know, before it becomes common knowledge!'

'Stop acting like a child,' she spat. 'Honestly, Luke, I wish you'd sort yourself out. You know what your problem is? You've been alone far too long, and it isn't healthy. Look at me, I've been with Noel for a good few years now and it's done me the world of good because it doesn't give me enough time to think things over too much in my head. Matt and Val aren't good influences on you either, so you could start by associating with classier people.'

I could feel myself filling with rage. It was so bloody typical of my sister to make her mouth go on the faults of everyone else's life and how they can improve it, whilst she remained oblivious towards her own imperfections. This had always been the case and so it didn't come as a surprise. I'd endured her endless lectures on the right way to live life ever since I was born.

'Have you heard yourself?' I barked. 'How can you criticise them when you're no prize, either? This must be why all your friends are never around when I see you and *I'm* the one with too much time on my hands? At least I've got a social life, Amber!'

'There's no need to go on at me like that.' There was a distinct tremble in her voice, which was a good indicator that things weren't going her way and she was irritated.

'There is when you ring me purely to pick a fight. Jesus, I can't remember the last time you phoned just to see how I was or to catch up.' I distracted myself by looking around the room and my eyes landed on Osiris, who looked confounded. 'Look, I'm a little busy right now. Can your bloated sense of entitlement take a break? I really have to go.'

I could practically hear her eyes rolling as she said, 'I don't know why I bothered ringing you; I knew you wouldn't care about what I had to say.'

'You were right, I don't care.' And, with that, I hung up.

'Who was that?' Osiris asked.

'My sister,' I replied, stuffing the phone back in my pocket. 'She gets into a mood over anything and I guess as her little brother I bear the brunt of that anger. Sorry you had to hear that. I hope it didn't frighten you.'

'It's alright, I've never gotten on with my sisters either,' she said.

This statement took me by surprise. I had been so focused on thinking about Osiris as an individual that I'd never given a single thought about her family, but of course she must have had one. It was this that helped me calm down and I sat on the spare armchair.

'You have sisters?' I asked, hoping to get a discussion started.

'Three,' she said. 'And four brothers. I've never been close to any of them, though. I was always alone. None of them really understood me.'

'What's it like under the sea?'

'Boring,' she said, looking depressed at the mere prospect of thinking about it. 'Nothing but rules and endless swimming. It was never where I wanted to be. I suppose my detachment from it all made my decision a lot more straightforward.'

'Decision?' I said, narrowing my brow.

'To become human,' she clarified.

'Oh yeah.' I laughed at my momentary folly. 'How exactly did you manage that?'

She opened her mouth to answer when the words were drowned out by a loud knocking at the front door, which caused her to jump.

'Who's that?'

I checked the time. 'It'll probably be Val.'

I leapt to my feet and rushed to the door. Val was indeed stood there, holding a pizza box.

'Anyone order a large meat feast?' she giggled.

'Brilliant,' I said. 'Come in, you need to see this.'

She looked puzzled for a moment, but followed me into the living room regardless.

'Hello,' she said as she entered, eyeing Osiris with perplexity. 'Luke, who is this?'

'Val, this is Osiris.'

'The, err, the...'

'Mermaid,' I finished for her. 'Only she isn't anymore because, well, she was just about to explain that, actually. Osiris, this is Val – one of my best friends in the whole world.'

Osiris waved. 'Nice to meet you.'

Val was looking from one of us to the other, her eyebrows raised. I knew that she had believed me when I told her that I had met a mermaid, but I also understood her confusion at the fact that I was claiming she was now lying on my couch with a pair of legs.

'It sounds insane,' I said, taking my seat back down on the armchair and signalling her to do the same. 'Trust me, I know it does. But this is her and she's now a human. Did hear the news this morning about the woman washing up on the beach? It was her.'

Val lowered herself into the seat and put the pizza box down on the coffee table.

'It's true,' Osiris said.

'How did you become human?' Val asked her.

'That's something I'd like to know,' I said, facing Osiris. 'Do you have the power to change back and forth at will?'

'No, nothing like that,' Osiris said. 'Actually, it's quite a long story.'

'Why don't we move into the kitchen?' I suggested. 'Then you could tell us at the table while we eat the pizza.'

'Pizza?' Osiris questioned.

'It's food,' Val explained. 'I brought it with me.' She tapped the box. 'Are you hungry? Have you had anything to eat since you washed up?'

Osiris shook her head. 'No, I didn't eat at the hospital because I was too nervous. I've never eaten land food before.'

'What do you live on in the sea?' Val asked.

'Mostly seaweed and algae, but whatever plant life we can find really.'

'Sounds like actual solid food will be a completely new experience,' I said. 'I'm assuming you have a normal human metabolism now, so you'll have to try it at some point, but I'd rather you try something a bit safer to start off with.'

'Look,' Val said, viewing Osiris with concern, 'you're still in a hospital gown and it appears like you've been through hell. How about I go back home and fetch some spare clothes, then I could get you in the bath and help you put them on. Luke, you can warm up a can of soup or something, and then we'll sit down and listen to her story.'

'That sounds like a good plan,' I agreed. The fact that Osiris hadn't bathed and had no clothes hadn't occurred to me until that moment, but it made sense to address the problem now. 'I'll start running a bath. Are you okay with that Osiris?'

'Sure, but I don't actually know what a bath is.'

'It's to keep clean,' Val said, gently. 'It's something humans should do fairly regularly. You have a bath or a shower where you wash yourself in water and soap.'

Osiris nodded. 'Oh, okay then. Well, if it's a necessity, then it's fine by me.'

I smiled at Val and she returned it. I could see in her eyes that she was experiencing the same feeling of euphoria as me and was greatly anticipating learning all about what we would have considered at one point to be impossible.

'Right,' she said, getting to her feet. 'Luke, get that bath started – I'll be right back.'

Chapter 9

I stood in the kitchen, watching the microwave where the soup was now getting heated in preparation for Val and Osiris returning downstairs.

It had been just over half an hour since they'd gone upstairs. Val displayed surprising upper body strength and lifted Osiris with as much ease as I had done. She'd come back from her house with a pile of clothes for her that she had gotten from Alice's wardrobe – which I assumed was because they were a lot more conservative than her own.

Usually, Val and I would spend nights together drinking, though I suspected it would be unwise to allow Osiris to consume alcohol considering she had only recently become a human. Instead, I placed three glasses on the table and filled them with water. It wasn't like we wanted to get drunk when Osiris would be describing the exact process of becoming human. I wanted to remember every single detail.

There was a small cough behind me and I turned to see Val stood in the doorway. She had taken off her jacket, revealing a vest that showed off the sleeve of colourful tattoos consisting of feathers and swirls she sported on her left arm.

'Osiris is in the bath,' she said. 'I told her I just needed to come and talk to you, then I'd go up and help her get dressed. She says that she's starting to get a bit of feeling in her legs.'

'Great,' I said. 'So, what did you need to talk to me about?'

She pulled out one of the chairs at the table and sat down. 'This is all happening so fast, it's unbelievable. I mean, I believed you about meeting a mermaid – I really did – but seeing her in the flesh was a lot to take in.'

'How do you think I felt? I only went to her ward to be nosy when I was visiting my dad, I didn't expect for the woman to be her!'

'So, it was only by chance that you met her again?'

'Yep,' I said. 'Matt mentioned that someone had been found this morning on the beach and taken to the hospital, so when I heard a couple of nurses talking about her whilst I was there, I thought I'd go have a snoop around. Lo and behold, it was Osiris.'

'Hmm...'

'What?' I asked, sharply.

She appeared to be thinking things over in her head and vaguely responded, 'Seems almost like... well, fate. The person to find her was the same one who saw her on the beach.'

'When you put it like that, I suppose it does seem like it was meant to be.'

The words of Madame Malina suddenly came into my head: *'Perhaps fate will give you a helping hand.'* Was this what she was referring to?

'Good job it was you that found her and not that woman who you went to see a few days ago,' Val said.

I laughed at this last comment. 'Jodie? Yeah, I don't want her finding out about Osiris. Though now that she's human – and not some mystery from the deep – I guess we don't have to worry about Jodie having an interest in her.'

'But there'll be others,' Val pointed out. 'The police for example. I'm guessing you didn't discharge her from the hospital properly and she has no ID?' When I didn't reply, she continued, 'This will all look very suspicious, Luke, and they will find you quite easily as the hospital will have you on camera.' I opened my mouth to respond, but she quickly added, 'Don't worry, though, I can help you out there. I know a guy who can get you a fake passport and stuff. All I need is a photo of her to give to him and I'll go as soon as we finish up here. Where's Matt, anyway?'

'At the match,' I said. 'He said he was going to stay out afterwards, which means we won't be interrupted. And thanks for sorting everything out, you're a life saver.'

She smirked and stood up. 'Don't worry about it. I'm going to go get her out and dressed.'

Whilst Val went to sort out Osiris, I dished the soup into a bowl and put it on the table. I then helped myself to a slice of pizza before sitting down and pulling out my phone to pass the time.

After about ten minutes, Val tapped gently on the door.

'Are you ready?' she asked.

I nodded and she stood aside, revealing Osiris, who got up from her wheelchair and hobbled a short distance, before leaning on the door frame for support. She was dressed in a rose-patterned cardigan over a plain shirt and completed with a pleated skirt. Her legs and feet remained bare, but it suited the ensemble well. Her tousled platinum hair was now loosely curled into ringlets and it truly highlighted her natural beauty.

'How do I look?' Osiris hesitantly asked.

'Amazing,' I replied, without even having to think.

She blushed slightly and Val helped her back into the wheelchair before pushing her towards the table.

'This smells incredible,' Osiris said, her eyes visibly sparkling at the sight of food.

'Hopefully it will taste as good,' I said, handing her a spoon. 'Careful, it's a bit hot.'

She lifted the cutlery to her mouth and took a hesitant sip. We waited in anticipation for her to react and she thankfully broke into a massive grin.

'That's amazing,' she declared, wiping some from her lips.

'Something like tomato soup should be easy on your stomach,' Val told her. 'Have a drink – you need to have a lot of liquid to survive. Though having been a mermaid, I guess you're used to that.'

Osiris giggled and took a mouthful from her glass of water.

'Now can you tell us the story of how you managed to, you know, become a human?' I asked. I was very anxious to hear the story and didn't want any further delay.

Osiris looked a little uneasy, but took a deep breath and managed relaxed slightly. 'I was transformed after drinking a potion made by a very powerful sorcerer.'

Val and I exchanged looks then both asked, 'What sorcerer?'

'Mermaids aren't the only secret that the ocean has to offer,' she said. 'Out of the entire population on this Earth, humans seem to be the most blind when it comes to seeing what is right in front of them. Magic does exist and it is a very real force of nature. Hundreds of years ago, though, things began to change. Don't ask what happened exactly, because I obviously wasn't alive back then and what I know comes from hazy second-hand stories told to me by others over time. All I know is that mankind began to slowly forget that magic existed and merfolk, along with others, hid away to avoid them. They had already bore witness to the cruelties they could inflict and the sense of power people seemed to desire.'

'So, humans and mermaids used to co-exist?' I said.

'Sort of. Mermaids were still confined to the ocean, but they used to regularly come to the surface apparently and interact with humans. That hasn't happened for centuries, though, which is why I was shocked when you knew what I was, Luke. I thought that stories of us would have long-since died away.'

'Like we were saying on the beach, though,' I said, 'it's possible that other mermaids have been sneaking above water for years, which is why legends of them have prevailed.'

'Hang on,' Val interrupted, 'don't the mermaids we hear about in mythical stories all lure sailors to their death? I'm sure that in some cultures they're an omen of bad luck or something.'

Osiris looked rather sheepish. 'That could be true, I don't know. I suppose some of them are bad like that.'

'Humans can be just as bloodthirsty,' I pointed out. 'Please, Osiris, go on.' The constant intermissions were building up far too much suspense for my liking and I just really wanted her to get to the part where she turned from being a mermaid.

'Well,' she went on, 'when I said that other beings hid as well as merfolk, I meant that there are a lot. I never really encountered many of them, but I heard about them for as long as I can remember. A lot of those that are hidden are capable of extraordinary magic. I knew that to get what I'd always wanted, they were the ones who I needed to talk to.'

'You always wanted to be human?' Val said.

'Yes. All my life I have felt... wrong, but I never knew exactly why until I started coming to the surface. Seeing humans and their world made me feel at home and meeting you that day, Luke, made me realise that I wanted a life like that, too.'

I was touched by her honesty. 'So, where exactly did you go when you made the decision to have that life?'

'After talking to you that day, I went straight to where the most powerful beings were last rumoured to be living. They would be the only ones who would be able to help me – and it was in the deepest, darkest part of the ocean where I finally found them.'

She went silent for a short while, so I prompted her by saying, 'And they gave you a potion?'

'No,' she said, eventually. 'Not the ones I spoke to at first. They didn't want to be seen and instead spoke to me from the shadows. They said that they would not use that kind of magic and certainly not to aid a mermaid. However, they told me of someone who would and what I could do to find him.'

'Who was it?' Val asked.

'They did not dare speak his name for it apparently heralds a powerful curse. They informed me of where he lived, in a cavern not far from where they were. I had to pass unthinkable evil to get there, but I was determined. In the end, I entered his... home, you could call it, and, although I was more frightened than any other time in my life, I asked him for help in turning me into a human.'

'Did you see him?' I said. 'The person in the cavern, did you see what he looked like?'

'Yes,' she replied. 'He was sort of... human, and yet not quite.'

'And he helped you?' Val said. 'I mean, you're human now.'

'Yes, he did help me. I explained my situation to him and I think he saw how genuine I was about ceasing existence as a mermaid. He quickly crafted a potion and encased it inside a small glass bottle.'

'He made it – just like that?' I asked. 'There was no price or anything?'

This seemed to be the most difficult part for her as she was now avoiding our eyes and staring intently down at her now-empty plate. 'Not a price... as such. Well, maybe it was. He agreed to turn me into a human.... but gave me a warning. You see, merfolk are meant to live for a very long time. *Centuries*, even. I would be dramatically sacrificing my life span which, in turn, would be given to him. That was the payment if anything.'

It took me a moment to recover from this before I asked, 'Then what happened?'

'I was instructed to swim to land and drink the potion, but not to do so lightly, for the process was irreversible. Once I was human, I would never be allowed to return to my family again.'

Val gaped at this last part. 'And you chose to still become human?'

'I had to,' Osiris said. 'I couldn't live that life anymore and I knew my family would never understand that. When I left with the potion, I swam for days trying to find where I had met you Luke. You were the only human I'd ever spoken to and I could never have imagined such kindness. If I was to become a human, then I knew that I needed to be in your company.'

I felt a rush of emotion, flattered by her words. 'So, you took the potion on the beach?'

'Yes, once I was sure I was at the right place. I just hoped I'd be able to find you. It was a great risk, I know, but I'd taken so many up to that point that I figured I may as well continue.'

'But you passed out, didn't you? You were found on the beach the next day,' I said.

Osiris shuddered. 'Yes. The drink was foul and I was in great pain for a while without being able to scream for help. I could feel my entire body changing, though I blacked out shortly afterwards. When I woke up, I was in a bed with loads of humans around. Some began questioning me and I was scared.'

Her hand sat limply on the table and I gave it a squeeze. 'It's alright now. I found you.'

'Thank you,' she whispered.

Val and I spent the next few minutes eating more pizza, though I don't think either of us were particularly hungry. We kept glancing at one another, both silently marvelling at the sheer astonishing proceedings that had occurred. Osiris seemed to be going through the motions, the events that led her to gain legs taking their toll on her mind.

When we had eaten and drank as much as we could, I walked Val to the front door.

'Thanks for everything,' I said. 'It's nice not to be keeping all of this a secret.'

'Don't mention it,' she said. 'Just give me a few hours and I'll come back with the fake documents.'

'Can you get them that fast?'

She rolled her eyes. 'Do you really doubt me? Look, before I turned eighteen, I had ID to get us drink with, remember? I can get them a lot quicker than most other people. After I got her dressed, I took a photo of her face and that's all this guy will need. Once her alias is set, we should be able to blag our way through any questions the police will have. When I get back, we'll think of an alibi for why she was on that beach and why you snuck her out of the hospital without permission.'

'You're remarkable, you are,' I said.

'I know,' she said, opening the door. 'Where would you be without me?'

Chapter 10

Early the next morning, I decided to make Osiris breakfast. Like with the soup the night before, I knew I needed to give her something easy to start the day with. Luckily, I managed to find some porridge at the back of the cupboard which I knew would be perfect.

As I prepared it, she sat watching me and we talked as if we had known each other our entire lives and the conversation flowed with unbelievable ease. I explained to her exactly what I was doing in order to make the oats edible and why it was a good choice for starting the day with.

'This smells nice,' she said, as I placed the bowl in front of her. 'Just like the soup did.' She followed this by taking an almighty spoonful. 'It tastes just as good, too!' she exclaimed, shovelling as much of it into her mouth as possible.

'Calm down,' I laughed. 'You'll end up with a stomach-ache.'

She finished her food and looked up at me. 'I could definitely get used to having that every morning. I can't wait to try all the different foods you have to offer.'

I placed the bowl in the sink and then assisted her into the living room.

'I'll get you a glass of water to wash your breakfast down with,' I said. 'We can decide on something to watch after that. If you're going to be human, then you must get used to the telly. There's a lot to choose from.'

I walked back into the kitchen and opened the cupboard. I was about to reach for a glass when there was a loud knock at the door. I jumped when it happened, but tried to remain calm and stick to the plan. I had held out hope that they wouldn't be able to track us down, yet I knew that they would. The police couldn't possibly be incompetent enough not to be able to identify me quickly, especially with the footage of my face. Before this, I had never been in any form of bother with the authorities, so the experience was horrifying for me. I knew that I had to remain strong for Osiris's sake, for it must have been just as bad (if not worse) for her.

I made my way through the living room where she was sat, also looking terrified. She had been reciting what she would say all night and had been intermittently doing so since waking up. Her face looked even paler than normal and there was a notable absence of enthusiasm in it, which was now replaced with nothing but fear.

'What's going on?' Matt grumbled sleepily, descending the staircase in nothing but his boxer-shorts. He hadn't gotten home by the time we went to bed the night before, so I was forced to leave him a note telling him that the police could be coming by to ask questions. I wasn't sure if he had read it or not, but that was irrelevant now.

I pressed a finger to my lips and opened the door.

Two police officers were stood. Though both male, they were visibly opposites of each other. One was quite young with a smooth face and cropped dark hair, whilst the other one was middle-aged with thin, receding hair and tired eyes. The older one stood in front and it was clear that he was the one in charge. He was looking at me as though he suspected me of murder.

'Good morning,' he said, a distinct gruffness in his voice. 'May we come in?'

I hesitated for a second, then nodded. 'Yes, of course.'

'I'm PC Maguire and this is PC Thomas. We're here about the taking of a young woman from hospital who has yet to be identified.' His gaze lingered on Osiris before returning to me. 'Are you Luke Holden?'

I swallowed and replied, my voice slightly cracked, 'Yes.'

'Are you aware, Mr. Holden, that you have been identified on CCTV escorting said woman from the care of the hospital?'

'Yeah, well I did, but –'

'And are you also aware that she was under investigation by police for being the presumed victim of a crime?'

'Err, well –'

'I asked him to,' Osiris said, suddenly.

Both officers turned to look at her. The youngest one, PC Thomas, looked surprised and repeated, 'You asked him to?'

She nodded, more confident this time. 'Yes, I did. I wasn't the victim of an attack. I'd went to the beach the night before I was found because I was feeling depressed and thought some skinny dipping might cheer me up. You know, let my hair down a bit. I guess I lost track of time and fell asleep. I was embarrassed that people found me the next day. Luke saw me by chance at the hospital when he was visiting his dad and I decided I wanted to be discharged. Sorry I didn't do it properly, that was at my insistence, not his.'

PC Maguire scowled. 'Skinny dipping? That kind of activity can be considered a form of indecent exposure. Take that as a warning, young lady.'

'I understand,' she replied, even though I knew she didn't have a clue what any of that meant. I gave her a wink for encouragement.

'Now,' he said, stepping forward, 'do you have identification or not?'

'Yes,' she said, reaching into a bag on the floor.

Val had returned the night before with a passport, a birth certificate, a National Insurance Card and a provisional driving license. I was impressed by how authentic they looked and thanked her wholeheartedly for being able to get a hold of such genuine-looking fake documents. We both then sat with Osiris and made sure she knew exactly what to say if the authorities did ask questions.

The officer took the phoney passport and read before passing it to his colleague who said, 'Osiris Jenkins?'

'That's me,' she lied.

'Why didn't you just tell the hospital staff that when you woke up there? It was very bad practice to withhold that information.'

'I was really ashamed about what happened and didn't want my name associated with it.'

'You don't get to decide that,' PC Thomas said, handing the passport back to her.

'You've acted very irresponsibly, Miss. Jenkins,' PC Maguire said. 'And you're not innocent in this, either,' he added, glaring at me. 'But as you've explained the situation and you aren't a repeat offender, we'll let you off.'

'Thanks,' was all I could think of saying.

They headed towards the door. PC Maguire stopped short and turned back to us.

'I don't want a repeat of this behaviour,' PC Maguire warned. 'Any more out of either of you and we'll be forced to take more serious action.'

We both nodded and they stepped out, closing the door behind them with a snap.

'Christ, you've been lucky,' Matt said, stifling a yawn. 'What's for breakfast?'

'I was going to make myself a couple of bacon sandwiches if you want some,' I said, resting my head against the door in relief. 'I'll be through in a minute to start them.'

He appeared satisfied and walked away into the kitchen.

I looked over at Osiris and her eyes met with mine. The glimmer in them sent a stream of warmth through me.

'Is everything going to be okay now?' she asked. 'They won't come back, will they?'

'Everything is going to be fine,' I said. 'We answered all their questions and, as long as we stay out of trouble, they'll never bother us again. I promise.'

I wheeled her into the kitchen so we could chat as I cooked.

That morning, Osiris had been able to stand up for a few seconds, but she was still not strong enough to manage on her own, so I had decided that I would go out later and look for some crutches. I was pleasantly surprised at the progress she was making, and I was confident that she'd be walking without the need for assistance by at least the following week – an amazing achievement considering she had only recently gotten legs. I had been worried that she may never be able to properly use them, perhaps it being an unspoken side-effect of the transformation process, but luckily that wasn't the case.

Matt sat at the table, his hands against his head as if was suffering from a bad hangover, which he probably was. 'I read your note,' he said, his eyes peeking out from behind his fingers. 'Why exactly did you take this girl from the hospital?'

'She's an old friend,' I said, scaring myself at how easy it was for me to lie. 'When I saw her at the hospital, she explained the whole skinny-dipping incident and I got her out of there. Sorry I didn't tell you sooner, but you were going out so there wasn't any time and I knew the police would most likely be coming today so I quickly wrote the note.'

He dropped his hands away from his face. 'It's fine,' he said, accepting the sandwich that I passed to him. 'But next time you break some chick out of the hospital, make sure it's not when I'll be suffering from a major hangover because that knocking on the door was too much. Anyway, I'm going to take this upstairs – put me down for a Full English tomorrow.'

'Yeah right,' I said. 'Tomorrow should be your turn.'

He gave me the finger as he left the kitchen.

I was just plating up my food when my phone started to ring. A panicky voice spoke straight away when I answered. 'Have the police been?'

'Yeah, they have, but –'

'How did it go?' Val cried. 'Did you tell them everything as we agreed? How did Osiris do with remembering the story? And were the documents convincing enough for them, because if they weren't –'

'Val, relax,' I said, grinning to myself. 'Everything went smoothly. They said that we acted irresponsibly but, because we've never done anything illegal before, they would overlook it and just give us each a warning.'

This caused Val to snigger. 'That's because they don't know about the weed you used to smoke with me when we were teenagers.'

'Very funny,' I replied. 'Anyway, all that fake stuff was great. They didn't question them at all. I owe you so much.'

'Are you kidding?' she said. 'Thanks to you, I know that there is such a thing as freaking *magic*. I owe you so much more.'

'Don't mention it. What are your plans for today, anyway?'

'Alice wants me to go to some museum opening with her,' she groaned. 'Kind of seems pointless when you've just had a conversation with a former mermaid who made a deal with some powerful sorcerer, you know? But I guess I'll have to go through with it if I want to get lucky tonight.'

'Have fun,' I smirked. 'Speak to you, later.'

I hung up and Osiris said, 'I know this might sound really greedy, but can I have another bowl of porridge? Your food is so much better than what we have in the sea.'

Happy with how pleased she was, I began preparing her more food at once.

Afterwards, I watched her eating it and thought about how incredibly fortunate we had been so far and the extreme lengths we had gone to in order to assure that we would be safe. Never had such a thing happened to me, but I knew that I would do it all over again in a heartbeat. I knew that the hard part was over now, and I felt nothing but joy at the prospect of how I would be spending my next few weeks.

Before this had happened, I would normally focus on my job or arrange more parties with Matt and Val in order to distract myself from painful memories and the overall boredom I felt with life. However, none of that was a priority for me anymore. These were things that I would have worried about in the past. Now, I would be doing something much more enriching – showing someone the world that they had always dreamed about.

Just as I was thinking over what an extraordinary opportunity I was being given, the landline phone started to ring. It was never usually anything important when someone used that number to contact us, but with everything going on with my dad I decided to answer it just in case. Excusing myself from the table, I jogged through to the living room and picked it up.

'Hello?'

'Who is this?' the person on the other end asked. I immediately thought it was a man, but it was also clear that they were using some sort of voice changer, so I was unsure.

'Luke,' I replied. 'Who is this?'

He didn't answer straight away, and I almost put the phone down when he said, 'You can consider me a friend.'

'Err, okay, and why would I do that?'

'Because I only have your best interests in mind,' he said.

'Who are you?'

'I told you,' he said, breathing heavier, 'I'm a friend. I need to warn you.'

I thought that it must be a joke. 'Warn me about what?'

'You need to be careful. When you interact with Jodie Grayson, you never truly leave her radar. If she thinks you have something she wants, she won't give up until she has it.'

'What the hell are you talking about?'

The person hung up.

I tried dialling the number back, but they had apparently withheld it. I was now left with nothing more than a mysterious warning that put me in even more unease.

I decided to push the incident to the back of my mind because it was the last thing I needed on top of everything else that was going on. Yet, as I returned to the kitchen, I couldn't help but wonder who it could have been on the phone. One thought I had was that maybe Jodie herself had arranged someone to call me in order to make herself appear more threatening, but what would she get out of that? I was almost certain that she didn't know about Osiris and there'd be no other reason for her to set up the phone call. And even if she did suspect something from my initial encounter with her, there was no way she could possibly know that a mermaid I'd spoken to was now human.

The niggling question kept running through my mind: if it wasn't Jodie, then who was it?

Part 2

Chapter 11

The next week passed without much incident. I managed to get hold of some crutches from my neighbour, who had bought some when her leg was broken and decided to hold onto them in case of any future injury. These helped Osiris a lot as her legs became stronger and she was able to stand for longer periods of time. It turned out that her ability to walk improved spectacularly within only a few days. Every night, I helped her up the stairs and into the guest bedroom, then doing the same with her the next morning. However, she was soon able to do so by herself and didn't need the crutched as much.

Val came over regularly to check on Osiris's progress and to lend her more clothes, which she assured me hadn't aroused any suspicion from Alice. It seemed that she had accumulated so many generic shirts and trousers that she failed to notice when they began to vanish from her wardrobe. I guaranteed Val that this arrangement would only be temporary as I intended to take Osiris shopping as soon as she could walk confidently, though she brushed off my concerns, telling me that it was no inconvenience to her.

In the meantime, Osiris was constantly asking me questions regarding everyday human life. She frequently joined me in watching television and was always wondering out loud about things that I would take for granted, but which needed explaining to her. Although we had not been able to go outside due to a mixture of bad weather and her legs, she had nonetheless found countless items around the house to study and enquire about. It was quite amusing to watch her go from analysing a murder scene in a documentary (where she made comparisons with shark attacks) to marvelling over the workings of a teapot.
*

One morning, we were sat in the garden because the weather had taken a surprising upturn. The sun was blazing down upon us and so I made sure to tell her the importance of sun lotion and to never look at the sun directly.

I prepared a few slices of buttered toast for us and we sat eating them with a cup of tea on a pair of deckchairs. These were normally used by me and Matt during the summer months when would sunbathe, even though most of the time we would burn instead of tan.

'Luke,' Osiris said, finishing her food and licking the remaining crumbs off her fingers, 'can I ask you something?'

'Of course you can. You always do anyway,' I grinned.

She laughed then said, 'It's just... you never talk about your family, how come?'

I had been waiting for her to ask me something like this. From the moment she mentioned having brothers and sisters, I suspected that I would eventually be questioned about mine. I had briefly mentioned my sister when we first arrived home from the hospital, but I hadn't spoken about her since and I hadn't mentioned my brother at all. It felt unfair to withhold this information from her when she had been upfront with me on how exactly she had become human, yet at the same time it was a big step because it wasn't a subject that I usually discussed with anyone.

'There's a lot of bad blood there,' I admitted.

'What does that mean?'

Her naivety towards the phrase made me warm inside, despite the topic of conversation, as I remembered how new she was to everything around her. 'It means that there are still some... not-so-good feelings between me and certain members of my family. I get on well with my dad – *really* well, in fact – but others, my brother and sister in particular, not so much. There's been a lot of stuff said over the years that make things difficult.'

There was a pause afterwards in which Osiris digested what she had just heard, and I took this opportunity to polish off the rest of my toast and have a sip of tea.

'Can I ask what happened?' she said, timidly.

I smiled at her reassuringly. 'It's fine. I guess it's natural for you to want to know more about me, just like me and Val wanted to know more about you the other night. What you need to understand, though, is that I'm going to be bias towards a lot of the events. If you were to ask other members of my family the same questions, then they might have completely different answers for you. That's life, I suppose.'

Osiris reached over slowly and squeezed my knee, which shocked me slightly in that it was obviously meant as a caring gesture as opposed to the more sexually suggestive meaning it would normally carry. 'Your side of the story is the only one I'm interested in,' she said. 'From the very first moment we spoke, Luke, I heard sincerity in your voice. That's the reason I knew it was the right decision to become a part of mankind. You helped me finally realise the path that my life had to take, so I will always believe what you say.'

There was a small catch in my throat at these words and I remained quiet for several minutes before I said, 'If we're going to be spending a lot of time together from now on, then it's only right that you know my life story.'

'You don't have to if it's going to make you feel too uncomfortable,' she said, quickly.

'Don't be daft, it's not like I haven't been asked it before. Val and Matt have both commented on my lack of, well, *affection* for my siblings. You were bound to ask about it sooner or later.'

'As long as you're sure,' she said. 'I was just curious because you seem so close to your friends and yet never mention your family. Like I said, I didn't get on with mine either, so I'll understand if you feel distant from them.'

'Distant, that's a good word to describe it,' I said. 'I've always felt distant.'

'Why though?' she asked.

'Well, there's quite an age gap between us. When my parents first got together, they were married within six months and my brother was born not long after that. Just under two years later, they found out that they were expecting my sister. So, in no time at all, the family they'd always wanted was formed. My parents had a little boy and a little girl; they had a nice house and good jobs. I guess life for them was perfect.'

It felt rather odd to be saying this out loud considering I tried my best not speak of it. Osiris was watching me with anticipation as it was clear that there was more to my story. I finished my tea and continued.

'About ten years later, my parents went to the wedding of one of their friends and spent the night... doing what humans do to reproduce. Err... well, nine months later, I was born.'

'But that's good, isn't it?' Osiris said. 'I thought they'd have liked having another child.'

'I think it came as a bit of a shock to them at first,' I said. 'They already had two children and they'd only planned on having them. It took them a while to get their heads around having a baby in the house again.'

'They eventually got used to the idea though?'

'Yeah, they did,' I said, though doubt began to creep in. 'Well, my dad says they did. I don't know, maybe they were always anxious about it, but I guess that's normal because babies cost a lot of money. Anyway, they were going to have me and I was going to be their new little kid.'

'So, what happened?' Osiris asked, cautiously. I could tell from her expression that she knew the topic was sensitive for me.

I exhaled slowly and looked up at the sky to distract myself away from her eyes, then said, 'My mam died giving birth to me.'

A silence hung in the air. I glanced at Osiris to see that she now had her head bowed and looked extremely uncomfortable. I reached over and touched her shoulder to let her know that I was fine to go on talking. She looked at me and I nodded, which caused her to give me a small smile in return.

'I think that's what caused the rift between me and my siblings,' I continued. 'They never said anything, but I think they held me responsible for killing their mam.'

'It wasn't your fault though,' she protested. 'You were a baby.'

'I know, but I think they felt like if she hadn't gotten pregnant with me then she never would have died. Don't get me wrong, they've never actually said anything... but I could always tell from the way they treated me that there was a definite tension there.'

'You said that you get on really well with your dad?'

'Yeah, I do. I think he had the opposite reaction to my brother and sister. With my mam dead, he pretty much had to take on the role of both parents and once Phillip and Amber moved out, it was just me and him. It was like I was the last part of his wife left, so he took me being alive as a good thing and didn't resent me.'

'So, you're close with your dad but not with your brother and sister,' Osiris said. 'That explains why you don't really talk about family a lot. Have you never tried to make it up with them? Maybe now that you are all older, things will be able to change.'

'I've thought about it... and tried loads of attempts that haven't worked. I guess my brother is too different from me for us to ever really get along and my sister, well, she's just a nasty person in general. I don't enjoy spending time with either of them. If they weren't family, I doubt I'd make any effort at all to keep in contact.'

'Your sister is a nasty person? I can't believe that. You're the nicest person I've ever met. Surely a member of your own family couldn't be so different from you.'

'Once you've met more people, I won't be the nicest,' I said.

Osiris looked slightly hurt by my remark. 'No matter how many more people I meet as a human, none of them have helped me as much as you have. I don't think many people would have taken the risk you did in rescuing me. Not only that, not a lot of them would have followed that by taking me in.'

'I was doing what I felt was right,' I replied.

'That's what makes you such a good person, Luke,' she said, beaming. 'And that's what makes me doubt that your sister can be the monster you portray her as. I'm sure some of your compassion must have rubbed off on her.'

'Trust me,' I laughed, 'you haven't met her yet, but when you do, you'll think she's just as bad as I describe.'

There was a slight pause, followed by Osiris saying, 'You mean you do intend for me to meet your family at some point?'

'I do. You need to remain in and around the house until you're fully able to walk, then I want to take you everywhere. We'll go shopping and eat out at restaurants and, yeah, meet my family. I was going to go over and see my dad today, but I think I'll wait and then we can both go see him together.'

'That sounds incredible,' she said. 'Thanks for everything. And, Luke, thanks for telling me about your family. I really appreciate that it was a hard thing to talk about.'

'Any time,' I said.

I stood up and took our plates and cups back inside, whilst she remained in the sunshine for a bit longer. It was true that my family was a difficult subject to broach with me, but I felt at that moment an immediate sense of relief. I was also pleased that Osiris was now able to understand me better. Just like with Val, I felt like I could tell her anything.

'Hang on,' Osiris suddenly blurted out as I returned to the garden. 'In your story you said that your parents had you by doing what humans do to reproduce.'

'Yes...'

'How exactly *do* humans reproduce?'

Again, her naivety of the world made me chuckle and I sat back down in the deckchair to explain something that I didn't think I'd have to until I had children.

Chapter 12

The next day, I awoke to find Osiris already downstairs and chatting brightly with Matt. Two bowls of cereal were in front of them. It was quite a surprising turn as she had not felt confident enough to walk a considerable distance without me up until this point. And yet there she was, striding around as though she'd been doing it her whole life.

'What's going on?' I asked, walking into the kitchen.

They both stopped talking and turned to face me.

'Osiris made us breakfast,' Matt said, abandoning his spoon completely and lifting the bowl up to his mouth in order to drain the remaining contents.

'I was up early watching the TV when Matt got up,' Osiris explained. 'You've done so much of the food preparation that I thought I'd try my hand at it. Don't worry, though, I made sure it was something that didn't involve the oven or anything.' She smiled nervously and then continued, 'Sit down, Luke, I'm going to pour you some.'

'Thanks,' I replied, taking a spare seat.

It was amazing to see her so confident walking around the kitchen. I realised at that moment that she was ready to face the outside world a lot sooner than I had anticipated.

Matt suddenly got to his feet and dropped his cutlery loudly into the sink. 'Right, I'm going to get ready then I'm out for the day.'

'Alright,' I said. 'Well, we're going to visit my dad so there's a chance we might be out when you get back.'

'No problem, mate. Let me know how he's doing, yeah?'

Matt left and I turned to see Osiris stood gaping at me, the bowl of cereal she was holding almost slipping out of her hand.

'Visit your dad?' she said. 'You mean... both of us?'

I grinned. 'Of course. You seem a natural at using those legs now.'

She passed me my breakfast and returned to her chair, smiling from ear to ear. 'I can't believe it. I'm going to be walking around outside, experiencing things like a real human.' Just as I was about to make a start on my food, she leaned forward and pulled me into a tight embrace. 'Thank you, Luke! Thank you, thank you, thank you!'

'Seriously, don't mention it,' I said. 'Anyway, what have you been talking to Matt about this morning?'

'Well, when he first got up, he had a girl with him. She left pretty much straight away, and I asked why she wasn't staying. Anyway, it turns out that what you told me about how humans make children – he does it all the time with random strangers! Though he says he's being seeing this one regularly. Emmie, I think she was called. I asked him why he has no children yet and he said it's because he's always safe.'

Osiris said this all very fast and it took me some time to get my head round it.

'Do you do the same?' she asked.

'Err, well, I have done in the past, but I don't feel as good about it as he does,' I admitted. 'Anyway, we best get ready to go visit my dad. Thanks for breakfast.'

I drank the last of the dregs and made a swift exit from the kitchen. For as much as we were now close, there were some things that I just did not wish to talk about with Osiris.

*

My dad lived at the other end of the village to me, meaning that I usually just walked over to his house, unless it was raining. However, despite the fine weather, I did not want to risk Osiris overdoing it when it came to exercise.

I called him shortly after breakfast saying that I would be paying him a visit that day, along with a friend of mine. Osiris was delighted and, as we made our way in the car, she was practically shaking with excitement. This in turn made me feel happier as well.

'Right, here we are,' I announced, pulling up outside.

His bungalow was detached from the others in the street. He had moved there for ease once his old age began taking affect – this was shortly after I'd left home to start living in the house I now occupied with Matt.

I walked around the car and opened the passenger door to help Osiris out. She did not need to lean on me for support anymore, but still held onto my elbow.

'I'm a little nervous,' she admitted.

'There's no need to be,' I said, putting my arm around her. 'I explained to him over the phone that you're a mate of mine. He's not going to bombard you with questions.'

This seemed to relax her somewhat as I gave a short knock on the door and opened it.

'Dad, we're here!' I called.

Inside, there wasn't a lot of room, but this was ideal considering that he lived by himself and was unable to get around a lot. Upon entering, there was a very small passageway for shoes and the like, then a door that lead to an open plan living area.

My dad was sat on the couch when we walked in, looking noticeably more vibrant than he had at the hospital. He smiled as I approached. I bent down and hugged him.

'Dad, this is Osiris,' I said, getting up and walking over to her.

She smiled and gave a small wave. 'Hi, Mr. Holden.'

'Please, call me Rory,' he said, attempting to straighten himself up with slight difficulty. 'It's nice to meet you, Osiris. Forgive me, but Luke's never mentioned you before.'

'That's not a surprise, I'm new here,' she said. She looked from him to me, and then back again. 'You know, you really do look like each other.'

'So I've been told,' I smirked, sitting down. I patted the space next to me.

She sat down, beaming as she did so, linking her hands together in her lap. 'You have a beautiful home, Rory. And you live in such a nice neighbourhood.'

'Well, *usually* a nice neighbourhood,' he corrected her.

'What are you talking about?' I asked. 'You get on well with everyone, don't you? I thought Maureen from next door was going to come over to check on things.'

He rearranged his cushion and replied, 'She is, but that's not what I mean.'

The worried look on his face concerned me. 'Dad, what's going on?'

'I didn't want to say anything,' he sighed. 'Amber said I was probably being paranoid.'

'I don't care what Amber said. What's got you so uneasy?'

'Two nights ago, I fell asleep here on the couch and when I woke up... when I woke up, I thought I saw someone looking at me through the window.'

'What did you do?' I asked.

'I tried to get up,' he said. 'It took me forever, though... you know, with my leg and everything. By the time I'd got to the window, I couldn't see anything. It was pitch-black, so maybe it was just a shadow or something.'

I walked over to the window at once and looked out. There were trees and a shed in the garden; I could see how anyone caught spying would be able to hide with ease.

'Did you report this to the police?'

'When I suggested that to Amber, she said it would be pointless,' he said. 'Maureen and Phillip agree with her. I've been under a lot of stress lately.'

'And that means you're imagining someone watching you?' I responded with disgust. I couldn't believe that everyone else would be so calm about such a happening. 'Sorry dad, but I think you should take it seriously. An injured man living alone is a perfect target for burglars.'

His look of apprehension changed to a forced smile as he said, 'Nothing's happened yet, so please don't worry. Maureen will be keeping a look out at night.'

I still wasn't convinced, and my mind flashed back to the strange phone call I had received on the morning the police had questioned us. I had a feeling that the two may somehow be connected, but, knowing that my persistence wouldn't help matters considering that everyone was brushing the incident off, I returned to my place beside Osiris.

'Could I please use the bathroom?' she asked.

'Of course,' my dad said. 'It's just through that door.'

Once she had left the room, my dad turned to me with a genuine smile that stretched from ear to ear. 'She's seems like a nice girl.'

I wasn't quite sure what to reply so I simply mumbled in agreement.

'Just a friend, is she?' he went on.

'Yes,' I said, firmly. It was clear what he was hinting at and it was not something that I wanted to encourage. For as long as I can remember, my dad had been suspicious of females whom I had introduced as friends only. Though, in fairness, a lot of them had in fact been a lot more than that. However, it was different with Osiris because I didn't want her to become the focus of such rumours.

My dad didn't seem convinced but said, 'Fair enough, son, if you say so. Can I just give you one bit of advice?'

'Go on then.'

He leaned over to me as much as his body would allow and said, 'If you have feelings for her, don't ruin it by being all…. brooding. I know you, Luke. You'll let her walk right out of the door instead of admitting that you like her.'

'Dad, things are different with her. I don't *like* her in that way. Believe me, we met under some pretty exceptional circumstances.'

My words weren't having any effect and he kept on smirking to himself. 'Sometimes, I know you better than you know yourself. True, I don't know how the two of you met or anything like that, but I know when you walked through that door, I saw a happy couple. And take it from me, she certainly has feelings for you.'

'What are you talking about?' I demanded.

Before he could reply, Osiris exited the bathroom. She sat down and immediately began gushing about the interior to my dad who happily began a conversation on how he went about decorating the house when he first bought it. I was barely listening and only took in select snippets every now and again for my dad's words were still echoing around in my head.

Did I have feelings for Osiris? There was no denying that she was pretty, anyone could see that. But she was extraordinarily kind and didn't seem to have a bad bone in her body. I watched her chatting away and felt an undeniable tug in my heart.

*

It was dark by the time I pulled up back home. Matt's car was parked in the small driveway and a flickering light from the television could be seen in the living room window, meaning there would be no privacy once inside, so I unbuckled my seat belt and faced Osiris, who hadn't stopped smiling all day.

'What's the matter?' she asked.

'Nothing,' I replied. 'It's just I wanted to ask you something.'

'That's funny,' she laughed. 'Usually it's me who has all the questions. What is it?'

'Well, I'm at work tomorrow and... the rest of the week too, but this weekend I was thinking we could go shopping.'

Her eyes lit up. 'You mean where we can buy clothes and things?'

'Exactly,' I said, happy that she seemed so enthusiastic. Then I reminded myself that this was to be expected when she had barely ventured outside the house. 'I thought we could make a day of it. You know, shop and then go for a meal. If you think you're ready for that, of course.'

'Yes!' she cried. 'I'm ready for it, really I am. It sounds like a lot of fun.'

'Great, I'll sort something out for then.'

We both exited the car and Osiris practically skipped to the front door, whilst I hung back and studied my reflection in the glass. With everything that had happened in the past few days, I hadn't been taking very good care of myself. Most of my time was spent worrying about other things – Osiris, my dad, my job – and I had again neglected my own well-being. That night, I decided I would trim my stubble, and then when I had time during the week, I would go to the barbers. Hopefully then I would feel better about my appearance.

I thought about our plans for the coming weekend. No matter what I could say to try and convince myself of the contrary, I had just asked her out on a date.

I went to follow Osiris into the house, but just as I was about to walk through the gate, I heard the faint sound of footsteps behind me that made my ears prick up. I didn't look round right away as I waited for them to get fainter. Instead, I could hear them coming up right behind me. Before I knew it, a hand grasped my shoulder and I forcefully wrenched myself out of their grip, only to then turn and see who the person had been.

It was Val.

'What did you sneak up on me for?' I grumbled.

'Sorry,' she laughed. 'I didn't think you'd freak out. What's the matter?'

At that moment, I needed to tell somebody about my problems. I figured that there was nobody better than Val to do that. After all, a problem shared is a problem halved. So we stood for several minutes as I explained what was happening and what was worrying me: my dad and the mysterious person watching him through the window, my date with Osiris and my growing feelings for her, the fact that I had received an anonymous phone call from someone about Jodie. Val listened intently and nodded along with what I was saying, until I finished with, 'So, what do you think?'

'It sounds like you have too much going on, Luke.'

I pulled a face. *You think?*

She evidently picked up on what I was suggesting for she groaned with exasperation and went on, 'There's no need to be piling all this crap up. Your dad, I understand you're worried about him, but I'm sure that guy looking in on him was nothing and, like you say, you don't want to be the one to involve police – not after they already have you on their radar. Osiris, well it's only natural for you to be developing certain feelings for her after what you've been through, but just take things slowly. That day out you have planned sounds like a good idea; just see how you feel after that before thinking about it anymore.'

Already, the weight on my shoulders was lessoning. 'Thanks,' I said. 'That clears things up a bit, but I can't help feeling weird about the whole Jodie thing. It was a mistake getting in touch with her in the first place. I can't have the world knowing about mermaids.'

'You were doing what you thought was right at the time.'

I groaned. 'I suppose, but I still have a feeling she could be malicious. If she somehow knows about Osiris, then who knows what could happen.'

'How can she possibly know? You didn't tell her anything.'

'I know, but still...'

'It's no use thinking hypothetically. All we know is that some weirdo is messing you about. Some crazy internet woman isn't going to be a threat.'

She smiled and I smiled back. I was grateful to have a friend like her.

'What are you two yapping about?'

We both turned to see Alice walking over the road towards us. She looked as properly dressed as ever, with a stylish cream jacket that she really shouldn't have been able to afford given the financial situation that Ruby had let slip they were in.

'Just discussing things,' Val answered, quickly. 'Where've you been anyway?'

'Been helping Warren with some paperwork he didn't understand,' she said. 'I was just heading home. Are you coming, Valerie?'

'I guess so.' She patted me on the shoulder as she passed by. 'I'll talk to you later.'

'Yeah, see you.'

I watched them both walk off and then finally made my way indoors. I felt the desperate need for a drink that I hadn't done since Osiris had come into my life. I managed to subdue this craving though because I was determined not to get myself into a mess around her.

Chapter 13

I could barely concentrate at work the next day.

Ever since I had begun to really consider my feelings for Osiris, I started to think even more about how building her future could possibly work. Now that she was human, she needed to know all the basics – and getting a job to maintain a living was a massive part of life. She already knew through watching television the concept of work and had asked me about it, but I had figured that she wasn't ready yet to even consider getting one herself. I wouldn't even know where to begin when it came to her employment – should Osiris be given an education first, or would that end up arising more suspicion?

I was so absorbed in my own thoughts that it came as a surprise when I managed to shake myself out of them in time to realise that a man had approached the counter and was talking away to me. He stopped and looked expectantly at me.

'I'm sorry?' I stammered.

He responded, in a distinctive American accent, that he was looking for one of the local newspapers. 'I've just checked the shelf and couldn't see any.'

'Oh, right. Yeah, we keep them back here.'

It felt as though I'd just awoke from a deep sleep and everything still had a strange hazy quality to it as I tried to work out what was real and what wasn't. I hadn't felt this way in a long time, since it usually only occurred when I was drinking. I guess the stress of everything was having more of an impact on my body than I thought. I told myself that I needed to buck up and that I should concentrate on work whilst I was there. Anything else could wait until afterwards.

I grabbed one of the newspapers from the small pile beside me. Even in my bleary state, it occurred to me as unusual that someone not from the area would want to keep up on local goings on. Perhaps he was getting it for a friend or something.

As I was making the transaction, it suddenly occurred to me that I'd seen this person somewhere before. He didn't look too familiar, but there was something in the back of my head telling me that I should recognise his face. His accent made me question this, as I didn't know anybody from America… and yet I couldn't push this thought away.

'I'm sorry, do I know you?' I asked.

The man smiled and shook his head. 'I don't think so. Have a nice day.'

'You too,' I replied, still certain that he wasn't a total stranger.

I watched out the window as he got into his car and drove off. I was focused so much in doing so that I didn't even notice that my co-worker had walked in. Thankfully, this meant that my shift was coming to an end.

'You alright, mate?' he asked. 'If you want to close the shift now, you may as well. Best do it whilst we're not swamped.'

'Will do. Cheers, Stephen.'

After sorting everything out, I started to pack my stuff as Stephen made his way to the till. 'Here's Emmie,' he said, staring out at the forecourt.

I looked up and saw that Emmie had indeed just entered the garage. She appeared to be deep in thought, and her overall demeanour didn't sit right with me.

'Is everything okay?' I asked her, as she approached the counter.

I couldn't help but notice that she was looking at me strangely, like she was struggling to say something. 'Actually, I came to talk to you about something, Luke.' She cast a glance at Stephen. 'Privately.'

'Okay, well I was just about to leave anyway. See you later, Stephen.'

'Yeah, bye guys.'

Once we were outside, Emmie turned to me. 'It's about Ruby.'

This wasn't what I was expecting. 'What about her?'

'I'm not supposed to say anything, but she wanted to be alone and I didn't think that was wise. You deserve to know as well considering it could affect you.'

'*What* could affect me?' My throat went dry and I could feel myself beginning to shake.

'Ruby thinks she might be pregnant.'

'That can't be right,' I protested. 'I used a condom – I know I did.'

Emmie shrugged. 'All I know is what she's told me. I probably shouldn't have said anything, but I thought about it and decided you needed to know. Ruby's taking the test today if you wanted to go and see her.'

I couldn't believe what was happening, yet I knew she was right. 'Okay, yeah, of course. Where does she live?'

*

Emmie gave me directions, but I her words sounded out of focus and I had to ask her a few times to repeat what she had said. Thoughts of parenthood and all the new sets of problems it would bring, just when I was trying to brace myself for the ones I already had. Then Osiris kept coming back into my head. She was sat at home, completely oblivious to what was happening. This would ultimately affect her like it would me.

I found Ruby's house fairly easily. It took me a while to pluck up the courage to knock on the door. As soon as I arrived, I spent a while sitting in my car, thinking everything over in my head. I wasn't ready to be a father. And I certainly wasn't ready to have to face that possibility due to a one-night stand with a woman I barely knew.

When I thought about the people I knew with children, most of them had been teenagers during the conception. Though I didn't honestly know how I'd be able to handle the situation should Ruby turn out to be pregnant and choose to keep the baby, at least I was an adult. My mind immediately went to the hundreds of photos my former schoolmates posted endlessly on social media displaying their supposedly happy families and I felt a twinge of dread that this could soon be what was in store for me.

Eventually, I took a deep breath and knocked on Ruby's front door. As I waited for a response, I began to think that maybe she would ignore it – perhaps because she knew Emmie would tell me and didn't want me anywhere near her. Not now, or during the pregnancy itself. However, just as I was about to knock again, the door opened.

Ruby stood with a completely blank expression on her face, which was free of any make-up and mostly covered with her uncombed hair. 'Hi,' was all she could say.

'Hi,' I said. 'Emmie told me everything and where I could find you.'

She nodded and stood back to allow me inside the house. I stepped in and followed her through to the living room, where we both sat down on a small sofa.

'Do you want a cup of tea or anything?' she asked, her voice croaky.

I shook my head. 'Nah, I'm alright. Have you taken the test?'

'Yeah, we just need to wait a few minutes,' she said. 'It was nice of you to come over, by the way. I didn't want you to know yet in case it was a false alarm.'

'I was a little freaked out when I was told, but I knew I needed to be here.'

'Thanks. That means a lot.'

We waited in silence until Ruby leaned across and retrieved the pregnancy test, to which she immediately burst into tears. My heart began to race, and then I noticed she was smiling.

'Negative,' she declared.

A rush of relief swept over me and I pulled Ruby into a tight hug, which she returned with much enthusiasm. We parted then looked at each other, both looking extremely happy, though there were still tears streaming down her face. For a moment, our lips almost touched before I came to my senses and pulled away.

'I can't,' I told her.

She looked confused. 'Why not?'

'There's kind of someone else.' I don't know why, but I felt ashamed to admit this – even though I never particularly had any feelings for Ruby and very much liked Osiris.

'Kind of?' she asked.

'It's complicated.'

She nodded and turned away. 'It's okay, I think I just got caught up in the moment, I'll go make us a cup of tea and we can talk.'

Even though it had not been my intention to stay, I could see the positive side to talking to someone who wasn't Osiris, Val or Matt. Sometimes, I felt a little trapped and it was nice to have a break for a change. This was something I kept in mind for Osiris, which is why I was pleased that she was having a day where I wasn't constantly in her presence.

Suddenly, I heard a loud snap sound from outside, as though somebody had just broken a twig in the garden. Yet from what I could see out of the patio windows, the garden appeared to be empty.

'Do you have a dog outside or something?' I shouted through at Ruby, having to raise my voice over the sound of the boiling kettle.

'No, why?' she called back.

I didn't answer. Instead, I got to my feet and stared out at the garden. It wasn't very large and mainly consisted of hedges, with a large tree at the bottom. Behind this, I caught a glimpse of a hand peeking over the edge.

'There's someone in your garden!' I cried, but she didn't reply.

Without waiting, I opened one of the doors and edged out onto the patio. The hand shuffled out of sight and I immediately heard feet hitting the ground, which made me realise that the person (whoever it was) had just hopped over the fence and into the alleyway behind. I dashed over as quickly as I could and heaved myself up on the railing so I could peer out at the path, where I could just see a figure running behind a nearby house. They went by so fast that I couldn't identify a single thing about them.

'What are you doing?' Ruby asked. She was now stood on the patio, holding two cups of tea and looking completely perplexed.

I hopped down from the fence and walked back to the house. 'There was someone stood behind the tree and they've just ran off.'

Ruby's mouth dropped open. 'What the hell? Who was it? Oh my God, what do they want?'

'Don't panic,' I said, taking one of the mugs from her. 'I don't think they were here for you.'

We went back inside and sat down on the sofa. The good feeling I'd had when I found out that I wouldn't be having a child had now completely vanished. I now felt like I'd been kicked in the stomach.

'What's going on?' Ruby enquired.

'I honestly don't know myself,' I admitted. 'I went to see my dad yesterday and he told me that he woke up a few nights ago in the living room and saw someone watching him from the window. I thought maybe it was a burglar or something looking to see if they could rob him, but now I'm thinking it's to do with me.'

Ruby didn't look convinced. 'Or maybe it's the same guy and he's just scouting around the area looking for potential houses.'

'It seems like a bit of a coincidence for him to target two people who just happen to be associated with me, though. Look, I wouldn't worry about it, but call the police if you think that will help.'

She looked thoughtfully for a while then put down her drink. 'So, there's kind of someone in your life? Who is it?'

'It's hard to explain, really,' I said. 'It's a person I haven't known long but how we met was... unusual. And I really like her.'

Despite how understanding she had been about not embarking on a relationship the morning after we had slept together, I noticed that Ruby looked deflated at what I was telling her. This made me feel guilty, though at the same time I could not deny the fact that I did not feel the same way about her that she apparently did for me.

'That's great,' she said. 'It's probably for the better that I'm not going to have a baby, then. It would have just made things a lot more complicated.'

'You looked pretty upset when I arrived. Why does it sound like you sort of wanted to be pregnant now?'

It looked like this question had stumped her and there was a short silence as she mulled it over. 'My life hasn't exactly been the best lately. As much as it wouldn't be ideal to fall pregnant after a one-night stand, I can't help but feel like a baby would've given my life a bit of meaning, you know? You obviously don't feel the same way.'

'I can see what you mean,' I said. 'A baby would not be good for me right now, though. I've got way too much going on. I nearly had a heart attack when Emmie told me what had happened.'

Ruby laughed. 'I stand by what I said before. You are cute.'

'You're not too bad yourself.'

I finished the rest of my tea, then told Ruby that I needed to head home. She probably wanted me to stay a little longer, but understood and walked me to the door.

'Well, it was nice seeing you, Luke,' she said, hugging me. 'I really am happy that you've found someone. Don't worry, I won't bother you anymore.'

'Ruby, I'd like to still keep you as a friend.'

'You're too sweet,' she said. 'Thanks for coming today, I'll see you later.'

And with that, she closed the door and I began to make my way home.

I couldn't quite work out how I was feeling. On the one hand, my talk with Val had limited my problems and now I didn't have to worry about the possibility of a child. However, the worries about my dad and Osiris were still there in the back of my head, meaning that I was just as conflicted as I had been all day.

*

'So how has your day been?'

I had been expecting this question from Osiris and still had not thought about how I would answer it. I settled for, 'It was okay.'

We were sat either side of the couch in the living room with the television on, though neither of us was paying any attention to it. Osiris had assisted me in making a chicken salad and cheerily told me how she had occupied her time whilst I was gone. I remained quite apart from the occasional 'aha' and 'yeah'.

'Is that it?' she pressed. 'What happened at work?'

'Not a lot,' I muttered, unable to meet her gaze.

'How come you were gone for so long anyway? I thought you said you'd be eight hours at the most, but I kept checking the clock and I'm sure you were gone for much longer. Maybe I'm mistaken – the whole concept of telling the time still confuses me.'

'You're not mistaken. I guess time got away from me a bit.'

She stopped asking questions and I could tell she wasn't completely satisfied with the answers I had given. This wasn't what I wanted – for my other problems to get in the way of the bond that I was developing with Osiris, and it was becoming evident that she was growing more instinctive towards my lies.

A shot of guilt ran through me at the thought of how I had not been entirely truthful to a lot of people, even though that was not normally in my nature. My dad always said that what he detested more than anything was a liar. Yet here I was, casually telling them left, right and centre. Keeping things buried had been a speciality of mine for quite some time. It had used to be just one big secret I was keeping – now it was a lot of little ones.

'Osiris, I'm not being honest with you.' The words came out of my mouth before I could even think them over and she perked up with curiosity. 'Things aren't going well for me right now and I've been trying to keep you in the dark about a lot of it. Now that you've become such a big part of my life, I think you deserve to know everything.'

'What's the matter?' She sounded worried.

'Well, I've been getting really paranoid about that story my dad told us – the person looking in on him through the window. I have a feeling it wasn't just an isolated incident, especially after something that happened today.'

'What happened?'

'After work, I had to go see Ruby – a girl I know – at her house. While I was there, I noticed someone skulking around in the garden and they ran away once they realised that I'd seen them. I don't know, it just kind of freaked me out a bit after what happened with my dad.'

There was a silence before she asked, 'Who is Ruby?'

I knew this would be the part of the story she would question, and I didn't want to stop my honesty. 'She's a girl who I had sex with a few weeks ago.'

Osiris looked genuinely sad as she asked, 'Sex... that's what humans call the process that leads to reproduction, right? But it's not just for that, is it? Matt does it with the random girls. Or at least he says he did before Emmie.'

'Yeah,' I muttered. 'We were together just one night and agreed that would be it. While I was at work today, Emmie came and told me that Ruby thought she might be pregnant. You know, having a baby.'

Osiris gasped. 'And is she?'

'No, she took a test and it was negative.'

There was an uncomfortable stillness as she took in the news and I played with a loose bit of material on the couch.

Finally, the tension was broken by Osiris. 'Do you... like her?'

'Just as a friend,' I answered, quickly. 'And barely even that. I don't know her very well. Sleeping with her was a mistake and I regret it, but there's nothing I can do. The whole pregnancy scare just added to my worries. Now that it's over, I'd like to get back to trying to stay in a good mood. Are you still up for the shopping trip at the weekend?'

I met her eyes again to see that she was smiling. 'Of course I am,' she said. 'You don't have to feel bad about what happened between you and Ruby. I'm not going to pretend like there's something between us. We aren't a couple or anything.'

My heart sank as I replied, 'Yeah... exactly.'

For the rest of the evening, we stayed in the living room and continued to watch a marathon of a sitcom we both enjoyed. There was still an uneasy feeling between us, but I was determined to push past it. I had been brutally honest with Osiris that night and was going to do what Val suggested. That weekend, we'd be spending the day out together and I'd just have to see how that went before thinking about my next move.

Chapter 14

The train pulled into the station just after ten o'clock on Saturday morning. Osiris and I then made our way into York, where I had planned for us to spend the day together.

The journey from Hartlepool had been a success, with Osiris having very much enjoyed the experience of a different sort of travel to the car. She had sat beside the window so she could have a clear view of the landscape as we sped past it and was constantly asking me what various things were. I was more than happy to answer.

One aspect of the day that she had been anticipating was the fact that we were going to a city, which I knew would be a major change from her growing familiarity with village life. It was something, however, that I suspected she would adapt well to considering that I'd told her all about what to expect and what our plans for the day were. Mainly, it would be looking around the shops, with a small snack break around lunchtime, and then going for a meal at a nice restaurant later in the evening. Other than this, I was looking forward to seeing how the day would pan out and how I would feel about Osiris at the end of it.

'Where are we going first?' she asked.

'Let's just have a look around and see what takes our fancy,' I suggested.

It was a breezy day, but it wasn't forecast for rain until later, so I wasn't too worried about spending most of the time going from place to place.

We walked from the station to the main shopping area, which was about as crowded as I had expected it to be considering that it was a weekend. This seemed to add to Osiris's excitement though as she watched all the different people bustling around, clutching bags and announcing where else they were going to shop at.

'Do we buy things like that?'

'Maybe, it depends what we see,' I said, leading her to the nearest clothes shop. 'Let's try in here. You said you wanted to wear stuff like people you see on the telly? Well, have a look and see what you like – then you can try it on, and we buy it.'

Her face broke into an almighty smile as she raced around and began to take in everything that the place had to offer. A shop assistant came over and complimented how beautiful Osiris's hair was before asking if we needed help. I'd made sure to work out Osiris's exact sizes with Val before we set off and so gave these to the woman. She took her time deciding on what exactly Osiris would look best in, before leading her to the changing room with a pile of clothes. I sat and watched as she came out modelling various outfits. She looked good in everything. I didn't exactly have a great bank account, but she still came out with two bags of new things to wear.

Next, I took the chance and we browsed through a bookstore. Reading had been a tricky subject with Osiris as it was difficult for her to grasp the concept, even after I'd tried explaining it numerous times. She was intrigued by the very notion. I wasn't sure if she'd ever be able to learn; she was well past the age at which it was easy to pick up, but she spoke fluently in English, so I assumed it was still possible. I thought it was worth a try and so purchased several children's books for her to try out.

After that, we went to an art gallery, where I spent the best part of an hour explaining to Osiris what paintings were and why a lot of the time people were just as curious about the artist as about the piece itself. She enjoyed the various sculptures on show, even if she didn't fully understand a lot of them, and she particularly liked the ones involving water. They used rich blue and green colours that must have seemed very familiar to her.

'There's so much beauty on land,' she commented, whilst focusing her attention on a large painting of a pond at night that was illuminated by the moon. 'Can we ever see anything like this?'

I tried to imagine where such a place would exist and decided that we could eventually find a place to replica the picture. 'We can look around sometime for somewhere similar,' I promised.
*

When it got to lunchtime, we stopped to grab a sandwich. Osiris had never seen so much food laid out in one place and was enthralled at all the cakes on display. I had to warn her that such delicacies were bad for humans if consumed too frequently.

'I don't understand,' she said, as we left the shop. 'So, some stuff is bad for you when you eat loads of it, yet they allow loads of it to be sold to anyone who wants it?'

'People know the health risks, so it's up to them if they choose to continue eating.'

She still didn't seem to get it. 'But... shouldn't there be a law or something? I mean, it's delicious, but if it can kill you...'

'It's to do with free will,' I said. 'Everyone has the right to do what they want... within reason, of course.'

'Do... do I have free will?'

'Absolutely.' I noticed the look of shock on her face at my reply. 'I'm guessing that you didn't have free will when you lived in the ocean?'

'I guess not,' she mumbled. 'Our society had to be such a big secret that we were really... repressed in a way. There wasn't much room for something like free will.'

'We aren't exactly completely free to do what we want. We have laws and rules and all that stuff, but it must have been difficult to be so limited. You know, the ocean is so vast and yet you're forced to keep everything so tucked away. Humans suck, eh?'

Osiris shook her head. 'Not all of them.'

Her fingers brushed against mine which made them tingle. I tried to ignore this for the time being, though, and diverted the situation by saying, 'Is there anything else you'd like to see while we're in the city?'

She thought about it and then answered, 'How about one of those bridges that were in a lot of the photos you were showing me?'

'Okay then,' I said, leading her in the direction of the nearest one.

Before our trip, I'd gotten pictures up online for her too look at so that she knew exactly what kind of place we'd be going to. Typing the name of the city onto a search engine had resulted in dozens of pictures showing up for the many bridges that went over the River Ouse, so it came as no surprise that it was this that had stuck in her mind.

We arrived at one after walking a short distance and stood so that we had a view of the sparkling water as it stretched out into the distance. I could see Osiris's eyes were soaking up everything, from the birds flying overhead to all the people walking by the side of the river.

'What do you think, then?' I asked her.

She did not reply, but instead began crying softly into her hands.

This completely threw me. 'What's the matter?'

'It's just a lot to take in,' she said, wiping her eyes. 'It's so... incredible. All my life I felt like I didn't belong and seeing all of this just makes me realise that I've finally found a place where I fit in – here, with mankind.'

From what I could gather from how she awkwardly ended it, she had meant to finish the sentence off differently. *With you*, perhaps. At least, I hoped that's what she would say.

'It must be so different,' I said. 'You've handled the transition really well.'

'You think so?'

'Of course. The two worlds are completely different so for you to go from one extreme to the other and get used to it in such a short amount of time is remarkable.'

'Maybe it's because I didn't fit in there that I do so well here,' she pondered, and I agreed. Osiris was clearly happier as a human than she'd ever been as a mermaid.

Suddenly, her attention was caught by a pigeon on the railing and she slowly approached it. Birds had fascinated her since she first saw them out in the garden, and I had to talk her through the concept of flying and all the questions that came with it.

As I stood and she posed for some photos on my phone, a voice called my name. I turned and saw the man who had spoken to me the day I'd visited Jodie Grayson.

'Hi,' I said. 'It's Sam, right?'

'Yes, what are you doing here?'

I was still bewildered by why he kept approaching me, but I decided to be courteous and talk to him. 'Just came for a day out.'

He nodded, but his attention seemed to be elsewhere. 'Very pretty girl that one,' he said, looking intently at Osiris.

'Yes, she is,' was all I could think of saying as he had become suddenly quiet, watching Osiris's interest when the bird flew to another part of the bridge.

After staring some more, he commented, 'Her hair is so blonde it's almost unnatural, wouldn't you say?'

'It must be the type of dye she uses,' I said. Surely her appearance alone wouldn't arouse so much suspicion from a stranger, yet he seemed oddly allured by her.

'Maybe,' he muttered. 'Is she with you?'

'We're here together if that's what you mean. We aren't in a relationship,' I clarified.

'Pity,' he said. 'You shouldn't let someone as unique as her get away. Sometimes people show up who are one in a million and we may never get the chance with them again if they have to leave us.'

'I don't think she'll be leaving any time soon.'

'You'd think that, but again, sometimes things are out of our control. Like I told you a few weeks ago, there are bad people in this world. They won't care about the feelings of others.'

Osiris was now using some breadcrumbs it to coax the pigeon down. I watched her before bringing my attention back to Sam and asking, 'Why were you so keen to talk to me that day, anyway? Do you know Jodie or something?'

He too tore his eyes away from Osiris and said, 'I just needed to do something, it wasn't important. Anyway, I must go. Take care, Luke.'

I watched him walk away and expected him to turn back at least once, but he didn't. Instead, I saw him simply fade into the distant crowd.

'Who was that you were talking to?' Osiris asked when I caught up with her.

'I don't really know,' I said, still a little shaken up about the encounter. I wasn't sure why, but something about him didn't sit right with me. 'He says his name is Sam. I met him briefly a few weeks back and I guess he must live around here or something. He was talking about how unique you were.'

'Why would he think that about *me*?'

I did not answer straight away. I wondered about all the possibilities. He'd made a comment on her hair, which could be why he'd been so captivated. After all, it was unnaturally light in comparison to a lot of humans, though most people would have passed this off as some sort of crazy hair colouring and thought no more of it. The one chilling idea was that he somehow knew that Osiris had not always been human, which was a possibility that was causing me some discomfort. Before I met Osiris, I would not have believed anyone who said that they could sense the paranormal. This was no longer the case.

'It doesn't matter,' I said, firmly. 'Come on, let's go have a look about the city, there's still loads I want to show you. Then when we get hungry again, we'll go for a meal.'

We made our way back towards the shopping area, though I intended to take her in a different direction at some point so that we could see the other sights.

Osiris had a skip in her step as we went. 'Where will we be going to eat, then?'

'I'm not sure,' I replied, mulling the options over in my head. 'There are a lot of restaurants here. You can choose from a good selection.'

This seemed to satisfy her and, as we made our way down by the river, she focused her sights on all the visual splendours going on around her. Building on the learning experience, I told Osiris about the many cultures around the world and how different aspects were brought over into other countries.

She could clearly not believe all the things she was discovering and questioned me further on everything. Meanwhile, I was still thinking over what Sam had said on the bridge.

'There are bad people in this world. They won't care about the feelings of others.'

Chapter 15

'This way,' the waitress said, picking up two menus and walking towards a small table next to the window.

We took our seats and ordered drinks, which we decided would be non-alcoholic. The main reason for this was because Osiris had tried some a few nights before and did not react well to it, though I promised to buy more for her to try at a later point. I was also still determined not to go back to drinking heavily again now that she was around.

'I can have any of this?' Osiris questioned, flicking through the menu. It was nice to still see such wonderment in her expressions, even at something as simple as the range of choice in what food she could order.

'Yeah, well the meal will be separated into different parts,' I explained. 'You choose a dish for each course.'

Her eyes widened. 'That sounds like fun.'

I laughed and nodded in agreement. 'It does.'

With this all cleared up, we went silent as we read through the menus. I could hear the chatter of the other customers and smiled to myself when I thought about the fact that, no matter how many happy couples were here on dates, I was guaranteed to be the only one with someone who had once been a mermaid. That was special.

Having deliberated on a few options for dinner, we had finally decided on a small Italian restaurant that I had been to once before. It was somewhat hidden away from the more mainstream eateries in the area, which was a shame because it was beautifully decorated and provided the perfect backdrop for our date.

The time waiting for the food wasn't awkward as such, but I didn't know exactly what to say to her – which was unusual because usually the conversation came so easily. Instead, I sat and stared at her as she watched the rain lightly tapping against the window. Her looks were so distinct and so beautiful that I couldn't believe that it had taken me so long to realise how desirable she was. Val had come over that morning to style Osiris's hair in preparation for the day and the way she braided it so that her face was without cover brought out the true attractiveness in her looks. There was no way I could let her go on thinking that I wasn't interested, especially now that she knew about Ruby and probably thought that I was going to eventually go after other women.

'Have you thought about us?' I asked her.

She took her gaze away from the weather and turned to face me. 'What do you mean?'

'Like, have you thought about what we are? Am I just a friend to you or have you thought about us becoming more than that?'

'I don't think I've ever really considered you "just" anything. You changed my life from the moment I saw you. That day on the beach, I couldn't believe that after so many years of dreaming about it that I was finally experiencing what it was like to not be underwater... but I was also nervous about what would happen if I was seen. When you approached me, I was taken by surprise. I knew you were a good person and that I could trust you with my life, as crazy as that may sound.'

Her story was touching, though it hadn't really answered my question. 'That doesn't sound crazy,' I replied, 'it's very nice of you to say that. What about when you made the decision to become human and we met again, how did you feel?'

'When I was given the potion that would turn me into a human and told that I needed to swim to the surface before I drank it, I knew that I needed to be near you, which is why I swam to the area where we'd spoke even though there was a risk that I wouldn't actually be able to find you again. I've never felt happier than when you walked into the hospital room. It was the greatest feeling in the world.'

The waitress returned and placed our starters in front of us.

'Thanks,' we both said, without much as glancing at her.

'What do you mean when you say that you knew you needed to be near me?' I asked.

'Well, if I was going to be human and learn about everything, then I needed someone to be there to guide me through it all. Not only were you the only person I'd met, but I also knew that you were an uncommonly kind one.'

'You talk like I'm someone special,' I said. 'Really, if it wasn't me who found you then it very well could've been another decent human being. I think you're letting the fact that it was me and I was nice cloud your judgment.'

'*No*,' she responded, firmly. 'Luke, you put yourself down way too much and I don't know if I'll ever understand that. Remember that I was a mermaid who could live for centuries and merfolk have a lot more that differentiates them from mankind than just their physical appearance. They have the power to sense things that humans can't. When we met and I was a mermaid, it was clear that I was talking to a person with a very special aura.'

This revelation took me by surprise, and I thought it over in my head. It hadn't occurred to me that merfolk could be different from humans in a mental and spiritual way, but if what she said was true then maybe Osiris and I did have an extraordinary connection after all. Therefore, maybe it wasn't by chance we'd met again against all odds.

I did not reply to her comment straight away and instead filled the silence by finally getting a start on my food. She followed suit and several minutes passed.

When enough time had gone by, I eventually I managed to speak again and said, 'Err, so when you say you saw my aura and stuff... did it ever occur to you at the same time that I could be anything other than a friend to you in the future?' I could feel my mouth drying up as I spoke and took a drink to wash down the last of my bruschetta.

Osiris smiled. 'I was attracted to you – that much I know. Over the past few weeks, I think that's developed more and I got really jealous when you mentioned that other girl.'

'Like I said, Ruby was a mistake. Osiris, it killed me a little inside when I found out that she might be pregnant. And, yeah, it was partly because of the responsibility and the nerves about having to provide for another living thing, but mostly it was because I was afraid that I would lose you.'

'Why would you lose me?'

'A person with a kid isn't exactly the most desirable,' I said. 'It made me think that you'd go off, start a life with someone else.'

She looked thoughtful for a second and then said, 'Would that bother you?'

'Yes, it would,' I answered, truthfully. 'I want to be the person you start a life with.'

'Oh.' She finished off the remainder of her olives then bowed her head, just about hiding the smile she had on her face.

At that moment, the waitress came over and took our empty plates from the table. 'Was everything okay for you?'

Again, I did not make eye contact with her for my eyes were focused purely on Osiris. 'Yes, thanks. Everything's great.'

She shuffled away and Osiris raised her head.

'Would you really want to be with me... like that?' she asked.

I reached over and grabbed her hands, caressing her fingers with mine. 'Yes, I really would. Look, I'm not saying that it will be easy... but it's worth giving it a shot, isn't it?'

'I'd love to try it,' she admitted. 'If that's really what you want.'

'It is.'

We sat for a while with our hands interlinked. The sound of everyone else in the restaurant had disappeared as my focus became aimed entirely towards Osiris, who was now staring directly into my eyes.

Suddenly, we were both taken by surprise by the arrival of our main courses. The waitress put our plates down in front of us and we thanked her. She beamed at us, as if she knew how well our date was going and was pleased on our behalf. It seemed like we both realised what an appetite we'd worked up with such an intense talk about relationships and so we immediately tucked into our food.

It had been a very, very long time since I'd felt so comfortable in my own skin. I still wasn't completely sure how much I'd be willing to admit about myself to her, but I knew that I was closer to her than to anyone - even more so than with Val and Matt. And what she'd said about my aura was nearly enough to bring a tear to my eye. Perhaps I wasn't as useless as I'd always thought.

*

We didn't talk much after finishing our food and making the journey back to the train station, aside from occasional observations on what was going on around us. On the ride home, though, I eventually managed to speak again about the two of us.

'So,' I began, choosing my words carefully, 'should we tell everyone about us starting a relationship then?'

'Yes,' she said, taking my hand. 'I think everyone will be happy for us and it would be easier than hiding it, don't you think?'

I thought about it and decided that she was probably right. Matt had suspected from the beginning that she and I were more than just friends and Val had seemed supportive when I told her about my true feelings. And it certainly would be a lot easier to tell them instead of sneaking around and pretending that we weren't together. I wanted to be openly affectionate with Osiris and didn't want to sacrifice that by having to disguise it from anyone.

We continued to hold hands as the familiar landscape signalled that we were nearing home. I was trying to pass the time by looking around at the various passengers on the train when I suddenly noticed one person in particular, sat a few places in front on the opposite side.

It was Sam.

My chest tightened and I tried to pretend like I hadn't seen him, but this didn't work. For a second, it looked as though he had turned his head just enough so that he could see me out of the corner of his eye. I chose not to alert Osiris about him because I wasn't completely sure whether it was something we should be worried about.

The rest of the journey was spent with me attempting to distract myself away from the fact that someone who made me uneasy just happened to be on the same train and trying to rationalise the situation. I had not been too worried when I'd thought that perhaps meeting him again had been a coincidence, but now that he was also travelling back at the exact same time, something just didn't sit right with me.

'What's the matter, Luke?' Osiris asked me as we got up to leave the train.

'Nothing,' I said, not taking my eyes off Sam, who was also exiting through the open doors. 'I was just mulling things over. Come on, let's get home.'

We walked arm in arm, and I made sure to keep a tighter hold of her than normal.

Chapter 16

When I woke up the next day, I looked over at Osiris (who was still in a deep slumber) and smiled. Although she had slept in my bed, we were resolute to take things slowly – but even just having someone to cuddle up to had made a nice change from all the nights I'd spent alone.

It was a great feeling to know that I no longer had to hide how I truly felt about Osiris. Immediately upon arriving back from York, we told a rather tipsy Matt that we were in a relationship, only for him to comment on the fact he'd guessed that from the start. I'd also sent Val a text, to which she expressed her delight that it had all worked out for us.

Despite this great feeling, my mind was still working overtime thinking about how exactly I would manage to keep Osiris's true origins a secret for the rest of our lives. What if we had children, would we tell them eventually? I wouldn't seem fair not to. Could we even have children given that her body was created through magical means? I knew that she went through the menstrual cycle like an ordinary female, but that was no guarantee that she would be able to safely carry and deliver a human baby. I had the sudden image of one coming out with fins or some other aquatic identifier.

I realised that further research was necessary, so grabbed my laptop and headed downstairs, where I could look up what I needed to in peace.

There was no milk in the refrigerator when I went to pour some in my tea, nor was there any bread left when I went to make some toast. Doing the grocery shopping must have slipped my mind in all the excitement of the lead-up to the date. Matt was useless at anything like that and had spent most of the week with Emmie, anyway. My laptop loaded up, so I decided that I would flick through some websites first and then head out.

My thoughts immediately went to Jodie Grayson and her site *Belief in the Impossible*. It unnerved me that apparently there were people from all over the world who believed in all sorts of myths and legends, including mermaids. I knew how powerful the internet could be and if any of them found out about Osiris then who knows what they could do with that sort of information. Sam's warning was still echoing in my mind. I went back onto the site out of curiosity and began sifting through the forums to see if there was anything notable.

There were a lot of topics dedicated to ghosts, which was by far the most popular subject amongst this site's users. They were something I'd never given much thought to, but I guess I couldn't rule out their existence – there would definitely be more people who believed in them than in mermaids. Another prolific one was on sasquatches, whilst other threads seem to be dedicated to a specific myth and usually garnered quite a few responses. There was one about Loch Ness, Mothman, the Bermuda Triangle, and even the Amityville case. I was about to give up when I saw one for "sea monsters". I figured it was my best bet.

The first post, from a user known as CRaistrick, featured numerous examples of creatures rumoured to dwell beneath the surface, alongside images of what they supposedly look like. I scrolled down and read contributions from other users, who were mostly just speculating on which ones could exist – all of them, apparently, if these people were to be believed. They seemed positive that the likes of the Megalodon shark were still lurking about somewhere, though none of them provided any evidence whatsoever. I couldn't disprove any of them, of course, but it was a relief to find that not one of them was able to offer up photographic proof to back up their claims.

My mind began to wander as I drifted through the rest of the replies, until my eye was caught by someone bringing up mermaids. They were asking about whether anybody else had any information on them and their existence. The original poster then left a comment directing them to a thread that was apparently discussing the subject of merfolk. When I clicked on it, I saw that it was a recent thread with ongoing posts, so I must have missed it in my initial scan of the forum topics.

The first post was dated just a few days after Osiris had become human and the user talked about how they'd heard rumours from "close sources" that a mermaid had been spotted in the north east coast of England. I could feel my heart starting to beat faster and the beads of sweat drip down my forehead. I kept reading as the user posted a link to a news article about a young woman found naked on the beach and rushed to hospital. This person speculated that it could possibly be a mermaid transformed and, of course, I knew that they were right. What really scared me, though, was when I read the username: JodieAGrayson, listed as the forum administrator.

I couldn't sit still and began pacing, going back to the screen every now and again to read through the replies that her post had gotten. Unfortunately, every contributor seemed to agree with her theory, and they were enthusiastically discussing the possibilities. I couldn't believe this was happening – how could Jodie have possibly figured it out?

Deciding that I needed a break, I shut down my laptop without further ado. I then pulled on some old clothes and quickly made a run to the shop over the road.

'Just these please,' I said to the hard-faced woman behind the counter, putting down a loaf of bread and carton of milk.

She began to scan the items when the door opened and Val walked in, looking worse for wear in a pair of tracksuit bottoms and an old coat. I smiled at her and she returned it weakly.

'What are you doing out so early?' she asked.

'Woke up to find the fridge nearly empty,' I replied.

I paid for my purchases and waited while Val bought some cigarettes, then walked with her outside, where she stopped to light one up.

'I'm sick of her,' she suddenly declared. 'She keeps throwing my tabs away.'

I wanted to laugh but stopped myself. 'Alice has your best interests at heart.'

Val snorted with derision and took a long drag. Up close, I could see that there were heavy bags under her eyes. I wondered how much toll her financial situation was taking on her. I didn't bring it up in case it made her feel uncomfortable.

'I wanted to talk to you about something anyway,' I said. 'Have you got time to come in?' I asked, signalling towards my house.

'Yeah, sure.'

Val finished her cigarette and put it out with her foot, then followed me inside. I told her to take a seat in the living room whilst I sorted everything out.

'Matt and Osiris not up yet?' she enquired.

'You must be joking,' I said, placing my laptop on the coffee table, 'Those two will probably still be asleep this afternoon.'

'So, what is it you want to show me exactly?'

'Just stuff I've found online.'

I opened the browser and shifted the laptop so it was facing Val. She leaned forward and began reading – her expression gradually went from intrigued to shock the further she read on. I began tapping my knee anxiously as I waited for her to finish.

'No way,' she said, finally. 'There's no way anybody could have figured out the whole mermaid thing on a whim. I mean, this person must know something!'

'Look at the name of the person who started it.'

'Jodie A. Grayson... is she that woman you said you'd gone to see?'

'Yep,' I groaned, burying my face into my hands. 'I shouldn't have contacted anyone. Who knows what this could lead to?'

'You're being too hard on yourself,' Val assured me. 'You were doing what you thought was right at first. Hell, if I'd seen a mermaid on the beach, I'd probably have taken a photo or something so people would believe me – imagine the frenzy *that* would cause! No, you acted perfectly naturally, and you never actually told her what you'd seen, so you can't blame yourself for the stuff she's spreading round.'

I allowed myself to calm down and replied, 'Cheers, maybe I am overreacting a bit.'

'What do you reckon, then? What are you going to do?'

'I don't know,' I answered.

There was a creak from the staircase as Osiris made her way down and into the living room.

'Hi, Val,' she said, joining us on the couch. 'What's going on?'

Now that we were a couple, keeping secrets from each other was not what I wanted, so I decided that she needed to know about my concerns. I carefully explained to her what I'd read online and why I felt like we shouldn't ignore it. I had dreaded what her response would be, and her look of fear made me somewhat regret telling her everything. It was only fair that she be kept in the loop, but I just hated seeing her this way.

'This can't be real,' she said. 'That woman, she must be lying.'

'The only problem is that when I went to visit to Jodie, I got the feeling that she knew I wasn't just randomly taking an interest in her site's conspiracy theories. She even commented that I wasn't the usual sort that trawled her forum. And there's no way that she could just randomly jump to the conclusion that you are a mermaid based only on the fact that you washed up on the beach.'

'How about checking it out?' Val suggested. 'You could do some poking about and see how serious this site of hers really is when it comes to finding stuff.'

The idea sounded tempting, but it just didn't seem worthwhile. 'No, I don't think that would be a good idea. I don't think she could realistically do anything. She'd just look like a nutcase if she tried to involve the authorities.'

Osiris didn't seem convinced. 'What if she's planning something, though?'

'Okay,' I said, 'maybe we should just keep an eye out for any more updates and, in the meantime, just try and forget about it. For now, it isn't affecting us.'

The two women nodded in agreement.

'Well, to take your mind off things,' Val said, 'there's an idea I'd like to run by you both. And Matt, too, once he wakes up. Alice keeps going on about camping and she wants to make it as soon as possible since she only has this week off work. I was thinking, the only way it will be any fun is if a group of us go. Are you guys up for it?'

I looked at Osiris, who was confused. 'What's camping?' she asked.

'Oh, sorry,' Val replied with a laugh. 'It means we go on a little holiday to this field where you sleep in a tent. That's a sort of shelter thing made up from fabric attached to poles. I'm not describing this very well because, well, usually I don't need to explain what that kind of thing is. Anyway, it will be fun – there's a forest and a lake nearby.'

Osiris gasped. 'A lake? Luke, that's what you said that thing was in the painting at the art gallery. Can we go, please?'

'Of course,' I said. 'We have a tent in the shed we could use. Yeah, why not. We'll have to be back on Friday though because it's Phillip and Daisy's engagement party on Saturday.'

'Yes, we'll be back before then,' Val assured me. 'We got an invite to that, too.'

I'd forgotten how well Val and my brother used to get on. Even though he and I had a rather strained relationship due to our age gap, he'd always gotten on well with her and once she was a teenager, she'd spend a lot of time with his group of friends on their nights out. I suddenly felt a rush of gratitude that I'd have another friendly face at the party to counterbalance against my family, especially Amber.

'Do you think Matt would be up for camping?' Val asked.

'He might be,' I said. 'And he's been seeing Emmie an awful lot – he could bring her if he thinks it's serious enough.'

'Excellent!' Val beamed. 'It's going to be great with all of us there. I don't think I could put up with Alice in that type of situation without anyone else.'

I laughed. 'Honestly, you love her really.'

'Yeah, yeah,' Val answered, getting to her feet. 'Look, I have to go. Try not to worry about the whole Jodie thing. We'll discuss it later if you want, but you're right – we don't have to think about it now.'

We said goodbye to her, and she left. I'd forgotten to tell her about Sam and what he'd said, so made a mental note to tell her about it as soon as possible.

There was still no sign that Matt would be getting up yet, so I would just ask him about the camping trip later. Knowing that we'd be going either the next day or the day after, I would start packing soon, but not until I'd had some toast. With all the commotion brought on by running into Val, I'd almost forgotten how terribly hungry I was.

As if she'd read my mind, Osiris asked, 'Should we have breakfast?'

'Yeah, I was thinking of having toast. I bought a fresh loaf this morning.'

'Sounds good to me, come on then!'

I watched her dance into the kitchen with her hair bouncing behind her and a sensation tingled from my stomach through to my chest. If Jodie was planning something, I would just have to hope that it wouldn't lead to any serious problems. After all, she had no proof for her accusations, despite their accuracy. I ignored these worries because at that point, I was exactly where I wanted to be – with Osiris. Nothing else seemed to matter.

Chapter 17

'Who do you think he was?'

I shoved the tent into the boot of the car and slammed the lid down. 'I don't know, maybe someone who knows about mermaids. Like I said, he commented on how unique Osiris was.'

Val buttoned up her jacket, looking thoughtful. 'He could have just been a random nutter who was pointing out how pretty she was. She's a good-looking girl, Luke.'

'But it wasn't just that. Like I said, the guy has approached me twice and the first time was just after I spoke to that Jodie woman, which was once I'd met Osiris. And this time he made a comment on how unnatural her hair colour was. It was as though he knew it wasn't human.'

'And what was his warning again? There are bad people in the world? Anybody could tell you that, it's not exactly rocket science.'

'Yes, that part sounds generic, but I swear from the sounds of it that it was like... like he had been through what I have.'

Val looked confused for a moment then said, 'You mean, the in love with a mermaid part?' As soon as she said that, the idea became almost ludicrous.

'Probably not,' I said, though there was doubt in my voice. 'That's just how it sounded. He told me not to let Osiris get away and seemed to speak from experience.'

'Still, that could be important. Are you sure he didn't give a surname?'

I went to respond, but quickly closed my mouth when Alice approached.

It was mid-morning and we were preparing to set off for camping. Matt had looked online and estimated that it would probably take us no more than a couple of hours to get there. Each couple would be driving down separately, though setting off together to avoid getting lost on the off-chance that something went wrong. With everyone distracted and knowing that there'd be little room for privacy once we arrived at the camping area, I'd taken this opportunity to finally tell Val about both my encounters with Sam and what he had said.

Osiris exited the house, followed by Emmie, and then Matt, who locked the door behind him. Emmie had been delighted to have been invited along on the trip with us – I'd initially had my doubts about Matt's ability to maintain a steady relationship, but I was willing to concede that I had been rather hasty in my judgement because they really were great together.

I watched as the others got into their respective cars. Alice departed first, followed by Matt and then me.

'Did you tell Val about that Sam guy?' Osiris asked, as I drove onto the main road.

No sooner had I pulled out than I hit a red traffic light. I cursed, then replied, 'Yes, I did. She didn't think too much of it at first, but when I suggested that he may have known a mermaid she seemed to find it more noteworthy. I'll have to discuss it with her later, maybe during the trip if we have some alone time.'

The light turned green and I picked up the pace, hoping to catch up quickly with the others. My mood was suddenly brightened when I saw Osiris reach over and felt her hand on my leg.
*

Halfway to our destination, we stopped at a service station.

We'd skipped breakfast and I was now extremely hungry, so I made sure to stock up on supplies. I left the small store and was making my way back to the car when I noticed Val rushing over. Osiris rolled down the window of the car and I passed her the snacks as Val approached.

'Hey, I just thought we could talk a bit more while they're all in there,' she whispered, even though there really wasn't any need. I doubted any of them could hear us from where they were. 'So, this Sam person – did he give a surname?'

'No,' I answered, having already gone over in my head a thousand times what he had said, and I was positive that he hadn't. 'And he didn't even say his name was Sam, just that it was what I could call him. Bit of a strange way to introduce yourself, don't you think?'

Val sighed and turned her attention to Osiris. 'Are you sure you don't know of any mermaids who might've had contact with humans before you?'

Osiris shook her head. 'I've told you, the idea of any mermaid going to the surface before me was something I'd never even considered. Trust me, wanting to swim away from the safe areas of the ocean was not something to shout about.'

'It doesn't matter anyway,' I said. 'Maybe you were right the first time, Val, about him just being a creep. He saw us on the bridge and just approached us because he's weird.'

She didn't look convinced, but nodded. 'I guess. Ah well, there's Alice, I better get going. I'll see you both when we get there.'

I got back in the car and smiled reassuringly at Osiris. 'No point worrying really, is there? Let's just enjoy our weekend away.'

She beamed and responded, 'That's exactly what I'm planning to do. I can't wait to see the lake and everything. It's going to be fun.'
*

We arrived at our destination in good time. The field wasn't large, but it would do for what we needed. It was surrounded by trees, so it looked like we'd have plenty of privacy. Our cars were able to park up on the dirt road leading up to it and we all got out to view the area.

Emmie was the first to speak, declaring, 'It's perfect.'

Matt put his arm around her and kissed her on the cheek. 'I'll say. How about we put the tents up straight away and then get started on the booze?'

'Sounds good to me,' Val laughed, ignoring Alice's disapproving look.

Even though each couple had their own tent, everyone helped each other in putting them all up. Osiris didn't have a clue about any of it, yet was happy to help. Alice and Matt turned out to be the best at it, with Val, Emmie and I being more hindrance than help.

At last, the tents were finished, and we all sat round in a circle. Matt pulled out a cooler from his car and handed everyone a drink. I wasn't drinking so as not to get drunk whilst Osiris remained sober, meaning that only half the group were going to get wasted. I didn't mind this, though, as I wished to experience Osiris's enjoyment to the fullest. My day had been enhanced simply by her anticipation during the drive.

'Are you sure I can't tempt you?' Matt said, dangling a can of beer in front of Alice.

She rolled her eyes. 'Get lost.'

Val laughed and said, 'Pass it over here, Matt. I'll need a second one in a minute.

Emmie turned to Alice, looking inquisitive. 'Why is it that you don't drink?'

'I just don't like the taste,' she answered. 'Or what it does to people,' she added, with an unmistakeable side glance towards Val.

'Fair enough,' Emmie replied, with a small laugh.

Matt leaned over and put his hand on her arm. 'Best not antagonise Alice, or she'll murder you with a look.'

Alice shook her head and chose not to retaliate.

To divert the conversation (which I could tell was heading into rocky territory) I looked over at Emmie and asked, 'Are you going to be coming with Matt to my brother's engagement party on Saturday?'

She looked at Matt and said, 'I'm not sure. Am I, Matthew?'

I panicked for a moment, questioning how serious he was about her given that he hadn't asked her about it yet, and worried that I'd put him in a difficult situation. The tension swiftly passed with Matt's look of confusion.

'Yeah, you are,' he said. 'I mean, if you're up for it that is. I just assumed I'd asked you!'

She grinned and gave him a kiss on the cheek.

'Anyway,' Val said, compressing the now-empty beer can in her fist and getting to her feet, 'am I the only one who's hungry?'

'If you are, does it matter?' said Alice, tartly. 'I'm guessing you're going stuff your face regardless.'

Ignoring her comment, Val dragged a bag from her tent and brought it over to the group. She rummaged through it and pulled out a plastic container full of sandwiches.

'Are they all ham?' Alice asked, wrinkling her nose.

With a groan, Val pulled out another box. 'These ones are cucumber. Go nuts.'

Alice took it from her but continued to glare.

'Why won't you eat the ham ones?' Osiris enquired.

'I don't eat meat or any other product that comes from an animal,' she said. Then noticing Osiris's thoroughly confused look, continued, 'You do know where your food comes from, don't you? How old are you?'

Val suddenly let out a chuckle and said, 'For God's sake, Alice, she's messing with you,' before shooting me a look.

It had not occurred to me that I hadn't explained the way humans killed animals in order to eat meat. Considering that she had once been part-fish, I knew not to offer her any seafood out of respect, but never even thought that she may be put off by eating the flesh of life that came from the land.

'So, what's the plan for tonight?' I asked the group, hoping to get the topic away from anything relating to Osiris's lack of knowledge.

Luckily, everyone immediately began offering their own suggestions. Their words didn't matter to me, though, as I had my eyes on Osiris, who had not touched the ham sandwich she had been handed. I took it from her and offered her a cucumber one instead, giving her a reassuring smile.

*

'I'd not given a thought to where human's got food from. Though the ocean was filled with predators seeking other species to eat, so I suppose it shouldn't be a surprise.'

Osiris and I were walking through the woods. It was a rather warm night and neither of us was tired, so with everyone having retreated into their tents, we left the field in order to find the nearby lake. Now that we were alone, I was finally able to discuss the subject of food without the others getting suspicious.

'I should have mentioned it earlier,' I said. 'I'm sorry.'

She nudged me with her elbow and started walking closer to me. 'Don't apologise, Luke. I'm sure there isn't a handbook on how to tell a mermaid-turned-human everything they need to know about life on Earth.'

I smirked and nudged her back. 'I suppose not, but that would be useful.'

We continued for a short while until the trees began to thin out and we reached the edge of a small lake. The moon was bright and there were no clouds in the sky, which allowed for us to see clearly without the need for any electronic devices.

Osiris bent down and tapped the water. It began to ripple and glistened in the silver glow of moonlight. 'It's so pretty,' she commented, then glanced back at me. 'Could we... could we possibly go in?'

I considered her question for a moment. We had previously discussed the issue of swimming, which is when it dawned on me that Osiris would not know how to do that now that she had legs as opposed to a fish tail. However, I believed the lake would be okay if we kept to the shallow end.

'Okay then,' I said.

She stood up, looking shocked. 'Seriously?'

'Yeah, why not?' I replied, unzipping my jacket and throwing it onto the floor. She watched as I took off my socks and dipped one of my toes into the water. 'It's a bit cold, but we should be fine.'

'Do we keep our clothes on?' she asked.

'I wouldn't advise it,' I said, taking my t-shirt off and allowing it to join my jacket. 'We're going have to do what you were supposedly doing on your first night here. *Skinny dip.*'

'They said that was illegal though, didn't they?'

I unbuckled my belt and stepped out of my jeans. 'Well, there's nobody around and no cameras or anything. Everyone back at the tents will probably be asleep now. Who's going to know?'

I hesitated for a moment, and then removed my underwear. Osiris blushed and averted her eyes at first, but then returned her gaze when I began to make my way into the lake. It was a lot colder than I had thought, but I took the plunge and swiftly dived under the surface. My body initially seemed to scream at the temperature, though after a few minutes I calmed, apart from the occasional chattering of my teeth.

'Come on,' I called to Osiris, who was stood nervously at the edge.

She checked behind her shoulder to see that the coast was indeed clear. It looked like she was debating the situation in her head, but I could see the glint in her eye and knew she wanted to join. Eventually, she removed her shirt and jeans, so we stood in just her lingerie. Her bra was something she removed with ease, presumably because I had clearly seen her breasts the first time we met. She seemed a little more uneasy about taking off her underwear, though.

'Don't do anything you don't feel comfortable with,' I advised her. The last thing I wanted for her at that moment was to feel like she was being forced to do it.

'It's okay, I want to,' she said, slipping out of them.

As she slowly entered the water, I couldn't help but admire her body. She was so beautifully slender and her skin, which whilst still extremely pale, was now a lot more vibrant than it had been. Mimicking my earlier moves, she allowed herself to fall under the water then returned to the surface laughing.

'I've never felt the cold like this!' She declared.

'How does it feel?' I asked, holding her in my arms.

'Amazing,' she said. 'This is how I was meant to spend time in the water.'

'So, you don't miss having fins?'

She shook her head. 'Not at all. I always hated knowing my tail was there. But I didn't know it was legs that I wanted until I finally saw humans.' She then wrapped an arm around my waist and began to splash with her feet.

'Watch it!' I laughed.

Osiris giggled and made sure I got hit by more water. I stretched out my spare arm and caused a wave that hit her. She looked shocked then kissed me.

'I have a question,' she said.

I kissed her back. 'Ask away.'

'How do we get back to our tent? We're soaking.'

Getting back now that we were wet was not something I'd thought about in advance. Now, however, it became a real concern that we'd need to return, but not dampen our clothes.

I decided to see the funny side of it, though.

'We run,' I said, simply.

Osiris looked puzzled, but I winked at her and began to make my way out of the water. She followed, keeping a hold of my hand. I reached down and picked up my clothes in a pile and she did the same with her other hand, keeping them tucked next to her side. I squeezed her hand and encouraged her to pick up the pace, making sure not to overwork her legs.

We dashed through the trees, keeping a tight hold of both our clothes and each other. It felt exhilarating being naked and running through the open air, especially having Osiris there beside me. We managed to make our way back to the field and hurriedly got into our tent.

'That was fun,' I said, breathlessly.

Osiris rested her head against my bare chest. My heart was beating fast and she placed her ear over the sound. I could feel her hand brushing against my upper thigh.

'I really like you, Luke,' she said.

'I really like you, too,' I said, kissing her neck.

We had yet to consummate our relationship and I made sure not to be pushy about it because I knew it would be all new to her.

Osiris leaned towards my ear and said softly, 'I want you to show me that you like me, and I want to show how much I like you.'

'Are you sure you want to do this?'

She nodded and looked at me. Her golden eyes stared directly into mine and, in that moment, I knew that everything that had happened so far had happened for this reason. The two of us being there in that moment was meant to be.

I kissed her on the lips and gently laid her back on to the sleeping bag that covered the tent floor so her head rested back onto a pillow. She stared straight up, and I leaned over her so I was now looking into her eyes before turning my attention to her breasts. I placed my lips against her nipples and gently suckled on them until they were erect.

Her hands played with my hair as I began to bring my tongue over her stomach. A small gasp emitted from her mouth as my stubble tickled her skin. I glanced upwards to check if I should continue and it was obvious that Osiris wanted me to.

Chapter 18

When dressing for my brother's engagement party, I made sure to wear something that wasn't too casual, but also didn't look too formal either. In the end, I stood in front of the bedroom mirror wearing slim-fitting dark jeans and a long-sleeved shirt. My hair was smartly combed and I'd spent some time trimming my beard.

Osiris walked in and stood by the door, her reflection showing just how glamorous she could be in a dress. I turned and beckoned her over.

'You look beautiful,' I said, kissing her on the lips.

She blushed. 'So do you.'

I joined her as she sat down on the bed. The morning after our night in the tent, I had awoken to feel the best I'd felt in years – which was something that not even the constant glares I received from Alice could take away from me.

'I'm excited about meeting the rest of your family,' Osiris said, her hand rested on my knee. 'Do you... do you think they'll like me?'

'How could they not?' I replied. 'And even if they didn't, I wouldn't care.'

I dreaded what my sister was going to say about my new girlfriend, not because I valued her views at all, but rather what her scathing words could potentially do to the confidence that had been instilled into Osiris since her transformation.

A knock echoed from downstairs, followed by Matt's voice calling, 'Hurry up, guys! I've told Emmie we'll be leaving soon!'

I shouted back, 'Give us a minute and we'll be down!'

His grumblings signalled a return to the living room. I knew he'd be cursing us, but I wanted to talk to Osiris alone before we set off. 'Don't worry,' I said to her, gently running my fingers through her hair, 'my family will love you.'

She leaned forward and hugged me. The aroma from her perfume met my nostrils and I embraced her tightly, not wanting to ever let her go.

*

I stood outside the venue with Osiris and Emmie as we waited for Matt to park the car and join us. The girls looked very elegant, though they appeared rather self-conscious as people passed by. I noticed several guys checking them out.

'You both look great,' I assured them.

'Thanks,' Emmie said. 'I just wish Matthew would hurry up; it's getting cold.'

The temperature had indeed dropped, and I regretted not bringing a jacket with me. I put my arms around Osiris to prevent her from feeling the chill too much.

'Have you heard from Val?' she asked.

'She texted me saying her and Alice may be a bit late.'

Emmie turned her attention away from looking for Matt and frowned. 'I wonder why – they didn't say they were doing anything before the party when I spoke to them yesterday.'

I shrugged. 'I don't know, but Val does get easily distracted.'

'Here's Matt now,' Osiris pointed out.

Sure enough, he came into view from the other end of the street, half-jogging towards us.

'Had a nightmare trying to get parked round here,' he said, grabbing hold of Emmie's hand. 'Are we going in then?'

Glad to be getting out of the cold, we all entered the building and up the stairs to where the party was being held. Music could be heard playing even from outside and it got steadily clearer as we approached the double doors. Through the glass panels, I could see that a fair number of people had already shown up and I made sure to keep a tight hold of Osiris because I knew that I'd feel more confident amongst my family with her next to me.

A few people looked in our direction when we entered, though more of them turned back to their own conversation when they realised we weren't particularly noteworthy. A man from near the bar, however, looked elated by our arrival and rushed over to greet us.

My brother Phillip was just a touch shorter than me, with fair hair. He gave me a small hug. 'Glad you could make it. You too, Matt,' he said, shaking his hand. 'Who are these two beautiful ladies?'

'This is Emmie,' Matt said, and she beamed as her hand was also shaken.

'And this is Osiris,' I said, putting my arm around her. 'She's my girlfriend.'

Phillip's shock was evident, and he immediately tried to recover, but not before his fiancé arrived wearing an expression of equal surprise.

'Did I hear right, Luke? You have a girlfriend?' Daisy asked. Her normally wavy red hair had been tied back into a loose knot for the occasion, and the colour was very striking amongst the sea of people. 'Blimey, you haven't had one of those in a while. It's lovely to meet you.'

'What's going on here?' said a horribly familiar voice and my heart sank as my sister approached us, looking like she was missing out on an undeniable treat.

Dressed in the most unflattering dress donned with a mixture of purple and lilac patterns, Amber resembled what I could only describe as a psychedelic nightmare. Her hair had been bleached, but it did not suit her at all. In fact, it came across as a pale imitation of Osiris's, who she seemed to be eyeing suspiciously.

'This is Luke's new girlfriend,' Daisy explained.

'I'm Osiris,' she said, brightly.

'Delighted,' Amber said, scanning her outfit from head to toe. 'Your dress, it's... well, it's a look, I suppose.'

Luckily, this comment completely went over her head and Osiris merely smiled back.

'Come on,' I said to my group. 'Let's find a seat.'

We walked to the other end of the room and sat down around a small table in the corner, making sure there were two empty seats for when Val and Alice arrived.

'That girl wasn't very pleasant,' Emmie scowled.

'I'll say,' Matt laughed. 'That was Amber, Luke's sister. She isn't exactly a ray of sunshine.'

'Never has been,' I added. 'Just try and ignore her if you don't want your evening ruined. I hope you're okay Osiris, I did warn you about her.'

'I'm fine,' she insisted. 'I really don't think she's as bad as you made out.'

I didn't argue, for I knew that Amber's spiteful personality would become more pronounced when the night wore on a bit.

'Right,' I said, standing back up, 'my round. What's everybody drinking?'

After memorising their desired drinks, I made my way across the room, taking the time to politely reply to distant family members and familiar faces who spoke to me on my way. I gritted my teeth and was as polite as possible, but noticed that my dad was now at the bar and I was eager to speak to him.

'How're you doing, dad?'

He turned and broke into a smile. 'Luke! I was worried you wouldn't show.'

'Don't be daft,' I laughed. 'I wouldn't miss my only brother's engagement party. Besides, it was you that I was worried wouldn't be able to make it. Are you feeling okay?'

He took a swig of beer and nodded. 'I am, actually. The doctors think my leg is improving. I need to go in for a follow-up in a few days, but I'm quietly confident.'

'That's great, dad, really it is.' I hesitated slightly, and then asked, 'You haven't noticed anything else strange, have you? Since that person who was watching you from the window the other week?'

My dad sighed. 'You haven't been thinking too much about that, have you? I shouldn't have mentioned it. I haven't had anything happen since, so it must have been an innocent mistake.'

I highly doubted that, but chose not to pursue the topic. There was a niggling feeling in my head that the person had something to do with me and not him, so I didn't feel it necessary to pester my dad about the issue. Instead, I ordered the drinks and said goodbye to him, before returning to my table.

'How's your dad doing?' Matt asked, as I passed his soft drink over.

'Well, he reckons his leg is getting better.'

We sat in silence for a few minutes, listening to the music. Osiris's eyes were transfixed by people on the dance floor. I looked from her to them, wondering whether she was soaking in the movement of their feet, when my attention was caught by my sister's obnoxiously loud voice.

'She's so monstrously obese,' she cried. 'I bet you anything she'll be dead within the next five years.' She kept glancing over at a large-framed woman wearing a cardigan that barely covered her arms and a loose-fitting dress that didn't quite disguise her stomach.

Noel shook his head. 'Don't be so cruel.'

'Oh, come on. Let's make a bet,' Amber replied. 'A tenner that she'll snuff it in the next few months?'

Noel merely rolled his eyes in response. Amber turned her attention to the next victim: a nervous looking young man with a pale complexion and dark, wiry hair.

'As for *him*,' she spat. 'He looks like a failed abortion.'

Evidently shocked, Noel responded with, 'That's Daisy's cousin, Elijah. He's actually really nice.'

'Oh, pur-*lease*,' Amber sniggered. 'I can practically smell the failure from here.'

Matt and Emmie both looked at a loss for my sister's words and Osiris seemed uncomfortable, so I put my hand on her knee. I guessed that perhaps up until now she had been denying to herself the belief that humans could be as cruel as the other mermaids had told her. Seeing Amber being so venomous would convince anyone that there are people in the world who lack empathy.

Emmie's eyes widened as she looked over the glass of wine she had to her lips. 'Look, there's Alice and Val,' she announced.

The entrance doors had indeed opened, and the pair walked in. Alice looked radiant in a frilly purple dress and long, wavy hair, complete with stilettos. Val, on the other hand, was wearing a rather nice, simple black dress and matching black shoes, but had this mostly covered over by her normal thick, brown jacket. They both spotted us and waved before making their way over to the bar, where Val immediately began talking animatedly to my dad, who looked thrilled at her arrival.

'She's so crude,' Amber suddenly declared, and I saw that she was glaring over at Val.

'Who is she?' Noel asked, leaning over to get a better look.

'That's Val – Luke's friend,' she said, grimacing. 'Honestly, there's not an ounce of class about her. Her girlfriend scrubs up pretty well, though, so goodness knows what she sees in her. And it looks like she didn't bother dressing up for the occasion, either. Check out that hideous charity shop jacket – it looks like she pulled it off a dead homeless man!'

'Why is she being so mean about Val?' Osiris asked me.

It was on the tip of my tongue to simply describe my sister in a cluster of swear words, but instead opted for the more tactful, 'Because she has no consideration for people's feelings.'

Alice and Val made their way over to occupy the empty seats we had left for them.

'What's happening, then?' Val asked, taking off her jacket. I noticed Amber's eyes peer over from the next table and land on her tattoos. No doubt she wouldn't approve of them, but I hoped she'd at least have the decency to keep her mouth shut.

'Not a lot,' Emmie said. 'We were just listening to the music.'

'Just as long as we don't have to dance to it,' Alice said.

'Oh, come on,' Val begged. 'Surely you can't deny me a little waltz.'

Alice narrowed her eyes. 'We've been through this, Valerie. If you want to go and make a fool of yourself, then feel free. Count me out, though.'

I leaned over and whispered to Osiris, 'Do you want to dance?'

She whipped her head round at once to stare at me. 'Can I? I mean, do you think I'll be able to?'

'Of course,' I said, getting to my feet and holding out my hand.

Osiris took it with glee.

'Right,' I said to the others, 'we'll be back shortly.'

I didn't normally dance at parties, even though I wasn't bad at it really and didn't get embarrassed easily or anything. With Osiris's look of longing at the dancers, this party would be an exception and we walked together over to the dance floor. It had thinned out considerably, which was better for us I thought given that it was her first attempt at dancing.

The music changed once we got there. I took both of Osiris's hands in mine and began to make movements for her to copy. She laughed and began to move her feet a bit more in a mimic of what she had seen earlier.

'That's right,' I encouraged. 'Just have fun with it!'

After a few moments, I twirled her under my arm, which made her smile brighter than ever before. We then continued until our attention was distracted by something happening across the room. Looking over, we could see that Amber and Alice were both stood looking fiercely at each other and talking with raised voices.

'I'd back off now if you know what's good for you!' Alice warned, whilst Val tried in vain to get her to sit back down.

Amber smirked. 'You'd like that, wouldn't you?'

'What the hell is going on?' I demanded. By the time I'd reached them, a small crowd was already gathering, including Matt and Emmie who looked sheepishly happy at the drama that was unfolding.

'This foul excuse for a human being has been criticising Valerie ever since we sat down,' Alice answered, pointing at my sister. 'Nothing but vile, disgusting things have come out of her mouth and if she won't stop it then I swear to God I'm going to make her!'

Daisy made her way over, visibly quivering. 'Okay, ladies, how about we take this outside? Let's not ruin the evening, please.'

'I'm not ruining anything,' Amber said, without taking her eyes off her opponent. 'She's the one with the problem. I only said a few home truths about her girlfriend and, well, I seem to have touched a nerve.'

'Come on, Amber,' Phillip said, attempting to grab her arm, but she brushed him off. 'If you want an argument then fine, but don't do it here.'

'He's right,' Noel said. 'Sit and finish your drink at least.'

Alice folded her arms. 'Yeah, go on, Amber – finish your drink! Hopefully someone's laced it with poison and do us all a favour.'

I had to stifle a laugh and, for the first time, admired Alice's way with words.

Amber was clearly up for a fight and hissed, 'I know more about you than I think you realise. You had a falling out with your parents, didn't you? No surprise, really. If they hadn't ditched you the moment you came out then they certainly did when you introduced them to the tramp you call a partner!'

With one swift movement, Alice punched Amber squarely on the nose and sent her crashing to the ground. Noel gasped and immediately went to help her up, whereas Alice looked particularly smug with herself and walked off.

'Come on,' she said to Val. 'We're going home.'

Val wisely chose not to argue and followed her out of the room. Amber shoved away anyone who tried to assist her. There was an immediate buzz about what had just happened, and the crowd began to disperse as people went to discuss the argument.

My dad let out a low whistle beside me. 'Christ, I hate to say it, but it might have done our Amber some good to get a smack. Sometimes she doesn't know when to shut her gob.'

'She really shouldn't have been saying bad things about Val,' Emmie piped up.

'I told you she wasn't pleasant,' Matt said.

Amber had gotten to her feet and was wiping the blood from her nose. '*Stupid dyke*,' she spat. 'I'll kill her for this.'

'No, you won't,' I growled. 'Just learn to shut your mouth.'

She looked as though she'd just received another hit. 'Excuse me?'

'You heard.'

'Okay,' Noel said, physically stepping in as though he was worried another actual fight was about to go down, 'I think we all just need to cool down.'

Phillip nodded in agreement. 'Yeah, let's all sit down and –'

Amber held up her hand. 'Oh, shut up. Go on then, Luke, take your best shot. What's the problem? I told them the truth, it's not my fault they couldn't take it.'

'You don't even know them.'

She rolled her eyes. 'I know enough. Anyway, it's not hard to guess what –'

'Enough!' I shouted, a lot louder than I had intended. 'Does it ever occur to you that maybe you can't just judge people based on your own assumptions? Do you ever stop to think that maybe people are dealing with things you might not realise? That you may be making horrible, cruel, vicious comments and not considering the damage you're doing? No, of course not, because you don't care! Nobody does! People have despicable things happen to them all the time and you and other clueless idiots think you can just openly make your mouths go! Well I'm telling you now to shut the hell up!'

There was a deathly silence following this, in which it seemed nobody dared make a single noise. Everyone was looking at me with complete disbelief – I had never blown up like that before in public. I could just imagine how I must look, my eyes ablaze and fists clenched. I don't think I've ever once witnessed my sister being lost for words.

'Let's go home, mate,' Matt interjected, placing a hand on my shoulder. 'We can pick up a takeaway or something on the way back.'

I took a few deep breaths and then nodded. 'Yeah, alright, sounds good.' I knew that I needed leave as swiftly as possible and the food at the party didn't look too appealing, anyway. 'Let's get out of here.'

Chapter 19

As the others unpacked the Chinese takeaway, I excused myself and swiftly went upstairs to the bathroom. I sank down to the floor and willed myself not to cry. I normally didn't allow my sister's toxic words affect me and always tried my hardest to ignore her. But hearing her openly criticising two people she didn't know personally had reminded me about how cruel others could be to a person without knowing the full story. It brought unpleasant memories flooding back, a dark time that I'd kept hidden for years out of fear of judgement.

There was a small tap on the door and Osiris's soft voice spoke up. 'Luke, are you alright? I'm really worried about you.'

'I'm fine,' I replied, yet not even I could believe the lie. My voice cracked as I said it, and nobody could fail to realise I was choking back tears. 'Seriously,' I continued, pressing my forehead against the door, 'just go and enjoy the food.'

'I'm not going anywhere,' she said, and I heard her sit down.

I pressed my hand against the wood. 'There's stuff I haven't been entirely truthful about. I mean, effectively I've been lying.'

'To me?'

'To everyone.'

There was a pause before she responded, 'You know that you can tell me anything. What's said between us won't be repeated. I'd never betray your trust like that.'

'I know,' I said. 'It's just hard for me to admit.'

'Admit what? Luke, what's happened?'

I didn't respond straight away because every time I tried to talk, the words got caught in my throat. For eight years, I'd kept my mouth shut about an experience I'd gone through, but something was telling me that it was time to admit it to someone. And I knew that that someone should be Osiris. It wouldn't really be fair on her to start a relationship with me if I was constantly carrying such an extreme secret with me.

I considered opening the door, but I didn't think I could allow myself to see her face when I revealed the truth. There needed to be some distance if I was to talk.

'It happened the night of my prom,' I said, finally. 'That's a gathering you attend to celebrate the end of secondary school. I went and it was good, then we went back to a party someone was putting on. It was a chance to drink and have fun without the teachers around. One of our friends had made arrangements with his cousin to use his house. It was at Hartlepool, so not too far away.'

'And something bad happened there?'

'Well, it started off really great. Me and Val and Matt and everyone were all messing about, having a few drinks and just genuinely winding down. A few friends of the cousins friends arrived, a big group of them; they were like late twenties, early thirties. I didn't think too much of it at first. Just made it seem like the party was getting bigger and better.'

For a few seconds, I stopped in order to compose myself. When it had first happened, I'd gone over the events leading up to it repeatedly in my head, but I'd suppressed it for so long that it felt all new to me again. I felt a shiver go to my core.

'Eventually, Val and Matt ended up collapsing from all the alcohol, but I was still feeling pretty decent. I went outside for a smoke and got chatting to these two guys. They were part of the gang that had arrived late. They seemed okay and told me they had some weed back at their place and wanted to know if I'd be interested in trying it out. I didn't think anything of it – I'd tried weed with Val loads of times and met strangers through nights out before, so I decided to go with them. I mean, all my friends were passed out by this point so I figured I may as well. Turns out they took me to a hotel room. I thought it was weird, but I still followed them. I feel so stupid, but I was sixteen and drunk. I was an idiot.'

'You're not to blame for whatever happened,' Osiris said. 'You were young and you were vulnerable.'

A tear rolled down my cheek and I wiped it away. 'When I was in the room, they offered me a drink and then a joint. It felt alright for about half an hour and then... I began to feel sick, like I had a fever. My heart was racing, and I just wanted to leave. They told me to lie down on the bed, which I did because I thought I could just sleep it off. I didn't have control... I could barely move. I could still tell what was going on but that was about it. Before I knew it, stuff was happening and I couldn't stop it.'

'What? What happened?'

It was on the tip of my tongue, the words I'd dared not say, even in my own head. The secret I'd tried to keep dead for nearly a decade.

'They raped me,' I said, in barely more than a whisper.

A solemn silence followed this as I let it sink in the fact that this was the first time I'd ever said that out loud. Osiris knew about the concept of rape due to some of the films and television programmes that we'd been watching. Tears were now streaming down my face and I knew it was futile to even attempting to stop it. I let out a choking sob and attempted to carry on the story.

'While it was going on, I tried to block out what was happening. I wanted to fight – I really did – but the drugs and the alcohol and everything meant that... I just couldn't. In the end, I just laid there and flopped. I guess it's a natural reaction. I don't know how long it lasted because I blacked out eventually. When I woke up a few hours later, they'd gone. The hotel room was a mess, like it was the scene of a burglary, and I just left. I walked all the way home, still in shock.'

Even though I couldn't see her, I could hear Osiris sobbing. 'You don't have to go on if you don't want to,' she wept. 'I'll understand.'

'It's fine, I need to talk about it. I need you to know.'

'Okay.'

'The journey home took ages – not that I noticed. So many thoughts were running through my head about what had happened. I could remember some of it. It's like when you wake up from a dream and you can remember certain details, but not the whole picture – that's how I felt. When I got home, it all hit me and I broke down after having a shower.'

'But you didn't tell anyone?'

'No, I was too ashamed. I burnt the clothes I was wearing that night and tried to forget that it ever happened. For weeks I couldn't look anyone in the eye, and I kept lashing out. I think everyone noticed how much I'd changed and probably just thought I was reacting badly to leaving school. I tried my hardest to give college a go, but it was no use. That's how I ended up working in the petrol station and not really having any goals beyond that. I remember the summer between school and college – I rarely left my room, let alone my house. My dad started to get scared and I'd spend hours crying, imagining how he would feel if he knew about what had happened. My sister started to say things to me about being selfish because I was closing myself off. I think that's why I was so angry at her tonight, because she'd made assumptions about me back then without knowing the full story.'

'I can't even imagine what state you must have been in.'

'I'm glad you weren't there to witness it. The whole ordeal resulted in me being horrible to my family and friends. I ended up chucking tables and chairs, losing control of myself, screaming in private that I wanted to die. Even when I finally left the house, there were days when I couldn't even get out for a cigarette because the anxiety would take over and I would start panicking. I guess by not talking about it and bottling it all in, I hadn't helped myself. That's what a lot of men do'

'But you started coping at some point, right? You don't resemble that person anymore. I've never witnessed you being truly angry before, and you have a great relationship with your friends and with your dad. You must have finally come around?'

'Yeah, eventually I did. In the early days, I contemplated suicide. If it wasn't for the thought of the devastation for my family and friends, I would've killed myself. I think it got to the point where I realised that if I was going to keep on living then I needed to do it properly and not close myself off. Not that I was completely cured – I began drinking a lot and sleeping with random girls on a regular basis. My way of coping, I suppose.'

'Luke, why didn't you tell anybody?'

'I was too embarrassed. I didn't want to admit it to myself, never mind anyone else. I felt ridiculous for putting myself in that situation and ashamed that... that...' I tailed off and had a small cry. It felt strangely exhilarating to have finally spoken the truth.

There were a few minutes when no words were spoken, and then Osiris said, 'It must have been awful. I don't think I could ever imagine what pain you've went through. Did you not consider telling the police? You could have brought legal action against the two men.'

It wasn't as simple as how she made it sound. I tried to think of the best way to explain it to her. 'Do you remember that film we watched the other night, about the woman who went to court against her attackers?'

'Yes, they got off, didn't they? The police couldn't prove anything.'

'Well that's what I thought would happen to me, which is why I convinced myself that coming forward about it would be pointless. I did research and in a lot of rape cases, it comes down to the issue of consent. I mean, it happened behind closed doors. I voluntarily went to the hotel with those men and entered the room of my own free will. What happened inside can't be proven. I know it happened and they know it happened, but that's about it. I barely remember what they look like. It scares me knowing that they are still walking the streets and that they could do this to someone else. I sometimes feel guilty when I think about it.'

'You shouldn't,' Osiris said, softly. 'If there's anyone who should be feeling that way then it's the men who did this to you. You did nothing wrong.'

Eventually, I stopped crying. My face was numb by this point, though I nonetheless felt like I had just made great progress. It took several more minutes, but I did manage to get to my feet and open the door. Osiris's face was as red and blemished by tears as I imagined mine must've been. Without saying a word, she pulled me into a tight hug and we stood like this for what felt like hours. I buried my face into her hair, never wanting to let go and taking in how soft and pure she felt. The only sound in the house came from the faint muffle of voices from the kitchen downstairs.

We ultimately broke apart and she cupped my face with her hand. 'What do you want to do?' she asked.

Instead of answering, I took her hand in mine and walked towards the bedroom. It had been an eventful and stressful day. I was extremely tired, but once we were under the duvet, Osiris and I engaged in the most intimate, gentle and natural lovemaking. It was the first time since our awkward night in the tent, when we had both been anxious and nervous – on this occasion, however, there were no such feelings from either of us.

Chapter 20

I thought that after finally unloading the countless worries that had been hounding me for years, I would've had the best night's sleep I'd had in a long time. Unfortunately, that was not the case and I found myself waking up only an hour after falling asleep. At first, I just laid in bed, listening to Osiris quietly snooze beside me. She always looked radiant and it was irrefutable that she was one of those people that looked good even when sleeping.

Doing my best not to wake her, I got slowly out of bed, shoving on a pair of boxer-shorts and a t-shirt. My room was a mess and I had to manoeuvre my way through all the junk before reaching the landing.

There was something soothing about the house being so silent and I crept downstairs so that I could make a start on the Chinese food I hadn't gotten around to eating yet. I hadn't realised before how starving I was, but my stomach was now certainly letting me know that it needed filling.

My head was still buzzing over my confession to Osiris. It seemed so surreal that I had willingly shared something so personal with somebody I hadn't known for very long, yet it felt so right to have done so. I wasn't sure where exactly we were going to go from this point in terms of truly tackling the issue because it was an extremely complex and delicate subject. I decided to not think about it for the time being.

I had just made a start on eating when there was a knock at the door. I went to answer it, perplexed at who could possibly be calling for a visit at this hour – it was Val, looking extremely gaunt.

'Hey,' she greeted me, 'can I come in?'

'Sure,' I said, and moved back so she could enter. I was slightly taken aback by her abrupt arrival.

'I've barely had an hour's sleep,' she muttered, as I closed the door. 'When we got home, me and Alice talked about everything. After that, I kind of just drifted in and out until I realised that I wasn't going to get so much as a nap. Thank God you're up, I'm sorry if I woke anybody up, I just needed to talk. I did send you a text.'

'Shit, sorry about that, I've left my phone upstairs. Do you want a drink or anything? I was just going to have water, but –'

'Waters fine,' she said. 'Here, I'll get it.' She walked over to the sink as I made to put the rest of the Chinese away. 'I just came over for a bit of a chat, you know. I'm sorry if what happened ruined the party for you guys. Alice has been going through a lot lately and she just sort of... snapped over what Amber was saying.'

'Don't apologise,' I told her, firmly. 'It's my sister who should be doing that – Alice punching her was the best thing that could've happened. Honestly, don't worry about a thing, Val. I'm here for you if ever you need to talk.'

She passed me my glass and we both sat down. 'Thanks. You're the best, Luke, I really don't deserve you.'

I took a long gulp of water, before saying, 'I'm pretty sure I'm the one who should be saying that to you. I don't know what I would've done without you during this whole situation with Osiris.'

'I'm just glad you came to me straight away instead of keeping it to yourself.'

'That's something I now know to avoid,' I said, swigging back the last of my drink. 'I think from now on, I'm going to be open about everything – less self-punishing that way.'

I knew Val wouldn't understand the full impact of my statement, but she smiled all the same and I was happy for her company.

She then glanced at the time and stood up. 'Anyway, I better get going.'

'No, stay,' I insisted, but then I realised how tired I was. I guess the lack of sleep was starting to catch up with me.

'You look a little drowsy to me,' Val said. 'How about you get yourself on the couch for a little nap? Text me tomorrow and we'll talk.'

'Okay,' I agreed. 'I'll see you later.'

She scurried off and I made my way into the living room, where I did what Val had advised and collapsed onto the couch. Before I knew it, I was fast asleep.
*

A ray of sunlight peeking through the curtains woke me a few hours later. Checking the time, I saw that it was a lot earlier than I would normally wake up.

There was noise coming from the next room, which I attributed to the others also waking up earlier than usual. After a quick trip to the bathroom, I went into the kitchen, where Matt and Emmie were indeed sat sipping coffee.

'Morning,' I yawned, walking over to pour one for myself. 'How come you two are up at this hour?'

'Bloody dog next door barking about twenty minutes ago,' Matt grumbled. 'I swear I'm going to have a word with Charlotte about it. Bad legs or not, surely she can keep the animal indoors until I wake up. Maybe waiting until sunrise would be a good start!'

'Don't cause trouble,' Emmie said, rubbing her eyes. 'I know it's not ideal, but she's just an old woman. Maybe the dog will settle down eventually.'

Matt didn't look convinced, but wisely chose not to argue back.

I made some toast and stood looking out the window as I ate. 'I'm going to hop in the shower after this. What have you two got planned for the rest of the day?'

Emmie walked over to put their empty mugs in the sink and shrugged. 'I don't know. The forecast reckons it's going to rain later so we might just have a day in the house. What about you and Osiris? If you don't have plans, we could all do something together.'

'Sure,' I replied, finishing off my breakfast. I wiped my hands on a tea towel then left to take a shower.

Luckily, I had some fresh clothes in the spare room, so I chose to collect those instead of risking waking up Osiris, who I assumed was still out for the count.

I had only been in the shower for around five minutes when I heard a knock from the front door. This was something I initially brushed off because I didn't think anyone would be making a house call this early, yet within seconds there were footsteps on the staircase and the wrapping of knuckles on the bathroom door.

'Luke?' It was Matt's voice.

'What's the matter?' I asked.

'There's someone here to see you,' he said. 'What should I tell him?'

I had no idea who could possibly need to see me at this hour. 'Who is it?'

'He says his name is Sam.'

It took a while for me to comprehend what he'd said. Once it began to sink in, hundreds of questions began to race through my head. Why would Sam be at my house wanting to talk to me? What could he want, and what would be so serious that felt the need see me about it? How did he find out where I lived?

'Luke, what should I tell him?' Matt repeated.

'Tell him I'll be down in a minute,' I said. 'I just need to finish up here then get dressed.'

I heard Matt go back downstairs then I stepped out of the shower and began to dry myself, all the while thinking over all the possibilities of why Sam was here. There was a horrible sinking feeling in my gut that something bad was happening. I got dressed in a hurry, debating on whether to wake Osiris. I decided against it as it might amount to nothing and I didn't want to disturb her slumber.

Sam was sat at the table when I came down. Matt and Emmie were stood, both looking thoroughly confused at his sudden appearance.

'Sam?' I said, tentatively.

He looked up. 'Morning.'

'Would you like some coffee?' I asked, not sure exactly what else I could say.

'No thanks, I'm alright,' he replied.

I turned to the others. 'Could you give us a minute, please?' They left and I took a seat opposite Sam. He looked quite worn out, as though he'd skipped several nights of sleep. 'Are you sure you don't need a drink or anything?'

He shook his head. 'I'm fine... it's just been a long couple of days. Sorry for just dropping in on you without any notice. There are some things I need to discuss with you, and I figured it was best to do it in person.'

'How did you find out where I lived?'

'I looked it up online,' he said, simply. 'Wasn't exactly hard.'

'How did you know my full name though?' I clarified. 'You must've needed it to look my residence up and I don't think I ever told you my surname.'

'I got it whilst I was doing some investigating. It's kind of what I came here to talk about. Please, if you could just listen and then you can throw me out or whatever, I just need to try and explain it to you.'

'Okay, then. Go for it.'

'Well, you found Jodie through her website, right?'

'Yeah, *Belief in the Impossible* or whatever.'

'And when you spoke to her, she told you about her interest in finding all these elusive creatures I'm guessing. That's what we call cryptozoology, have you heard of that?'

I shook my head.

'It's a sort of pseudoscience, basically aimed at proving the existence of stuff like Bigfoot and the Loch Ness Monster, as well as more obscure ones. It's what Jodie's dedicated her life to, but she isn't alone – and I don't just mean her online buddies. Have you ever seen this person before?'

At this point, he pulled out his phone and got up a photo of a man who looked to be in his late fifties, with shaggy grey hair and a short beard. I had definitely seen him before, but couldn't place where.

'Who is it?' I asked.

'A man named Casey Raistrick. He's an American, originally from North Dakota, but he moved to England a few years ago and has now set up a sect in London.'

Then it hit me. He was the man who had come into the petrol station a few days prior and asked for a local newspaper.

'He came to my workplace... it was just over a week ago, I think. I thought it was weird that some American dude would be interested in news about this area.'

'Right, well it sounds like he was deliberately confronting you. He probably wasn't content at watching you from a distance.'

'Watching me? Who the hell is this guy?'

'He and Jodie have been close for a long time.'

More pieces of the puzzle began to slot into place. In Jodie's house, there had been a framed photograph of her and a man – who, I now realised, was Casey. I knew there had been something familiar about him.

'I don't know the exact nature of their relationship,' Sam continued, 'but it's clear that they share the same determined drive. There are a lot of contributions from him on her forum if you know his username.'

My brain was working in overdrive. 'Yes!' I cried. 'I found a thread about sea monsters on there from someone called CRaistrick and he linked to one about mermaids. It had the news article on it about Osiris washing up on the beach.'

Sam grimaced. 'That doesn't shock me. Jodie will be working closely with him given that she very likely knows about Osiris... about her origins.'

'You know, don't you? That she used to be a mermaid.'

'Yes.'

'And you're certain that Jodie does, too?'

'Luke, you won't have just left her radar. She's meticulous when it comes to weird reports relating to possible mythical being sightings and she doesn't forget conversations she's had with people. You went to her and she won't let that go – the fact that Casey has been in your shop pretty much confirms that. She knows you have something she wants, and she won't give up until she has it.'

His words stirred something in my memory that made me question him. 'Were you the one who phoned me a few weeks ago?'

'Yes,' he replied. 'Once we'd spoken that day outside of Jodie's house, I thought it best to investigate who she was associating with, so I followed you home and eventually saw you with Osiris. It was obvious to me immediately what she was and so I thought I'd let you know the dangers you could be facing. I stuck around a bit and when you didn't show any sign of giving up your connection with her, I decided to approach you when you were out in York to give you another warning.'

'You've been following me?'

'I'm sorry, I know it must seem sinister, but I didn't want Jodie to try anything if she found out about Osiris.'

'Are we in danger?' This was the only thing I needed to know.

'Perhaps,' he said. 'My main concern is that all the research I've done into Casey and his background suggests that he's after a very different goal than Jodie. She mainly wants fame and fortune from the discovery of some figure from folklore, but Casey seems to be after power. He's very much into the occult and there would be great advantages in terms of magic to having something like a mermaid at his disposal.'

'Such as?' I asked, even though I dreaded hearing the answer.

In response, he reached down and picked up a satchel, from which he pulled out three leather-bound books that he slammed down on the table. They were all the same reddish colour and encrypted with lettering that was starting to peel off. The sight of them sent a prickle of uneasiness through my veins because they reminded me of the kind of tomes you'd see used for witchcraft. Correlating this with the statement he made about Casey wanting a mermaid made me want to run upstairs and keep Osiris close to me.

'These are filled with dark enchantments,' Sam explained. 'The kind of stuff you wouldn't even find online. These are some ancient and very secret works I've unearthed, and you can bet Casey has similar artefacts.'

'These enchantments, are they the kind of things that require mermaids for them to work?' I shifted nervously, thinking back to what Osiris had told me about the sorcerer making her trade in her mermaid lifespan for the potion to turn her human. It made me realise just how powerful the magic was that we were dealing with and the notion was tremendously overwhelming.

'Some of them.'

'But Osiris is a human being now. Shouldn't that, I don't know, *disqualify* her from being of use for whatever the book describes?'

'It's possible,' Sam said, though he sounded hesitant. 'Nothing about this is exactly guaranteed; it requires a lot of guesswork on the part of the reader. The wording for a lot of these are open to interpretation, but since Osiris was born a mermaid then technically, no matter what her current species clarification is, I could see her blood potentially being viable. In any case, I'd hazard a guess that it would be enough for Jodie and Casey to want to try it out.'

'Over my dead body,' I said, through gritted teeth.

'If necessary, I imagine,' Sam said. 'We can't know for sure, but I think it's likely that they know about Osiris and Jodie will no doubt guess from looking at her that she wasn't born a human. If I could work it out, then she will be able to as well.'

'How did you know, though? And how do you know she will? You know Jodie personally, don't you?'

'Just trust me that she'll know.'

He was being cagey, so I decided it was best not to query any deeper into how exactly he knew about all of this. It wasn't what was important at this point – I needed to find out what exactly Jodie was planning and how I could avoid any potential harm she may cause.

'What can we do to stop them?'

'Well, keep Osiris close by at all times. If they do know about these spells, then they might attempt to take her.'

'So, we don't know for sure that they're aware of them?'

'We can only guess. I have no records of their correspondence through email or anything, but from what I can tell through his cult and her website, I wouldn't put it past them to have some knowledge. That's why I came here to warn you in person. Where's Osiris now? She should be kept in the loop about all of this.'

'She's in bed,' I said automatically, but then my chest restricted.

I'd left Osiris upstairs when I woke up during the night and had not gone back up to check on her since falling asleep on the couch. Then Matt and Emmie had complained about the neighbour's dog waking them up – and yet this had not affected Osiris. Surely something that would disturb Matt's sleep would also do the same for her. A feeling of dread began to overcome me, and I dashed out of the kitchen and sprinted upstairs without a second thought.

I burst into my room, hoping with all my might that Osiris would be there. She would be startled and then I'd run over to cradle her, thankful that it was all going to be alright. However, there was no such luck to be had since I was greeted with only an empty bed.

Osiris was gone.

Part 3

Chapter 21

It took me a while to calm down. Once I had, I made sure that everyone was present for what I was about to tell them. We were gathered in the living room: Matt and Emmie on the couch, Val sat upright in one armchair and Sam on the other. I was pacing by the fireplace, trying to figure out the best way of breaking the news to them.

'What's going on?' Matt asked.

The answer to that very simple question was going to cause alarm amongst my friends and I was struggling to find the words to explain everything. However, the people assembled in the room at that moment were the ones I trusted most in the world and the ones I knew I could count on for help in getting Osiris back safely.

'There's something you need to understand,' I said, directing my attention to Matt and Emmie. 'Before I say anything, I just need to you to keep an open mind.'

Matt frowned. 'Okay, open mind in what way?'

'Think about Osiris – how effortlessly platinum her hair is right down to the roots and how her eyes are gold, considering she's never had anything dyed and never worn contact lenses. And the fact that that she just showed up randomly one day not so long ago and couldn't even walk. Think about how pale her skin was and still is.'

'I'll admit that it's unusual,' Emmie said, with a tone that showed she obviously wasn't understanding my point. 'What does that have to do with anything, though?'

'Just please accept that there are some things in the world that go beyond your grasp,' I said. 'I don't know if you'll believe everything that I'm going to tell you, but just let me finish and then it's up to you whether you do or not. I really need you two on board to help.'

They both nodded in unison.

'I guess it's easier just to say the most important thing first.' I paused, contemplating what was about to leave my lips. 'Osiris is a mermaid. Or, *was* a mermaid,' I corrected myself. 'She's a human now, but was a mermaid before.'

'What?'

'Osiris was a mermaid up until a few weeks ago. She'd never felt like she belonged in that world, though, and knew as soon as she saw a human that that's what she wanted to be. It's like she was born in the wrong body. I met her on the beach one day and it convinced her to seek the ability to transform into a human.'

There was a long silence until Emmie broke it by saying, 'Right, now I'm more lost than ever.'

I could see why. So far, I'd done a bad job of easing them into the truth.

I took a deep breath and told them everything, starting from my first meeting with Osiris on the beach. I recalled everything about the encounter in vivid detail, making it known exactly what we discussed and how we'd left things. I then went on to explain how I had gotten in contact with Jodie through her website and went to her house, where we'd discussed the possibilities about what secrets the ocean could be hiding and that she wanted desperately to find something no human had found before. I admitted that Osiris had been the girl the news reported as being washed up on the beach the morning after the party and how I'd found her when visiting my dad. I also told them how the only person I'd told had been Val and she'd helped in explaining human functions to Osiris.

'That's insane,' Emmie said, finally. I could hear the scepticism in her voice. 'Do you honestly expect us to believe that?'

Matt's expression seemed to agree.

'Look, I know it's crazy,' I said, trying to remain calm, 'but –'

'That actually makes a lot of sense,' Matt interrupted.

'You believe it?' Emmie questioned him.

'I'm not sure,' he said, slowly. 'Part of me doesn't want to, but another knows that it explains everything pretty well. Why she suddenly just appeared one day and why she was wearing a hospital gown when she first came to the house. I'm guessing she was in a wheelchair because she didn't know how to walk at that stage.'

I nodded. 'It's the truth, mate, I swear.'

Emmie looked less convinced. 'I'm sorry, Luke, I love you and everything, but this is just a bit too much to swallow. I stopped believing in mermaids when I was five.'

I exchanged a meaningful look with Val, who had remained quiet up until this point. I knew I could rely on her seeing as she knew the truth and had believed me that I had spoken to a mermaid even before she'd met Osiris. She nodded at me then turned to Emmie.

'It sounds unbelievable, but it's real – I know it is.'

'But you didn't actually see Osiris as a mermaid, did you?'

'Well, not exactly. Luke told me before she'd even shown up as a human and I knew in my heart that he'd never lie about something like that. And when she did appear, I got to know her and not even the world's greatest liar could say what she did with a straight face.'

Emmie sighed. 'I'll try to keep an open mind. But really, the whole thing sounds like something from a fairy tale.'

'Yeah, well something tells me this won't have a happily ever after,' I muttered.

Sam got to his feet and gripped my shoulder. 'Don't say that, Luke. We're going to get Osiris back.'

I tried to muster a smile but couldn't. 'I just want her back.'

'Osiris is missing?' Emmie cried.

'Since when?' Matt asked.

'I'm guessing she was taken early this morning – about the time you both heard Charlotte's dog barking. I think the reason it's been barking so much lately is because people have been watching the house. Today is just when they finally acted.'

'Watching the house?' Matt repeated, his eyes as wide as saucers. 'Luke, who the hell are these people and what exactly do they want?'

Judging from their faces, they were both finally taking the situation seriously, even if they weren't fully on board with all the specifics.

I glanced at Sam for support and he clarified, 'There's a man called Casey who Jodie is associated with and he's the leader of a small cult down in London. They focus on trying to find ways to harness power through dark magic. We think that he and Jodie are behind Osiris going missing since she could be of use given her background.'

Emmie shook her head. 'I thought this Jodie person only wanted some notoriety. Now you reckon she wants magic as well?'

'She wants fame, he wants power,' Sam said. 'They're helping each other out.'

'And Osiris is stuck in the middle,' I added, bitterly.

'Well, we're going to help you, mate. No matter what it takes,' Matt assured me.

Emmie nodded vehemently in response. 'Yes, we are. So, what's the plan? Are we going get the police involved? Maybe have those two arrested?'

'They won't believe us,' I said. 'Come on, there's no way they'd take any of this seriously. And we're already on thin ice with the authorities since Osiris mysteriously showed up out of nowhere and fled the hospital.'

Everyone seemed to agree with me and there was silence.

Sam sighed. 'Look, the only thing I can suggest is that you could come down to London with me. I'd happily have you all stay over in my flat for a few nights. We could draw up a plan to infiltrate Casey's headquarters.'

'I can't,' Val said, quickly. 'How would I explain that to Alice? I don't think she'd appreciate me jetting off right now. You know, with everything going on between us and all. Besides, things are really hectic at work lately with people being absent – I don't think I could get so much as a day off.'

My heart sank at her words, even though I could completely understand.

'It's alright,' I said, 'you've done more than enough, Val.' Not having her there would be a major blow, but I was sure that I could manage. 'What about you two?' I queried Matt and Emmie. 'Do you reckon you could manage a few days in London?'

'Well obviously we'd have to swap our shifts for later in the week,' Emmie pointed out. 'But if you can sort that out, then I'm up for it.'

Matt looked a little less enthusiastic, but responded, 'As long as I'm back by Thursday then I should be fine.'

'We should be back by then,' I assured him. 'And if it does on for longer than planned then I promise that you can just come home, and I'll stay.'

'Okay, deal.'

'Cheers, mate, you're a life saver. We'll set off tomorrow, once we've gotten everything worked out with our shifts and everything.' I wanted to go that instant, but knew that I needed to plan this all out. 'Sam, you can stay our spare room tonight.'

'Thanks, I'll just grab some stuff out of my car.'

'I'll get in touch with Stephen and Adam,' Emmie said. 'I'm sure I can get them to agree to change shifts with us. Let's hope so, anyway.'

Once everyone else had left, I took Val aside for a quiet word.

'What do you think? Am I doing the right thing here?'

It took her a moment to come up with an answer, but then she said, 'Yes. From what you've said, these people will stop at nothing to use Osiris for their own means. God only knows what will happen if they are successful at whatever they're doing.'

I shuddered at the thought. Almost instinctively, I went over to the window and peered outside. I wasn't sure what I was looking for, only that I kept getting images of people watching us from the street and it made me feel better to see that that was not actually the case. Paranoia seemed to have consumed me and I just couldn't settle.

*

My mood did not improve over the next few hours. The more time that went by, the more apprehensive I got about where Osiris was and what was happening to her. I was infuriated that I didn't have all the answers. Luckily, everything seemed to be going smoothly in terms of the plan and we were all packed ready for our travel down south the next day.

I was stood washing the dishes that night for something to try and take my mind off it all, looking out the window at the dark skies and not paying attention to what I was doing. A sharp pain shot through my hand and I looked down to see that I'd cut myself on a knife. I swore loudly and grabbed a towel, using it to press down until the bleeding subsided.

'*Last goddamn thing I need,*' I growled.

It took all I had not to just give up and join everyone else in the land of nod. The bags under my eyes felt heavy and my muscles were aching. All the thoughts whirling round in my head weren't helping. I checked the time and saw how late it was. Yet I knew that, despite feeling tired, I'd be tossing and turning as I was always the case when I was stressed. Even though it was nearly midnight, I decided to take a walk to clear my head.

It was a pleasant, cloudless night and I walked down to the beach, allowing the slight breeze to play through my hair and nip at my face. There was complete silence, until an almighty bark of laughter shattered it.

'Ssssshh!' someone hissed, before erupting into giggles.

'I'm not saying anything!' the other voice protested, whilst clearly trying their hardest not to laugh again. 'Hurry up, keep moving!'

As I continued down, two shadowy figures emerging from the opposite way came into view. A young man and woman, probably only a few years younger than me, stumbled out from beneath the railway bridge. They were both clinging to each other to avoid tripping over.

The girl suddenly dropped to the floor, managing to drag the boy down with her. They found this hilarious and staggered back onto their feet. I thought back to the many nights when Val and I would go drinking near the beach, which of course wasn't safe – but that wasn't something we concerned ourselves with, being so naive. Everything always seemed so funny, which often resulted in us falling over in fits of laughter.

The boy looked up at me and called, 'Oi! You look troubled, mate! Have a drink!'

This caused the girl to snigger and mumble something unintelligible. I simply gave them a nod of the head and kept on my way, aware that I would get no sense out of them and they'd need all their energy to manage the uphill climb towards the main street.

Eventually their drunken voices became fainter and fainter until I could no longer hear them. The silence returned. I found a bench overlooking the beach and took a seat. My head didn't seem any clearer.

I thought back to how much I'd revealed to Osiris, even though we'd only known each other for a few weeks. In comparison, I had kept everything a secret from my closest friends and family for years. That's how I knew that my connection to her was powerful – I could tell her anything. I imagined how terrified she must be at this point and felt sick. I needed to find her as soon as possible.

It helped to know that I had people to rely on, though I was still unsure as to how much Matt and Emmie believed. It was a lot to expect them to suddenly trust without question. I was just glad that Sam and Val were fully onboard with accepting that Osiris was a mermaid – it's not as though many people would so open-minded.

Then something finally clicked.

There might be one other person in the world who knew about the existence of mermaids, or at least who might be open to the possibility. Someone who had told me that I was destined for an incredible journey and that I had a unique path ahead of me. Madame Malina certainly seemed to imply that she knew about Osiris – or at least that my fate was strongly linked to the ocean. She'd also mentioned my past and that I needed to share it in order to start moving on from it. Whether or not she knew the specifics, she was correct about this as I'd felt like I could see a light at the end of a very dark tunnel since confiding in Osiris.

Madame Malina had predicted that the upcoming events in my life would be shrouded in darkness, but that this could just be temporary if I handled it right. Perhaps she could enlighten me a bit more about this aspect. It was worth another visit to her at least.

Chapter 22

We arrived at Madame Malina's shop early the next day, ready to confront her as soon as it opened. I'd sent her an email and received no reply, but there was no time to wait for one.

I hadn't managed to sleep at all that night. When the rest of the household finally awoke several hours later, I was sat up doing research whilst gulping down what must have been my sixth cup of coffee. I was shaking noticeably by this point and it took a while to convince them that it was worthwhile checking this person out.

Emmie had immediately rolled her eyes at my suggestion. 'Honestly, Luke, did you really go and see her? She's clearly a fraud.'

At one point, I would've agreed, but my last visit had convinced me otherwise – especially considering everything that had happened afterwards.

It wasn't an ideal situation given that I had hoped to start the drive down to London as early as possible, but I couldn't pass up the opportunity to pay Madame Malina a visit before we attempted anything. Especially since I figured she could be valuable in providing some insight.

I looked down at the card she had given me a few weeks earlier: *With Madame Malina, find out what the future holds.* I prayed that she could this time.

'Are you sure it'll be open?' Matt asked.

'Yes,' I said, firmly. 'She opens her shop every day and it should be opening any minute now.' I stared impatiently through the window, but couldn't see a thing behind all the furniture. 'Come on...' I muttered.

At long last, I heard movement from inside and ran to the door, where I began to furiously hammer my fist against it.

'Jesus, Luke, she'll call the police if you keep doing that,' Matt protested.

I didn't care though. I needed to get her attention and for her to understand how serious I was to speak to her. Thankfully, she opened the door within seconds.

'Luke?' she said, bewildered.

'I need to talk to you,' I said, barging past. The others followed me in as she stood looking thoroughly confused. 'Last time I was here you said some stuff that makes me think you might know more about my situation than you let on. Or at least that you do have some legitimate powers and can help tell me what's to come.'

'What on earth are you talking about?' she demanded.

I pulled out my wallet and through several notes on the table. 'There, if it's money you need then that should be more than enough. Please, we need to be in London as quickly as possible. All I want is for you to work your little crystal ball or flick through your cards and tell us exactly what we can expect from our trip.'

She let out a sigh of exasperation. 'Luke, it doesn't work like that. I can't just be expected to perform on a whim. I need the right atmosphere, the right –'

'Rubbish,' I interrupted. 'Your entire business hinges around customers coming in and you telling them what you can see about their future.' I held up her business card. '*Find out what the future holds* and all that.'

'Unless it's all a con,' Emmie pointed out. She was clearly yet to be won over regarding Madame Malina's credibility, despite everything she had been told to the contrary.

'It's not,' I said, not taking my eyes off Madame Malina. 'When I saw you a few weeks ago, you said that I had a certain path ahead of me, one that I'd be joined on by someone associated with the ocean. You also said that there was a darkness surrounding it all, but that this could be overcome if I made the right choices.'

Emmie scoffed, but otherwise remained quiet.

'You also...' I stopped and cleared my throat, then continued, 'You said that I needed to face my past by sharing it somebody else.'

'And did you?'

'Yes.'

She smiled. 'I can see that. You've changed so much in the short amount of time that I saw you, Luke. And you truly were a fascinating person to read.'

It seemed like she was starting to come around to assisting us and she quickly went over to lock the door, which I guessed meant she didn't want any other potential customers to interrupt us. I watched as she pulled out a single card from her deck and held it up. It was the one labelled *The Lovers* with the two naked people on it.

'Did this begin to make sense?' she asked.

'More than I ever imagined,' I admitted. 'Will you help me get her back?'

'I still don't understand what exactly it is that you want me to do.'

Sam stepped forward at this point. 'Look, we know that magic exists, and we know that there's a chance that there are people out there who have psychic powers. Luke has vouched for your authenticity and so we just want to know if you can do anything to tell us what path might be the best one to take. Someone very important has been abducted by people who may wish to do terrible things to her for their own selfish gain. I don't know how you go about reading the fates or foretelling the future, but please, just do whatever you can.'

I waited anxiously as Madame Malina looked to seriously consider Sam's words. After a long pause, she relented and said, 'Very well then, follow me.'

She led us into the back room with the round table, signalling me to sit in the chair opposite hers, whilst the others had to make do with leaning against one of the candle-lit tables against the wall. After not having a particularly pleasant experience last time, I felt a little uncomfortable, but kept telling myself that I was doing this for Osiris. I remembered our conversation in York about how mermaids could see people's auras and it made me wonder if Madame Malina was a rare human example of someone who possessed a similar quality.

'Now, please bear in mind what I told you last time – that the future is not set in stone.' She took her seat and began to adjust her crystal ball. 'I was able to predict certain aspects of your future, Luke, but you still had a choice. It's not like fate is unchangeable. You have free will and can alter your destiny. I can, however, try to provide you with a rough guide.'

'That's all I'm asking for.'

'And all I ask is that those who may... disbelieve,' she said the last word with a pointed scowl at Emmie, 'try to keep an open mind and not interrupt.'

Emmie held her hands up as a sign that she'd keep her thoughts to herself. Madame Malina seemed satisfied and then returned to gazing into the crystal ball. A few moments passed without her saying a word – though I wasn't sure if this was a good or bad thing. I just prayed she could foresee a positive outcome.

'Something's starting to come through,' she announced.

I could feel the others inching forward from behind me. I tried to maintain a sense of calmness as I asked, 'What is it?'

She frowned and then finally decided on, 'It's a person.'

'Can you be more specific?' I asked. 'Is it a woman?'

'I'm not sure... wait a minute, no... it's a man.'

I exchange a look with Sam, who I knew would be thinking the same as me. Could she be seeing Casey? It would certainly seem like the most likely option as I couldn't imagine which other man of importance could be involved.

'Is there anything else you can tell us?' Sam asked.

Her face was still furrowed, as though she was struggling to decipher exactly what it was that the ball was showing her. 'He's powerful. I can sense great power about him. More than I've ever seen before. It's like he's... I don't know... otherworldly...'

'There's a man who plans on harnessing magical powers,' I told her. 'Is it him? Is he successful? Please, I can't let this happen. I just can't.'

She shook her head. 'I can't tell who is. He may already have power or he might be going down a route of getting it – if so then you could stop him. Like I say, nothing is guaranteed about it. Though I must warn you that there's definitely still an air of darkness around it all.'

'But that's something I can stop, right?'

'It's possible.'

I didn't like the way she was talking because it sounded like she was unsure. If I had to hazard a guess, then she didn't think I was going to be successful. Desperate, I held my hands out in front of me.

'Read my palms,' I begged. 'They could give you more of an insight.'

She looked rather sceptical, but must have taken pity on me for she took my hands in hers and began to stroke her fingers across them. My heart was pounding, and I could hear my breathing getting faster and faster.

It seemed to take a while for Madame Malina to reach a conclusion. 'Everything about your near future is so... up in the air,' she said. 'It's as though all your lines are about to converge, and the outcome could go many ways. Depending on your actions, on your words, on your feelings – that's what will decide the rest of your life.'

I didn't feel like we were getting anywhere. 'So, you're saying that a particular event coming up is, I don't know – unreadable?'

'I suppose you could say that.' She gave me a look of sympathy and then pulled out her cards. 'I'll try one more thing; perhaps the cards will give some clarity.'

As she begun to shuffle the deck, I quickly glanced around at the others. They all looked enthralled – even Emmie seemed to be giving the situation the utmost attention. When they caught my eye, they each gave a reassuring nod, although I could tell they weren't pleased either about the ambiguity. I turned back around and saw that Madame Malina was beginning to lay out the cards face down.

'Okay, Luke, pick one.'

I stared intently at the cards and took my time in deciding which one. It seemed almost ludicrous that my choice of one could change that much, though I guess my decisions were going to affect a lot of what happened from this point onwards. At long last, I tapped a card and nudged it forward. Madame Malina smiled and flipped it over.

We were greeted with an illustration of a skeleton sweeping the floor with a scythe. Beneath it read *Death*. I heard someone gasped behind me, but ignored it and instead focused on Madame Malina's expression. She had a stony look on her face, which I was unable to decipher.

'Is someone going to die?' I asked.

'Yes,' she said, in hushed tones. 'Perhaps more than one. I don't know what is going to happen, Luke, I don't know what you have planned – but please know that death may be inevitable no matter what path you take.' She shuddered and stood up. 'I'm afraid that's enough for today.'

Nobody disagreed with her and we all walked back into the front room of the shop, where she unlocked the main door.

'Thanks for your time,' I said.

'I'm sorry I couldn't be of more use,' she said. 'I'm sorry to say that many situations cannot be foretold, especially those that are particularly unique.'

The others all began to make their way out and I was about to follow when Madame Malina grabbed my arm and I stopped.

'Good luck, Luke,' she said. 'I hope it all works out for you.'

'Thanks,' I said.

Then I left, hoping that I'd never have to encounter her again. There was only so much I could deal with when it came to magic and all the otherworldly goings-on. Reading the future was not something I planned on doing again in a hurry.

Chapter 23

We'd already made sure to pack our bags and everything the day before, so when we got back from seeing Madame Malina, it was simply a case of loading them into Sam's car and heading straight for London. I was thankful to find that he wasn't a particularly cautious driver, and this made me optimistic that we'd make it there in good time.

Whereas Matt and Emmie had waited to pack until it was confirmed that we could get out shifts altered with our co-workers, I'd pretty much done so without this go-ahead because I knew that I was leaving no matter what. Getting fired would have been worth it to get Osiris back safely. One thing I'd made sure to bring with me was my *The World's Greatest Mysteries* book, though I'm not completely sure why I chose to do so. It wouldn't exactly help; I just found it strangely relaxing to read accounts of otherworldly phenomena with the knowledge that some of it was true – maybe all of it.

Since I'd had no sleep, I pretty much dozed off as soon as we started driving. It wasn't the most peaceful slumber given how uncomfortable it was to sleep upright in a car. Plus, I was plagued with nightmares about Osiris at the hands of the cult. By the time I woke up from this, we seemed to have been considerable progress in our journey.

'Not long now,' Sam said, as I attempted to shake off the remaining fatigue. 'We'll be there in just over an hour. I just need to fill up, then it's full steam ahead.'

'Great,' I replied, rubbing my eyes.

Matt and Emmie were sat in the back, holding hands but not saying anything. Emmie looked wistfully out of the window, perhaps contemplating the exact nature of what we were doing, whilst Matt reached forward and placed a reassuring hand on my shoulder, which I appreciated. Nobody said anything for a while.

After several minutes, Sam parked up at a petrol station. We all took this opportunity to use the restroom, though I wasn't planning on using it for the toilet as such.

As Matt walked over to the urinals, I hurried into a cubicle and locked the door. I put the lid down and sat, taking my phone out to browse down my contact list. I was extremely nervous about confronting Jodie and Casey, considering how far I imagined they'd go in order to achieve their goals. And that was not to mention the power they could wield if they managed to succeed in harnessing magic powers. In any case, Madame Malina's lack of certainty on what could happen had spooked me enough that I needed to talk to someone in case the worst were happen to me. I waited until I heard Matt finish up and leave, then made the call.

'Hello?'

'Hi, dad.'

'Luke? Hi, son. I'm glad you've called. You just rushed off the other night – we never really got a chance to catch up.'

'I know, I'm sorry.'

He chuckled. 'It's fine, I was just disappointed we didn't get to see more of you. You should have seen Amber's face the rest of the party – she was furious after what happened. I've got to say, though, I was worried about you when you left.'

'There's no need to worry.'

I tried to hide the fact that I was on the verge of tears, but clearly wasn't successful as my dad immediately asked, 'Is there something wrong, son?'

'No,' I insisted. 'Everything's fine.'

'Well it doesn't sound that way.'

I hated how concerned he sounded because I didn't want to worry him. I just wanted a normal conversation. One we'd ordinarily have. I needed some normality if this was the last time we were going to speak. The thought made me feel sick, but it was an unfortunate possibility given how things could potentially go down when I got to London.

'Tell me something,' I said.

'Like what?'

'I don't know – anything. You must've done something today, tell me all about it. Did Maureen come to see you? Have you spoke to Phillip? Did you go to the shops? Just tell me anything, dad. Tell me.'

'Luke, you're scaring me.'

'I know, and I'm sorry. Look, when I get back, I promise that I'll explain everything. There's some stuff that I should've told you a long time ago.'

'What stuff? Get back from where?'

'I'm going to be in London for... a few days, I think. I'm not sure. I'll come visit you as soon as I come back. I'll come visit you more often.'

'You never told me you were going to London. What are you doing down there?'

'It was last minute thing, literally decided it yesterday. We're just doing a bit of sightseeing, you know. I got some time off work and decided I needed a change of scenery.'

'Are you there with Osiris?'

Hearing her name made my heart sink. 'Yeah, that's right. It's just me and her.'

'That's wonderful, I'm so happy for you both.' I could hear how sincerely pleased he was, and I tried to ignore the fact that he may soon get news of my death. 'You'll have to tell me all about it when you get back. You never know, Phillip might not be the only one who gets engaged this year.'

'Bloody hell, bit soon to be thinking about that, isn't it?'

'I'm just saying, from the feeling I got between you two, it wouldn't surprise me. I love to see you happy, Luke, and something tells me that she's made you the happiest you've been in a long while.'

I couldn't argue with him since he was one hundred percent correct. However, this wasn't something I needed to hear as there was no guarantee that Osiris and I would have a future together, or at all. I guess it was too much to ask to have just had a boring, everyday conversation with my dad. I just wanted a small slice of regularity. Maybe in a world of magic and mermaids, nothing was ever intended to be this way.

'There's a chance it won't work out,' I admitted, not that he would fully understand what I meant. 'I just hope we'll both be back up north soon.'

He didn't reply straight away, but finally said, 'I don't know what's going on, but please try and be safe, Luke.'

'I'm scared, dad.'

'Of what?'

I wanted to say that I was scared that she was going to be killed (hoping against hope that she wasn't already dead) or that I was, but decided this was too gruesome to divulge and might be unnecessary. Instead, I stuck with the technical truth and said, 'Losing her.'

'Unless you're the world's biggest idiot, there's no way that's going to happen. She looks at you like you hung the moon and the stars. That doesn't come along every day, Luke, and... and you need to appreciate someone whilst you have them. You never know when you might lose them.'

I made a small whimpering noise as I tried to stop my nose from running. 'Do you think mam would've liked Osiris? Do you think she would've approved?'

'I think she'd have loved her as much as you do.'

There were many times during my childhood when I'd ask my dad whether my mam would have liked me. I used to write her letters and would make cards for her on special occasions. He'd assure me every time that I would have been the light of her life.

'I need to go now, dad,' I said, aware that I'd been keeping the others waiting quite a while at this point. 'I love you.'

'Stay safe,' he said. 'I love you, too.'

I sat for a short while longer, contemplating everything in my head. There was a part of me that just wanted to run away from it all, but I knew I'd never do that – I was done ignoring my problems. There was no hiding from the world, and I was going to rescue Osiris... even if I was killed in the process. If she was still alive, then I owed it to her to get her back home safe and sound. I was also aware that Matt and Emmie were putting themselves in harm's way as well, and I was determined for them to make it out in one piece.

*

We arrived at the exact time we had estimated. I was thankful that everything was going according to plan and even more relieved just to be in London – the closer I was to Osiris, the better I felt.

'We're coming up to the building where Casey and his cult congregate,' Sam informed us, as he began to slow down. 'It's just through those trees.'

He pulled up against the curb and we all looked towards where he was pointing. It wasn't the best view, since it was quite obscured by all the foliage, but you could still make out a relatively decent-sized building with large blacked-out windows. The mere sight of the place gave me the creeps, with the knowledge that the people inside may have access to powerful magic. There was also the fact that this is where Osiris was being kept and all I wanted was to run in there at that moment and find her. I had to keep reminding myself that once everything was planned out, I had a better chance of getting her out safely.

'It doesn't look too hard to access,' Emmie noted.

'Yeah, there's not a big security presence,' Matt added.

'Not that we can see,' I said. 'I bet there'll be cameras and everything inside, though. You have photos of what it looks like inside though, don't you, Sam?'

He nodded. 'Yeah, we'll sort everything out as soon as we get to mine. I just wanted you to see it for yourselves in person before tomorrow.'

We stared at it for a few more minutes, then Sam slammed his foot against the accelerator and we were off again. I kept my eyes on the building as we passed by, wanting more than anything for Osiris to sense that I was here and that I was actively trying to rescue her. She was so close and yet so far away.

*

It only took around five minutes to get to the block of flats from Casey's building.

'Right, I'm on the third floor,' Sam said. 'Follow me.'

With our bags slung over our shoulders, we made our way to upstairs to Sam's flat. He'd warned us in advance that it was a little run-down and was rather cramped, but I was just grateful that he was allowing us a place to stay. I couldn't imagine what the house prices must be like London – I don't think I could've afforded even his place.

As soon as we entered, he led us into the living room. It was indeed very small. The kitchen looked as though barely two people could fit in it at the same time and I could see through an open door that the bathroom was even more confined.

'There's a bed in that room,' Sam said, indicating to the door close to the bathroom. 'It's not very big, but I think Matt and Emmie should be able to squeeze in together. Are you sure you're okay with the couch, Luke?'

'Honestly, that's more than fine,' I said, knowing full well that I most likely wouldn't be getting a good night's sleep anyway. 'Seriously, mate, thanks a lot for this.'

'Don't mention it,' he smiled. 'Anyway, I think it's best if we all get freshened up. We don't exactly look in our best minds, especially considering we're going to be planning an infiltration. How about we get cleaned up a bit and I'll order some food, then we can sit round and properly map out what's going to go down tomorrow?'

I nodded in agreement. 'That sounds good.'

The idea of breaking into this cult's headquarters felt both thrilling and terrifying. I knew that if it was to go without a hitch, then we'd have to make sure we discussed it fully and try not to leave anything to chance. I wasn't sure I liked our odds of succeeding.

Chapter 24

It took about an hour for everybody to get sorted. I was in and out of the shower within minutes, but the others took longer. Even though I was desperate to get started on fleshing out the plan, I tried to remain patient since I was just thankful that I had people on hand to help in getting Osiris back safely. And I knew that we weren't going to be doing anything until tomorrow, yet I still wanted everything finalised as quickly as possible.

Sam was the last one to use the bathroom and the rest of us made ourselves comfortable around a small table in the living room as we waited. He'd placed a pile of files filled with notes down on it, along with rolled-up blueprints and various other sheets of paper that were no doubt going to be of use. I wanted to know everything.

There was a knock at the door, and I jumped up to answer it. A rather scruffy guy was stood, holding two large pizza boxes.

'That'll be £18.50,' he grunted.

'Here,' I said, giving him the cash, 'just keep the change, mate.'

'Nice one,' he said, handing the boxes over and pocketing the notes.

I closed the door and pondered about the fact that he would be completely unaware of what we were planning. I guess it's true what they say about not knowing what goes on behind closed doors. He was just a typical delivery person, trying to earn some honest money, blissfully ignorant (as I had been mere weeks ago) to the fact that there was such thing as magic. I allowed myself to smile about this and then returned to the living room.

It wasn't too long until Sam came out and quickly sat down at the table. He rearranged the files and took a slice of pizza. 'Right,' he said, his mouth still full, 'here's everything I have about the members of this sect, including Jodie and Casey.'

We all took it turns to read through the individual descriptions. I scanned them all several times, determined to know everything about the people who now held Osiris prisoner. I felt the rage burning inside me when I thought about them possibly taunting her as we sat here enjoying food in the safety of these walls.

'There are only four people that Casey trusts enough at this point to allow in the building,' Sam told us, explaining why there were so few members. 'From what I understand, he's trying to expand, but remember that they're after harnessing magic and they want to make sure that only their closest allies are involved at this point. That includes,' he started pointed at the different papers, 'Graham, Harris, Tyrone and Shefali. All English, but I daresay Casey will want to look for people in America eventually as well.'

'Do they reside permanently in the headquarters?' Emmie questioned.

'During their initiation period, yes, but then they're free to go out of the facility once they can be trusted.'

'How does he recruit them?' Matt asked. 'Are they random, or...?'

'He's working with Jodie, so they're people who've expressed interest in the unknown and the supernatural through her website. I imagine there's a vetting process and then only the elite get asked into their little team.'

'Alright then,' I said, 'now we know *who* we're dealing with, but the question is: what are we going to do tomorrow? Osiris is definitely in the building, yeah?'

'It's our best guess. Obviously, we can't know for sure, but I daresay they wouldn't take her anywhere else. From what I could gather when I was doing my investigation into the group, all their major events take place there. Members are sworn in there, meetings take place there and any readings of dark magical texts are done there. If they are planning to use Osiris in this way, then they'll want to do it in their own facility.'

All the talk of dark magic and Osiris's involvement in such matters made me anxious. It was more than I wanted to think about. 'Okay,' I said, eventually, 'I'm going to say that they're definitely in there with her right now, then. So, is it just as easy as walking in or will we trip some sort of alarm?'

At this, Sam unrolled the blueprints and laid them down flat for us all to see. It was a two-story building with many rooms and corridors, any one of which could be housing Osiris. Vague notes had been written over the drawing with descriptions of what the various rooms could be used for.

Sam pointed to a large one and said, 'From what I've seen from my stake-outs of the place, this looks to be something of a meeting room. It's where they all gather to basically listen to whatever insane rant Casey is going on. I wouldn't imagine they'd keep Osiris there.' He then pointed to a few smaller ones, saying, 'These could potentially be where she is, or could also be where they keep their documents and books and other things. They'll all need to be searched to make sure.' He then indicated to the right side of the building. 'Down here is where they sleep, so again there's potential. I would definitely check out where I've shown you, though, because these are usually where the curtains are always closed.'

'When's the best time to go inside?' I asked, fidgeting nervously.

'I would say around midday since that's usually when Casey gathers to talk to them all in that meeting room. It could be our best chance of getting in and out without being seen. Now, I don't know whether the place has cameras, but it's very likely. In any case, we just have to hope that we're swift and they're all occupied by Casey's talk. They won't have chance to check the footage until Osiris is safe and they won't be able to do anything about it after that because they'd have to admit to the police that they abducted her in the first place.'

'Bloody hell,' Matt said, grabbing another slice of pizza, 'this is intense.'

'I know,' Sam said, 'but hopefully it'll be worth it.'

'What do we do after we've got her?' Emmie asked. 'Do we just come back here?'

'Well, I was thinking we should hightail it out of London, to be honest. I know I said they can't do anything, but these people are crazy – there's no telling what they'll be capable of, especially since we're stealing something very valuable from them. I think it's best to drive to a remote location. That's why I'm going to be waiting outside.'

'You're not coming with us?' I asked, quite shocked.

'We need a getaway driver,' he said, simply, 'and I know these roads better than any of you. If something goes wrong, we may need to get away fast. Plus, I've scouted the building before, many times, so I know what will look suspicious. I'll be keeping an eye out the entire time you guys are in there. And you can all keep in touch through our phones.'

What he said made sense, so I nodded. 'It's a plan, then.'

*

As I had predicted, sleep eluded me that night. I'd managed to nap for maybe half an hour before finally admitting defeat and sitting up. The sofa wasn't uncomfortable, but there were just too many thoughts going through my head for me to simply shut them out.

After a short trip to the toilet, I returned to find Sam sat on the couch with a lamp turned on to give a small bit of light. He smiled when I approached.

'Couldn't sleep either?' he asked.

I laughed and took a seat next to him. 'Well, I managed to close my eyes for a bit if that counts.' I tousled my hair and stretched. 'I've never been able to sleep if there's a lot on my mind. And there's a hell of a lot going on right now.'

'I'm the same. Fancy a drink?'

'Sure, what'd you have?'

'Got a few beers if you think that'll help send you off?'

I seriously considered taking him up on this offer. Alcohol was always my way of coping with stress and the only reason I hadn't turned to it recently is because I did not want to overdo it and get too drunk in front of Osiris. Considering she wasn't here at this point, I technically could've taken this opportunity to slip back into my old ways. In the end, chose to keep myself level-headed for the sake of our upcoming mission.

'Nah, thanks. I'm trying to cut back on stuff like that.'

'Fair enough,' he said. 'Wait here and I'll go make something that should help us relax. Non-alcoholic, I promise.'

'Cheers.'

He got up and went to the kitchen. I took this opportunity to check my phone and saw that there were no messages or missed calls, which I was glad about because I couldn't really focus on anything other than the job at hand and didn't need any distractions. I did a quick sweep of my social media pages and then put it away, just in time for Sam to return with two steaming mugs – one of which he handed to me.

I thanked him and took a sip. My taste buds were immediately hit with the sweet taste of hot chocolate. As I drank it, I thought about the fact that I'd never thought about making one for Osiris the whole time she'd been with me – yet it was a drink that I imagined she would very much enjoy. I tried to wave this thought away because it was no good to constantly be reminded of everything Osiris and I were yet to experience together.

'It's great,' I said, trying to distract myself.

'I'm good for some things,' he chuckled.

'So, are you going to tell me what your connection to Jodie is? Were you once a member of this cult? Were you in a relationship with her at one point?'

'No, nothing like that.'

'What, then?'

'She's my sister.'

I genuinely wasn't expecting this, and his words took me off guard. Not knowing what to say, I compensated by dinking a slurp of my drink.

Sam smirked and shook his head. 'It's not something I'm proud of.'

'Don't worry,' I said, 'my sister's no better.'

'I dare say she's not as evil as mine.'

I wanted to say that I wouldn't bet on it, but not even I could imagine Amber going as far as Jodie – she was an unpleasant person, but not pure evil.

'At least you're doing something about it,' I said. 'I really appreciate you helping me out with all of this. You could've just ignored the whole thing.'

'I can't let Jodie get away with this. Not after last time.'

'What happened?'

'Osiris isn't the first mermaid to have contact with humans, though I'm guessing you've already figured that part out. Well, many years ago there was one who came to the surface near where we lived. It wasn't too far from where you saw Osiris, actually. Jodie and I were always hanging out on the beach when we younger.'

'You both saw a mermaid?'

He nodded. 'We were only teenagers, but even then, my sister had a craving for fame and fortune. The mermaid spoke to us for the first time when it was just the two of us having a stroll along the shore. She told us that there were more like her in the sea. I was thrilled at the prospect, only because it made me realise how much grander the world was and the endless possibilities it presented. Jodie was only interested in making a profit.'

'So, then what?'

'We used to meet up regularly with the mermaid. Her name was Telanthera. Whenever she came to the surface, we'd listen to her stories about what it was like living underwater. But then Jodie started telling people about our encounters and they began to join us in the hopes of seeing her for themselves. They never did, though. We went to the same spot where we always saw her over and over, but Telanthera never came back. Jodie was made to look like a fool. That's what I guess fuelled her desire to set up her website in the hopes of finally proving the world that she wasn't lying.'

'If these people have been stalking me, then I'm assuming they took photos of Osiris. Do you think that once Jodie saw her, she knew what she'd been due to her appearance? That's how you said you worked it out.'

'Yes, Telanthera's hair and eyes were very similar – distinctly not human.'

'And so started this whole ordeal,' I mumbled, glumly.

'But this time it's not going to have an unhappy ending,' Sam added. 'I won't let her get away with taking Osiris away from you. I promise.'

'Do you really think we can get in there without getting caught? Do you really think I'm going to get Osiris back safely?'

'Yes,' he said. I looked for a trace of doubt, but he seemed to be honestly confident when he said it. 'Try not to worry, Luke. You've got a good team behind you.'

'I'm trying my best to stay positive,' I said, which was the truth.

We sat for a few minutes and finished our drinks, before Sam said that he was going to try and get some sleep, leaving me alone yet again with my thoughts. I got back under the blanket and began to imagine how Osiris and I would spend the rest of our lives once we were reunited.

Chapter 25

Against all odds, I managed to drift off for an hour or two after my talk with Sam, which helped me feel rather refreshed when I woke up. I glanced at the time to see that it was still ridiculously early – though the lack of sunrise had tipped me off about that. Once I felt fully awake, I went about getting dressed and making myself look somewhat presentable. I would have considered having breakfast, but my stomach felt far too queasy for me to even consider that a sensible option.

Since we weren't going to be starting our mission until midday, the others were bound to want to try and sleep-in for as long as they could. It was pointless for me to try and go back to sleep, so instead of making noise and running the risk of waking them up, I quickly grabbed my jacket and headed out. It wasn't a familiar neighbourhood, but I was sure I could navigate my way around the block and back again without getting lost. Besides, the fresh air would help me think. I left a note on the sofa just in case anybody got up and got alarmed by my absence, though I was certain this wouldn't be the case.

When I got outside, I saw the first rays of sun begin to peak out from the horizon and found myself strolling towards Casey's building. When I got close, I made sure to sit at a bench that was obstructed by a tree so I wouldn't be seen – though I doubted anybody else would be up at this time anyway,

I felt a powerful tug towards Osiris, who I just knew was behind those walls. I wondered if she was awake and what exactly she was doing. There was something telling me that she wasn't dead yet – I wasn't even considering that an option. But in what condition she was currently in was anyone's guess. I prayed that they weren't harming her, though I didn't trust any of them. Just the thought of her beautiful face stained with tears made me want to run in there at once and demand to have her back. I knew that it wasn't good to think about it and had to stop; I needed a distraction.

Before we'd left for London, I'd promised Val that I would keep her in the loop as to what was happening with the mission. However, everything had been so hectic that I hadn't had chance to. Now seemed like the perfect opportunity, despite the early hour. I knew that she was an occasional early riser and decided to take the chance.

I pulled out my phone and sent her a text asking if she was awake. She responded almost immediately that she was, so I quickly called her.

'What are you doing up so early?' she asked.

'I could ask you the same thing,' I replied.

'I've barely slept at all, to be honest with you,' she said, and it did indeed sound like she was exhausted. 'I've got a lot of things on my mind. It's crazy.'

'I know the feeling. Anything I can help with?'

'No, I don't think so. So, I take it you're in London?'

'Yep, got here safe and sound last night. We've planned out what we're going to do today. Sam reckons that Casey usually gives a little talk to his followers around midday so we're going sneak in then to get Osiris. We don't exactly know what all the rooms are used for, but we're sure she must be in one of them.'

'Sounds pretty dangerous,' she said. 'You best be careful.'

'I will be. It's Matt and Emmie I'm more worried about. If I get caught and something terrible happens, then that's on me — it isn't fair on them, though. They've just kind of been thrust into this whole thing. They've handled it pretty well considering.'

'I'm sure they'll be fine,' she reassured me.

'I wish you were here, Val. You always make me feel better about everything.'

'I'm there in spirit.'

'I guess so. This whole thing has really made me appreciate my friends and family. I mean, you've went above and beyond for me, as have Matt and Emmie. I made sure to ring my dad on the way down, too, just in case... well...'

'Don't be silly,' Val said. 'Nothing's going to happen to you.'

'I wish I could have your confidence. I keep thinking about me and Osiris and the future we could have. All I want is the assurance that we can have a life together.'

'You mean like marital bliss and all that?'

'I guess you could say that.'

'Do you think about starting a family with her?'

I gave this some thought. Having a baby did not factor into my immediate plans, but wasn't something I wanted to right off completely. I couldn't imagine getting to old age without having children. I thought about what it would be like a year or two down the line, and I pictured that I would be in a much better place for raising a child. The question of whether Osiris could even get pregnant was another matter entirely, though I was not opposed to going down the route of adoption.

'I think that's something to consider later on,' I said. 'Right now, all I can think about is getting her back safely. Anything else is a bonus.'

'Just focus on what's important,' she said. 'I'm sure it'll all be fine.'

'I'll try,' I said, glumly. 'What are you up to today, anyway?'

'Oh, err, I'm not sure really. I think Alice might have something planned, so I guess I'll just go along with whatever that is – nothing exciting, in other words.'

'I wish I was doing nothing exciting,' I said. 'Try to have fun.'

'Like I'll be able to concentrate knowing what you're doing,' she pointed out.

'Don't worry about me. I promise I'll get in touch with you as soon as we've got Osiris out of there and back to safety.'

'You really are a good friend, Luke,' she said.

'So are you,' I replied.

'Thanks,' she said, with a slight quiver in the voice.

'Is something wrong?'

'No, I'm just feeling a little guilty about not being there with you guys. I hope you know that I would've been if I could.'

'Don't worry about it. Seriously, you've helped me out enough as it is when it comes to Osiris – I don't know how I would have coped if it wasn't for you. I mean, I don't think I'd have been of much use when it came to... you know, the female stuff.'

She gave a small laugh. 'It was my pleasure.'

'Anyway, I better get going. I'll speak to you later.'

'Yeah, see you soon.'

I hung up and sat for a while in my own thoughts. I was immensely thankful that I'd manage to speak to both my dad and Val – probably the two people I cared most about in the world alongside Osiris – before I went through with what was planned for that day. Doing so over the phone wasn't exactly ideal, yet it would have to do under the circumstances. If the worst was indeed to happen to me, then at least I had the reassurance of knowing that they'd heard from me one last time. I was hopefully just being melodramatic.

Poor Val hadn't sounded quite herself and I made myself a reminder that the two of us would spend some time together when all of this had blown over. I'd also do the same with my dad, and maybe with Phillip, too, if I felt up to it. I needed to start making time for those closest to me and being caught up in something as drastic as what was going on now in London really made me realise that.

For now, I took advantage of some much-needed respite.

*

When I returned to the flat, there was only the faint sound of movement coming from the bedrooms, indicating that nobody would have noticed by absence. I crumpled up the note since it was no longer necessary and made my way back into the living room.

Sam stepped out of his room and smiled. 'Did you manage any sleep in the end, then?'

'Aye, I did. Thanks.'

He gave me an empathetic look. 'Big day, eh?'

'I'm petrified if I'm honest.'

'Don't worry, it's going to be fine.'

There wasn't much use in trying to debate if things were going to go well, so I nodded and thanked him for the encouragement. I don't think a single word anybody could say would sway me away from my feelings of anxiety. Yet there was a small part of my brain that kept reminding me to almost appreciate the unique situation I was in. How many people could say they were spending their day doing what we were? On the opposite side, however, there was the very real danger that we did not know what we would be dealing with nor how we'd properly handle the situation once we got there.'

'Are you feeling okay, Luke?' Matt asked, exiting the bathroom.

'Yeah,' I said, though in truth my stomach was in knots. 'Are you both absolutely sure that you want to go through with this?'

He sighed as he answered, '*Yes.*' I had been repeating the question several times the night before, mainly because I wanted to be certain that they understood the seriousness of our mission and were prepared for anything bad that could happen. I also couldn't believe that I had friends who were willing to go this far to help me out.

'Sorry,' I mumbled. 'I'm all over the place right now.'

'Don't worry about it, mate.'

The rest of the morning mainly consisted of essentially killing time. We went over the plan a few more times, but we'd gone over it so thoroughly only hours beforehand that it seemed rather repetitive. It was all well and good being meticulously primed; it was quite another thing to be constantly repeating the same information over and over again. This was especially true given that the nature of our mission revolved a lot around guesswork. There was no way of knowing what was in many of the rooms we'd have to look, or which one Osiris would be locked away in. Therefore, we sat flicking through the television channels, trying to make small talk and generally counting down the clock until midday.

The hours eventually whittled down into minutes and, before long, we were starting to get ready for our infiltration into the cult's headquarters. There wasn't a lot to necessarily pack given that the blueprint was a very rough guide and anything else could merely hinder us in getting around faster. We went over the plan one more time and voiced any uncertainties that we had about what was about to go down and what we hoped to accomplish. It seemed relatively straightforward – get in, look for Osiris, find her and free from any bindings if necessary, then get the hell out of there without being caught – but it was exactly the simplicity of it that had me worried. I couldn't help but think that something was bound to go wrong.

When everything was sorted and we were fully agreed on our task, Sam reached over for his car keys. 'Alright then,' he said, with one last check of the time, 'let's go.'

Chapter 26

Sam parked the car at the very end of the street so that we could just barely see the entrance to Casey's building. I could feel myself trembling and tried to relax my heartbeat. It was finally happening. We were going to get Osiris back.

'Right,' Sam said, 'I'm going to be right here throughout. Make sure you call or text if anything goes wrong. And remember, don't be afraid of aborting the mission if you feel like it's going wrong.' He directed his attention towards me. 'We *will* get Osiris back, even if it doesn't end up being today. I'm sure it will, but don't put yourselves in direct danger. Ideally, you want to be in and out of there as quickly as possible.'

I knew in my heart that I was not going to leave that day without Osiris, but I agreed anyway because I didn't want to look as though I was abandoning the plan we'd laid out. No matter what happened, I would always make sure to the best of my ability that Matt and Emmie made it out safely. If anyone had to go down for this, it was going to be me.

'Hopefully it will be less than an hour,' I said.

'Well, I'll be here as long as is needed,' he assured me. 'And I know it goes without saying, but be careful – all three of you. Don't forget, these people have the potential to be extremely dangerous.'

I looked at the others to make sure one last time that they understood the severity of what we were embarking on and they nodded.

'Come on then,' I said, getting out of the car.

I led the way over to the building, ignoring the primal desire to flee. There was something about approaching it that seemed eerily akin to a suicide mission. This was something I'd have to ignore if we had any hope of succeeding. It came more into focus and I could feel myself trembling as we approached it, though I tried to keep my nerve. Despite the numerous ways that everything could go wrong, I knew the only way to overcome my fears was to remain positive and tell myself that nothing would get in our way.

We crouched down behind a wall near the main gate, making sure we were concealed from anyone who might be watching.

'There doesn't seem to be anyone around,' I noted, peeking through the fence at the surroundings. I squinted and couldn't see much, so was therefore unaware of whether there was anybody stationed outside or not. 'We're going to have to just chance it.'

They both nodded in confirmation and then the three of us helped each other over the wall. Once on the property, we ducked behind some shrubbery. I glanced behind some branches at the main doors, but still couldn't see anyone.

'Now is as good a time as any to go for it,' I said, turning to face the others.

Without any further discussion, we walked over to the main door. In a stroke of luck, it was open, and we were able to slip in. We stood in a small passageway, trying not to make a sound. I put one finger to my lips and then signalled to the others to follow me. Unfortunately, this was the point in which the plan relied almost wholly on luck. We had no idea who or what we were going to encounter and no clue as to where Osiris was within the maze of corridors and multiple rooms.

I could see that there was a door leading to main part of the floor, but we'd have to pass by an open door to do so and we could hear a voice coming from it. I crept towards it and the others kept close behind me. I breathed a sigh of relief when I saw that the person closest had their backs to us. They were stood on a raised platform, so we couldn't make out who they were addressing, but it was presumably the other cult members. The person talking was undoubtedly Casey Raistrick – I could recognise him even from behind and his thick American accent would have given him away regardless.

'We cannot take for granted just how important this day is for all of us,' his voice echoed loudly, as I signalled for Matt and Emmie to very quietly walk past the door and follow me further down the corridor. 'By the time tonight is over, not only will all our lives have changed significantly, but it will also mean that we will be crucial in ushering in a new era for humanity. The dawn of the next great civilisation will have us at the front and centre, ready to guide everyone with the support of the power we will receive.'

Once we'd safely crossed without being seen, the others made a move towards the door at the end of the corridor and I was going to follow, but was also tempted to listen to more of Casey's lecture. Matt shot me a confused look, but I held up my finger to show that the delay was only going to be a minute.

'If there is one thing that we have learned over the last few weeks,' he continued, 'it is that the world is, as we have always known, much larger than people truly understand...'

When it became clear that he wasn't readily going to go into anything more specific about his plans, I continued to the other door. I opened it and made sure that the other two were through before closing it very slowly, making as little sound as possible.

'Sorry about that,' I whispered. 'I just wasn't sure if he was going to say something about Osiris. I thought maybe it would offer some insight into where she's at.'

'It's alright,' Matt said. 'Just remember that we don't know when his speech is going to end. When it's finished, we'll have to get out of here because those freaks will start walking around and they're bound to catch us.'

I knew he was right and now that we were here, our goal seemed more and more likely to fail, as much as I hated to admit it. I doubted Casey would go on for much longer, though I prayed that once we'd stopped listening, he'd gone on to go in depth about their plans – whatever they might be – and that it would take up a considerable amount of time. All I knew now was that we had to hurry up and search the building. From the snippet of his speech that we'd heard, it was obvious that Casey and Jodie were truly looking to start some sort of society with their newfound knowledge of magic – presumably with themselves in charge.

Emmie touched my arm and looked me in the eye. 'I know what he was saying was unnerving, but we're going to get Osiris back before they can do any damage.'

'Thanks,' I said.

I appreciated that my friends were so adamant in assisting me and glad that it seemed like they were both fully onboard with the fact that Osiris was once a mermaid. There were several times since the revelation that I wondered if they honestly believed me. Not that it mattered completely, as right now it was all about searching the building.

I spotted that the door closest to us was ajar. 'Right, we may as well look in here first,' I said. 'Come on, let's get a move on.'

It was a rather small room and the windows were blacked out, making it extremely hard to see properly and meant we had to use the light from our phones to see exactly what we were dealing with. The main feature of note was a large filing cabinet in the back corner that we immediately rushed to.

'We need to look inside,' I said.

'Why?' Matt asked.

'Because they might hold some information that we need. Damn, we need a key.'

'No, we don't,' Emmie said, fiddling with her ponytail. 'I know how to work these – my sister showed me ages ago.' She'd taken out a hair grip and was fiddling with the locks. Within seconds, all the drawers were open to our disposal.

'I could kiss you,' I declared, rummaging through the various files.

'And I actually will,' Matt added, planting a peck on her cheek.

'Can you see anything?' Emmie asked, holding her phone so that I had better light to see something with.

'Just a bunch of crap so far, but... hang on a minute... oh, no...'

'What is it?'

I had opened a rather thick file and was greeted at once by snapshots of all of us, taken at various locations and at many different times over the last few weeks. Most of them had clearly been from a distance and zoomed in, but others – such as one of Osiris and I in the York restaurant had evidently been done from much closer. I showed Emmie one of us in the petrol station.

She gasped. 'They really have been watching us!'

'Bloody weirdoes...' Matt mumbled, as I handed him a photo of us standing in our living room that had been taken through the window. 'This is beyond disturbing.'

'It proves that we were right, though,' I said. My stomach did a flip when I found further photos of my family. Amber and Noel walking the dog, Phillip and Daisy talking with their neighbour, my dad in his living room, even Ruby out doing the shopping – they had been keeping tabs on everyone I was associated with. I knew that people had been watching us all, but seeing it like this made it so much more real. These people meant business and certainly weren't messing around when it came to getting what they wanted. 'This has all been some elaborate plan for them, just so that they could get to Osiris.'

'Is there anything that says where they might have taken her or where she's been kept, that sort of thing?' Matt inquired.

I stuffed all the photos back into the file and shoved it into the drawer. 'Not yet, but let's keep looking. God knows what else we'll find out...' I glanced back to make sure nobody had discovered us. 'Emmie, could you stand by the door to keep a lookout? I should've thought about that earlier.'

'Yeah, no problem.'

I rummaged about quickly, determined to get as much information as possible and then move on to finding Osiris. I knew it was important to get as much detail as possible, but I also knew that we had a limited timeframe to act on. I searched the bottom drawer and saw that it was full of the same type of leather-bound books that Sam had shown me, the ones that contained spells for dark magic.

'These are what those nutters are using as their guideline,' I said, picking them up and ciphering through them. 'Maybe there's a clue as to what they want...'

'A page has just fallen out,' Matt said, pointing his phone to where he was looking.

I picked it up and smoothed it out. 'It's been torn out,' I noted.

'What does it say?' he asked.

'Guys, hurry up!' Emmie called, trying to keep her voice as low as possible.

'It's some sort of ritual,' I said, my eyes darting across the page as I tried to work out what it was saying. 'It's written kind of old-fashioned, but I think I can get the general idea. Okay, full moon... blood of a mermaid... it's all about resurrecting a demon, I think – it offers the chance for the summoner to harness his power. They need the victim to be purged of their blood so they can lay it out within a circle of people.'

'Wait, are you saying they're going to kill Osiris?'

'There not just going to kill her,' I croaked. 'Jesus Christ, they're going to cut her open whilst she's still alive and completely drain her of every last drop of blood.'

Chapter 27

I couldn't look away from what I was reading. When Osiris first told me about the magic that had helped turn her from a mermaid into a human, it seemed like such a whimsical thing to imagine existing in the world. Now, however, I was seeing the dark side to it and I felt disgusted. I tried not to let myself associate such a repulsive ritual with Osiris, but images of her being killed and laid out like a sacrificial lamb kept flashing through my mind. I was glad I hadn't had breakfast after all because I was likely to have thrown it up if I had done.

Matt tugged on my sleeve. 'Come on, mate, we need to get out of here.'

I tore my eyes away from the sheet of paper and nodded. 'We need to get Osiris – tonight is a full moon.'

'I know,' he said.

'We need to get move on and check elsewhere,' Emmie whispered. 'I just don't feel safe in this particular room. Judging from all this stuff, it's way too important for them to not come in at some point.'

I knew exactly what she meant. It wouldn't have surprised me if most of the rooms in the building were empty – that's certainly what Sam's blueprints appeared to suggest. It was likely that Osiris was being kept in one of those and we'd just happened to stumble across one that housed the cult's most important documents. Emmie was no doubt right in thinking that they'd be coming in here at some point, especially if it was true that they were planning on using these incantations that night.

'Should we take some of this?' I asked.

'What do you mean? Why?'

'Even once we get Osiris out, I doubt this is going to be the end of this whole saga. We need to make sure that they don't have any of this stuff at their disposal.' I began to pull various files out. 'Look at all of this; they have so many dark magic texts. And here are some plans to expand their inner circle. Jesus...'

Emmie walked over, grabbed the items from my hand and began to put them back. 'I know what you're saying, Luke, but if they come here whilst we're looking about then it's going to tip them off. We need to leave everything exactly where we found it. We can deal with all that later – you know, once we have Osiris back safely.'

'You're right. I guess I was just getting carried away. Come on then, let's put all this stuff back and get out of here.'

We placed everything back in its rightful place, making sure it looked as it did when we entered. When we were satisfied that we'd left no clues, we hurried away.

As we made our way back into the corridor, I couldn't shake away the feeling of dread that had swept across me. This was truly a life or death situation. Finding out about merfolk had at first seemed like a privilege, yet it was now feeling like more of a responsibility.

I closed the door behind us and then looked around. I wanted to get through the rest of the mission as quickly as possible to lessen the chances of getting caught.

'I think we should split up,' I voiced.

They looked surprised at my suggestion, which was understandable as we had previously agreed to stay together throughout.

'Why?' Matt asked.

'We can cover more ground quicker that way,' I explained.

'But this wasn't the plan,' Emmie insisted.

'We don't have time to argue,' I said. 'Look, what we just saw there shows us that these people mean business and the longer we're in here, the bigger chance we have of getting caught. We need to hurry – we don't know how long Casey is going to keep talking and we don't exactly know who else was in that room with him. There could be someone skulking about somewhere, so we can't dawdle.'

Matt bit his lip, but appeared to agree. 'Fine.'

'Okay, I'll check out the rest of this floor,' I whispered. 'You two go upstairs and text if you find anything – if you don't, then get yourselves out.'

'Are you sure?'

'Yes. I've asked too much of you already. These people are sick and the sooner we get out of here, the better. I'm not leaving without Osiris, but that's no reason for the two of you to get hurt.'

'But –'

'There's no time to argue, just go!'

They both looked reluctant, but nonetheless continued up the stairs. I hastily moved down the corridor and began checking through the glass panels at the side of each door. All I could see were empty rooms, with not so much as a person in sight.

I swore angrily and persisted in my search. However, no matter how many rooms I glanced into, there were no signs of anything untoward to be seen. Several doors lacked any glass and so I attempted to open them, to no avail. Beads of sweat were trickling down my forehead and I leant against the wall to catch my breath. I was going too fast for my body to handle and I knew that I needed to rest, but I didn't think the situation warranted it. Instead, I picked myself up and headed back to the staircase.

There was no word from either Matt or Emmie, and so, after checking my phone, I went straight up to the next floor. I was making my way up the steps and was almost at the top when I began to hear people talking.

'You should really know better than to go lurking around a place like this,' someone hissed. It sounded like a man. 'Just wait until they find out we've caught the intruders.'

A voice replied and my blood ran cold. 'Let us go!' It was Matt.

For a second, I considered running. Perhaps I could escape quickly and make it to Sam without getting noticed. However, I felt too much loyalty to my friends to just leave them there to suffer when the only reason they were in the situation was because of me. I kept my nerve as best as I could and persisted up the last few stairs.

I was met with the sight of Matt and Emmie in the grasp of two men, who I immediately recognised from the profiles Sam had shown us – Graham and Tyrone. Matt was sporting a bloody lip and Emmie a bruise across her left eye. Next to them, a woman – Shefali – was stood with her arms folded and was watching the proceedings with a scowl.

'Stop,' I said. 'It's not their fault, it's mine.'

'It's *him*,' Tyrone declared.

His eyes rested on something behind me and before I could even turn to see what he was looking at, I felt two arms grab my hands and restrain them behind my back. I tried in vain to get free, but the person was far stronger than I was.

'They're going to be very pleased about this,' growled the man who was holding me, presumably Harris.

'Put them somewhere until we get further instructions,' Shefali ordered. 'Come on, quickly.'

The men started to drag us away down the corridor. The one holding me changed his grip so that his arm was over my chest; I tried to bite his hand and successfully managed to sink my teeth into the flesh of his wrist. He howled like a wounded animal and I wrangled myself free. However, he clearly wasn't going down without a fight.

Shefali rolled her eyes. 'Harris, for Christ's sake – knock him out, will you?'

At that point, something hard smacked against my head and I knew no more.

*

'Luke! Luke, Wake up!'

I slowly opened my eyes, where I was greeted to complete blackness. I was lying down on a cold, hard floor, and there were two blurry shapes squatted down next to me. My eyesight gradually adjusted to the dark and I realised that I was in an extremely small room, with Matt and Emmie looking over me.

'What's going on?' I grumbled, rubbing the back of my head which was pounding.

'After those guys knocked us out, they dragged us here,' Matt explained. 'It's a storage cupboard I think.'

I stumbled to my feet and began to feel around for an exit.

'There's no point,' Emmie sighed. 'We've already tried the door. It's locked tight.'

I slammed my hand against the door in anger and then rested my head against it, beginning to sob silently. I should have known better than to attempt a rescue mission. Of course they'd be prepared for us.

'I'm sorry, guys,' I said. 'I really didn't mean for any of this to happen.'

'It's alright, mate,' Matt said. 'We knew the risk.'

'How long have we been in here?'

'A couple of hours I think,' he replied. 'It's hard to tell exactly – I've lost track of time. We tried to get you to wake up as soon as they left, but you were out cold. We kept checking to see if you were still breathing and when you finally began to stir, we tried to wake you again.'

'I guess I really needed to dream before I face what's to come,' I moaned. 'I guess it meant I saw Osiris one last time, even if it wasn't real.'

'I don't think we're going to be killed,' Emmie said, though the crack in her voice revealed that she wasn't completely sure about that.

I was about to respond when I suddenly heard a noise outside. 'Did you hear that?' I asked, trying hard to listen.

Matt whispered, 'What is it?'

'Someone's coming,' I announced, and we all jumped to our feet.

I was prepared to fight off whatever came out way, but as the door slammed open, we were immediately tacked to the floor, with absolutely no way for us to see what was happening. I felt myself being dragged across a hallway. It was still dark – the only source of light was coming from the crack of a door that was almost closed, which was where we appeared to be heading. We got closer, until the woman from earlier came into view, at which point she opened the door fully and we were taken into a spacious, well-lit room. My eyes stung at first from such brightness.

It looked like it some sort of study, with a large window concealed by curtains to the right and an antique desk to the left. Opposite us, there was an open door that seemed to lead into some pitch-black nothingness. Right in the middle, there something curled up on floor. With a pang of horror, I saw that it was Osiris, bound in chains and looking as though she'd been through torture.

'Osiris!' I cried.

Her head snapped up. 'Luke? Luke!'

She pulled at the chains as hard as she could, but they were far too strong, binding both her arms and legs with extreme force. The man that was holding me made sure there was no way I could loosen his grip and that my teeth could not find his skin.

'What's going on?' I screamed at nobody in particular. 'Have you brought us here to die?' I could hear someone walking in the next room. *'What do you want?'* I bellowed. 'Let me guess – now that you've got us here, you want us to talk? Maybe threaten us until we give you some answers?'

'That's an interesting hypothesis, Luke.'

The voice came from the open doorway at the other end of the room. A figure stepped out of the shadows and, for the second time in my life, I found myself in the presence of Jodie Grayson.

Chapter 28

The first time I met Jodie, she had greeted me with a smile. This time, no such fake courtesy existed. She was glaring at me with a burning hatred in her eyes, not unlike when she stared at me as I left in my car from her house. Donning a black blazer, with matching trousers and shoes, her hair clipped back, she resembled a serious businesswoman rather than a formidable cult leader.

'We meet again at last,' she sneered. 'It's taken long enough.'

I could feel myself quivering. 'What do you mean?'

She laughed. 'All in good time, Luke – I just need to make sure everything is in place so that we won't be disturbed.' She looked over at the man who was holding onto Matt. 'Graham, dear, you did inform Casey to bring our little informant, didn't you?'

The man gave a curt nod. 'I did. They should be here any moment.'

'Excellent,' she said, with a shady smile. I could tell that she was having fun making us wait and had everything planned out in an exact order that she wanted it to go in. 'Lock the door please, Shefali,' she added.

The woman obliged and the door locked with a loud clunk. It all felt real now: we were trapped, and I couldn't think of a way out. All I wanted was to sit down and think things over, the hundreds of questions I had in my head all bursting to be answered. I had to hope that Sam had realised something had gone wrong and would perhaps intervene. The minutes passed in excruciating silence. Osiris kept looking at me and all I wanted was to be with her, to comfort her in what must be a confusing and scary time.

'Just tell us what you want,' I said, when I couldn't take it anymore. 'Whatever it is that you're after, just tell us. We found that page for the potion back there; we know what you're up to. Why haven't you just killed us?'

'Calm down, Luke,' Jodie said, soothingly. I wanted to punch her. 'You're going to learn the hard way that you don't mess with me. I don't want you dead until you know exactly what I had to do to ensure I got what I wanted. You're nothing but a moron and you're going to watch the people you care about suffer for your selfishness. Besides, you are of more worth than you might think, and I consider myself quite the expert at bargaining.'

There came a small knock from the open doorway across the room and I looked up to see Casey stood there with an arrogant smirk on his face. 'Is it time yet? Should I –'

'*No,*' Jodie replied. 'Not quite yet.' She was savouring every moment. 'We don't want the surprise to come completely out of the blue for our guests. They deserve some kind of explanation before... well, before we get down to business.'

I winced. 'Just get on with it, you psychopath. Stop wasting time.'

She ignored me and instead turned her attention to her other prisoners. 'Well, aren't you pretty,' she said, stroking Emmie's hair. 'It's a shame you had to get involved with this, Emmanuelle – though I dare say some of our members would find use for you.'

I wanted to vomit at her words. I was truly dealing with monsters.

'Hello, Matthew,' she said in a horribly fake pleasant voice. 'I know you didn't ask for any of this. You were just being a loyal friend, weren't you?'

'Get lost' he retorted.

Rather than being offended, Jodie looked delighted at his response. 'Ho! He has fire within him, this one. Pity, perhaps in another life you could have been a part of this enterprise. You might have proved invaluable.'

'What are you talking about?' he asked, but she'd already grown bored of conversing with him and moved her attention back to me.

'Your friends mean a lot to you, don't they, Luke?'

I did not reply, but stared angrily back at her, hoping that all my hatred would radiate enough to give a hard slap across her smug face.

She held her gaze for a matter of seconds before saying, 'Well, Casey, I think now is as good a time as any. Let's not keep little Luke out of the loop.'

Casey grinned with delight and swiftly made his way back into the dark room, where he proceeded to whisper to someone. He exited a moment later with the person trailing behind him. Nothing could have prepared me for what followed.

It was Val.

'Ah, there's the person of the hour,' Jodie beamed, beckoning Val to join her near the desk. 'This young lady has been absolutely worth her weight in gold to us.'

Val walked over to her and looked as though she'd rather be anywhere else. I couldn't believe this was happening. Surely it was all a cunning trap and my friend was simply bluffing her way into Jodie's good graces in order to rescue us? Maybe Sam had convinced her to travel down to London after all and now she was here to help rescue Osiris. There was a throbbing pain starting to form in my head as I tried to work out what was going on.

'Confused?' Jodie scorned. 'I'd be surprised if you weren't. After all, Val is someone you trust unconditionally, isn't she?' She snorted. 'You know, Luke, you really should be more careful as to whom you choose to rely on in this life.'

I tried to catch Val's eye, hoping for some sort of sign – a wink, a smile, anything – that would confirm she was still on my side. However, she was very pointedly looking at the floor and attempting to ignore Jodie's lecture.

'Val, what's happening?' I called over, but this only caused her to turn her head away.

Jodie put her arm around Val and said, 'Don't hassle her, Luke, she's been through a lot. It wasn't easy for her to betray you – she drove a hard bargain.'

'I'm sorry, Luke!' Val suddenly wailed, shaking Jodie's arm off her and looking at me in the eye for the first time. 'You don't understand how hard it's been lately. I needed money and I needed it fast. It wasn't personal or anything, I promise!'

It felt like someone had kicked me in the stomach. Val had been involved with Jodie this whole time and had presumably been feeding her all the information she needed for weeks. This couldn't be happening. 'But... but how? When?' I spluttered. 'This doesn't make any sense!'

'Come now, Luke,' Jodie said, 'did you really not suspect this? We needed someone on the inside. After all, constant observation from afar could only accomplish so much.'

Her words didn't surprise me, but merely confirmed what I had already suspected. 'That person outside my dad's window and the one in Ruby's garden – you sent them to spy on me, didn't you?'

Jodie shrugged. 'I got a few people to loiter around your village and gather some information for me, yes. I needed a better understanding of how you worked and who you were most likely to trust. I must say, from what I was told about your sister, she'd have made quite the vindictive double agent. Unfortunately, it seemed like you were about as likely to trust her as you would me. But as soon as I found out about your best friend's financial problems, well, everything just sort of came together. It's surprising what the promise of a lot of money can do to someone's morals.'

I couldn't comprehend that this was happening. I had spoken to Val on the phone that morning and had trusted her with everything. No wonder we got caught so quickly – they'd been tipped off from the very start. I knew there'd been something off about her when we'd talked, though I could never have imagined this being the reason. All I had left in terms of hope was that Sam was still free and there was a chance, no matter how slim, that he could somehow save us all before it was too late.

I felt stupid for ever contacting Jodie and looked around helplessly at Osiris, Matt and Emmie, who were now all paying the price for what I had done. The only idea I could think of was to keep Jodie and Casey talking and just pray that Sam would arrive eventually.

'Why don't we just discuss what it is you really want,' I said, thinking up words from the top of my head. 'You said when we first met that –'

'No!' she screamed. 'Enough talking, it's time we got down to business!'

And with that, Jodie strutted over to me. She reached into her blazer and within seconds had placed a gun to my head. The cold metal hit my skin and my knees weakened at once.

'Let him go, Harris,' she ordered, and I felt myself fall to the floor.

Her gun dug deeper, and a trickle of blood ran down my face, mixed in with the tears across my cheeks. You could cut the tension in the room with a knife.

I had my eyes closed, but I could hear Jodie say, 'Now, I'm going to make things very clear, my little siren of the sea. You have a choice. Make no mistake – tonight is the full moon and we fully intend to take advantage of having your blood at our disposal. There's no way around that, I'm afraid. Or is there? You see, I think there's information we can get from your lips that could save us all that hassle. So, you have, oh I don't know – let's say five minutes – to tell us what we want to know and we'll set you all free. Or else it's goodbye to lover boy here and we will sacrifice you, too.'

Osiris replied in a shaky voice, 'What do you want to know?'

'We want to know how *exactly* you were turned into a human. There was magic involved, and you're going to tell us how we can harness that same power, or I will kill your boyfriend with no hesitation.'

I opened my eyes and saw Osiris watching everything in complete terror. 'Don't do it,' I warned her. 'It's not worth it!'

'Quiet!' Jodie screamed, smacking the side of my face with the gun. 'Ignore him, my dear. Of course it's worth it. Could you really live with yourself if you knew that you were the cause of his death? I mean, look around. All of this pain is because he met you.'

'She's lying!' I cried. 'Osiris, no matter what happens, meeting you was the best thing that ever happened to me!'

Jodie made a noise like she wanted to wretch. 'Oh, please, don't make me ill. Look, *Osiris*, Valerie has already told us the story you gave on how you were transformed from a mermaid into a human.'

'Only you were very vague on the exact details, weren't you?' Casey joined in. 'All we want to know is about the magic that this sea sorcerer holds. You could tell us where exactly we could locate him or perhaps just where we could find the magic he uses. We know that the sea holds secrets and if anybody knows them, then it's you.'

'Then we promise you that we will let you and your boyfriend and everyone else here go home safely,' Jodie tacked on.

'Don't believe them,' I sobbed. 'Osiris, you've seen what they're capable of – they're spiteful, vindictive, scheming nutjobs!'

Osiris shook her head. 'I'm sorry, Luke, but I can't watch you die.'

'That's right,' Casey coaxed her. 'This can all be resolved in a matter of seconds. Just tell us what we want to know, and you all go free.'

I knew it was hopeless to even try to stop Osiris from talking and I couldn't blame her. If the roles were reversed and they wanted to know something from me with the gun against Osiris's head, then I'd tell them everything I knew to keep her from being harmed.

Steadily, Osiris began to speak, 'Well –'

A sudden loud bang at the door caught everyone's attention and we all turned our heads to see what was happening. It was followed by an identical noise a few seconds later.

'*Who is that*?' Jodie snarled at her followers. 'Nobody is supposed to interrupt us!'

A third slamming sound erupted, and the door flung open. The first thing that drew my attention upon the person's entrance was the large rifle they were holding. Then my jaw dropped when I realised who it was.

Alice looked quite content with operating a weapon.

Chapter 29

'*Who are you?*' Jodie demanded.

'Never mind that,' Alice said, making sure she had everyone in the room within shooting range. 'I think you're the one who has some explaining to do, Ms. Grayson.'

Val looked as equally dumbstruck as everybody else. 'What are you doing here?' she asked. 'How did you know where we were?'

Alice's eyes didn't leave Jodie. 'I know more than you think I do, Valerie.'

'Enough!' Jodie cried, her revolver pressing into my head harder. 'Explain who you are, or I'll blow his brains out.'

'Shoot him and I'll shoot you,' Alice warned, without flinching. 'And don't think that I won't. Put your gun down and we'll talk.'

It was clear that Jodie was livid at been told what to do. However, with a rifle pointed directly at her, she had no other option but to give in to Alice. With visible regret, she took the pistol from my head and threw it several feet away before holding her hands up in the air. I immediately took this opportunity to crawl over to Osiris and embrace her.

'You found me,' she wept.

'I'll *always* find you.'

Osiris continued to tremble, but there was no time for us to talk properly for there were more pressing issues at hand and I wanted to get to the bottom of what was going on.

'Alice, how did you know where to find us?' I asked.

'I had help,' she answered, before shouting through to someone outside. 'I've got them all in place, come in!'

A moment later, Sam entered the room.

Jodie's face hardened. 'I should've known you'd make an appearance.'

'I see you haven't changed,' he said. 'Still craving that fifteen minutes of fame, I see. You've definitely raised the stakes a bit from when we were teenagers, though – I'll give you that.'

Jodie's lips were now pursed and her eyes narrow. 'Do you still blame me for what happened with Telanthera? I mean, how could I not want more? Looking at her all those times, with her tail, her webbed hands, her dazzling eyes – I could see the potential for extraordinary things. All I needed was for people to see her and attach my name to the discovery. Was that too much to ask?'

Sam glowered at her. 'You ruined my life, Jodie. You knew how I felt about her.'

'Get a grip,' she spat. 'She wasn't even human, you freak.'

He didn't respond, but you could practically see the crackling in the air between them. This had gone way beyond typical sibling rivalry.

'What's any of this got to do with Alice?' Val queried, eyeing her girlfriend who was still stood with a steady hold on the rifle.

This was something I wanted to know for myself as well. So far, everything was starting to add up, but I couldn't work out how Alice had any connection whatsoever to anything that had happened. Not even Val's association with Jodie made her relevance to events any clearer.

'I spoke with Sam this morning,' Alice said, which caused an immediate hush in the room. Even Jodie and Casey's lackeys looked like they were becoming invested in the backstory. 'I've been getting suspicious of Valerie's actions lately. It's no secret that we've been struggling with money recently and then suddenly she's pulling out money to pay the mortgage and buying me new clothes without letting me know how she could afford it.'

Val bowed her head in shame.

Alice continued, 'The other night, I heard her talking to someone on the phone. When she hung up, she refused to tell me who it was. I know it's not right, but I looked through her emails a few hours later and found that she'd been in contact a lot with a woman called Jodie Grayson. A little research showed me exactly who she was. Yesterday, she told me she was going out with friends. When she didn't come home, I grew suspicious. I managed to get into her emails again and saw that she'd been instructed to make her way down to London. I immediately made my way down myself.'

'But how did you know to get talk to Sam?'

'I caught her lurking outside this building about an hour ago,' Sam said. 'I knew she looked familiar, so I approached her. We got talking and that's when I realised that the cult would have knowledge of our infiltration. Sorry we didn't get here sooner, but Alice insisted on coming in armed.'

'Luckily, I have some connections in that department,' Alice said.

I was still digesting all this information. It didn't seem to make sense that Val, my closest friend since childhood, had betrayed me. She was looking extremely guilty, but this didn't take away from her disloyalty.

A single tear rolled down her cheek. 'I didn't think it would get this far.'

'Then how far did you expect it to get?' I snarled, angrily.

'I don't know. When Jodie told me about having met a mermaid in her youth, I assumed she'd want to talk to her. By the time I realised what she had planned, I was in too deep and I'm sorry, but I *really* needed the money.'

Alice let out a laugh of ridicule. 'No, you didn't. We've always managed, and we would have done without any help from such a horrible source. And I suppose buying me expensive clothes was necessary, or was that just a bribe in the hope that I'd not question you?'

'Of course not,' Val sobbed. 'I bought you stuff because I wanted you to be happy. I love you, Alice, I really do. Please don't hate me.'

'I don't want to discuss it right now,' Alice said. 'In case you haven't noticed, we have bigger problems to deal with. Sam, get Osiris out of those chains.'

'Where's the key?' I asked.

'Here,' Jodie mumbled, pulling a rusted one out of her pocket and throwing it nonchalantly at her brother. He grabbed it and set to work freeing Osiris, whilst Jodie turned her nose up at Casey's notable scowl. 'Don't look at me like that – I warned you we should've been more heavily armed. Now look what's happened.'

Everything seemed to be going calmly, until there was sudden movement from Harris, the man who'd been restraining me before. He had made a dive for Alice. We watched as the two struggled for possession of the rifle. Harris had the upper hand and had his finger on the trigger; Alice desperately tried to seize it back from him.

'Stop it!' Val screeched, running forward.

The gun went off and Val crumbled to the floor, her chest covered in blood.

Alice managed to secure a tight hold of the gun and smack it into Harris's nose, which caused him to back off. She then dropped the gun and ran to Val, who now had blood coming out of her mouth.

'Don't die!' Alice wailed. 'I forgive you, Valerie, I do!'

I knew that it was too late, though.

Val was choking as she spluttered, 'I'm sorry.' Then her eyes rolled back, and I watched in horror as my most cherished friend became nothing more than a lifeless body.

Alice glowered at Harris in anger. 'You...'

Sam picked up the rifle and bellowed, 'What the hell did you do that for? We were going to let you go in peace, you idiot!'

Harris didn't seem fazed and merely grunted back, 'I thought if I got in control, we could go back to the plan. We were fine before you two burst in.'

'I think it's gone beyond that now, don't you?' Sam shouted.

With Osiris now released, I rushed over to Alice's side. Val lay motionless on the floor, her pointed face paler than ever before and her eyes still wide open, with a blank, glassy expression. Despite her treachery, I never wanted this to happen.

Sam looked towards Jodie and her associates. 'Now someone is dead thanks to you lot and was it really worth it? Was it worth putting people through hell for? There were two people who only wanted to be together and weren't harming anyone, yet you decided amongst yourselves to get involved.'

Alice pointed at Harris and yelled, 'This is murder!' She went to say something else when she choked on her words and it became a heart-wrenching sob.

Jodie stepped forward and I felt uneasy at once when I saw the sly smile beginning to return to her face. 'Now, now,' she said, 'let's all stay calm. What's happened is a tragic accident, but we're all witnesses, and this could get really messy.'

Alice wiped the tears from her eyes. 'What are you saying?'

'Well, believe it or not, we're a powerful organisation. This tragedy could be swept under the carpet so easily. I mean, it's not like she'd really be missed.'

'*You cow!*' Alice shrieked. '*I'll miss her.* You aren't just going to pretend like she didn't exist and hope that we'll all just ignore what you've done here! You're a sick woman and I'm going to love seeing you locked away for the rest of your miserable life!'

This didn't seem to register with Jodie at all, who merely smiled wider and replied, 'But Alice, you're the one who has fingerprints all over that gun. And if you do alert the police, then not everyone in this room is going to collaborate with your story.'

'There's no way you're going to get away with anything like that,' I said.

'Do any of you realise the situation you're in?' she asked, staring around at us all. 'Look, I admit that I'm no saint in this.'

I made a noise of derision.

Jodie shot me a dark look then continued, 'I'm not just going to lie down and allow you to send us away to prison.'

She looked at Casey who nodded. 'We can offer you a lot of money to smooth it all over,' he confirmed. 'If you're willing, we can talk about this and come to an arrangement.'

Jodie began to slowly walk around the room. 'What do you say?'

I couldn't believe they had the audacity to think that they could talk their way out of the situation. 'I say you can burn in hell, you lunatics!'

'Very well,' Jodie replied. In one swift movement, she lunged at Osiris.

One arm wrapped around her so she couldn't move, whilst with the other, she pulled out a hunting knife which was concealed in the waistband of her trousers and held it to Osiris's throat. She had the blade so close to the skin that I could already see blood starting to ooze out.

A manic grin spread across Jodie's face. 'Did you really think I wouldn't have a backup plan? I always make sure to have this on my person at all times. It's so much more intimate than a gun, don't you think?'

'Let her go!' I begged. The look on Osiris's face made me feel as though my heart had shattered into a thousand pieces. I couldn't let her die. 'Please, take me instead – I'll do anything, I promise! Just don't hurt her, please!'

'Jodie... don't do this,' Sam voiced, quietly. 'It isn't worth it.'

'No! I'm in charge and you will listen to me!' she screamed back, her face now very red. 'Here's what's going to happen. This freak,' she grabbed a cluster of Osiris's hair with her teeth and tugged it, causing her to howl in pain, 'is going to tell us *exactly* where to look in the ocean and then we're all going to go on a little trip. Our discovery will be worldwide news in no time, and we'll harness more power than any other human on earth.'

There was nothing I could think of doing. Jodie was taller than Osiris, but from where we were standing, there was no way we could get a clear shot of Jodie to use the rifle on her. Not without risking hitting Osiris, in any case.

'Okay,' I said. 'Fine, we'll do that. Just let Osiris go.'

'Nice try,' Jodie cackled. 'No, no, she's going to stick with me just in case any of you try anything funny.' She loosened the arm she had wrapped around Osiris and used it to pull her head down so that she had a better view of her bare neck. The dagger smoothly drifted across the surface of the skin. 'After all, you wouldn't want her precious throat slit, which could so easily –'

Suddenly, a loud boom erupted from nowhere and the whole room shook. Everyone collapsed to the floor and I saw the Jodie's knife go skidding under the desk. The glass from the window had shattered, causing the curtains to tear away and reveal the shimmering light from the full moon outside. I quickly made my way across the shard-laden floor towards Osiris as the others scrambled away from the invisible threat.

'What's going on?' someone cried.

We all managed to get back to our feet and everyone sprinted towards the open doorway, which slammed itself shut. Matt tried the handle furiously, but it wouldn't budge.

'It's locked!' he shouted.

'Impossible!' Casey lambasted. 'I've got the only key for it!'

'For heaven's sake, try the other one!' Jodie screeched. 'Come on, can't you see that we're under attack!'

'It won't work!' Shefali said, slamming her hand against the door.

'Oh, move over,' Jodie snarled, but she couldn't get it to open either.

When it was clear that both exits were off limits, it seemed like everyone knew the best course of action was to try and use the window. We all made a move towards it, when suddenly a burst of cold wind swept the room and stopped us in our tracks. It was as though we'd been plunged into icy water as a frosty atmosphere enveloped us, and even our breath began to steam as if was a winter's night.

'W-w-what's h-happening?' I stammered, my teeth chattering.

Osiris's eyes widened. 'I think... I think it's *him*.'

We all turned to face her with looks of confusion when an ear-splittingly loud scream began to emit out of nowhere, forcing us to crouch down and cover our ears. I thought my ear drums were about to bleed when at last it stopped, though a distinct ringing noise remained. I looked around and saw that a large shadowy figure was now stood at the window.

'Sorry about that,' it said, with a loud authoritative male voice. 'I needed you all to stop. Now, are we all calm?'

I instinctively walked over to Osiris, who was backing off with a look of dread in her large eyes. Matt, Emmie, Sam and the four cult members all retreated to the furthest wall, whilst Casey and Jodie simply looked enamoured at the man who stepped forward.

I couldn't exactly describe him as human, even though that's what he may have resembled. He was good foot taller than me and I was probably the tallest one in the room and he had a noticeable crooked slant to him. His eyes were completely black, and his teeth resembled those of a shark, giving him a demonic look. Most of his face was covered my straggled hair, though from what I could see it looked like he was made up of skin mixed with crustaceous sea life. As for clothes, he was dressed in a combination of contemporary business attire and audacious whimsy, but was barefoot to reveal long, hand-like feet.

I registered Osiris's reaction and asked her, 'Is this who turned you human?'

'Clever boy,' the sorcerer said, grinning. He clicked his fingers and the ringing stopped. 'It looks like she's been quite a busy human.' He walked across the room towards Val and placed one of his feet on her, causing Alice to whimper. 'Tut tut, there's been so much death.'

'Only one person,' I insisted, as it seemed he was blaming Osiris for it.

'For now,' he muttered, ominously.

At that point, Casey stepped forward. 'This is incredible. Please, I want to know more. Your power... it's beyond what I could have hoped for. Let us harness your magic... please.'

The sorcerer whipped his head round to look at him. 'I know exactly what you've been up to. You've been messing with things beyond your comprehension. Do you really think a human like yourself could ever achieve the feats that I can perform? You have no idea just how much power I have at my disposal. You pathetic, insignificant mortal – reading a few books doesn't make you worthy.'

This didn't seem to go down well with Casey, who looked visibly furious. 'Tonight is the night we will perform one of the darkest uses of magic ever recorded and –'

The sorcerer interrupted him with a bark of laughter. 'Recorded? Yes. Darkest there is? Hardly. I can do things you couldn't even comprehend, so don't even try to talk big in front of me. Now, I've come to put things right.' He turned to Osiris. 'I'm afraid it's time you returned to ocean. I can see now that you clearly weren't ready for this life.'

'What?' I cried. 'No, you can't – Osiris belongs here!'

'She has risked far too much,' he retorted. 'I was quite clear when she came to me that she was not to let anyone know about where she came from. Instead, she allowed it get out amongst the humans and now look – so many people are in the know.'

'It wasn't her fault, she –'

'*Silence!*' he roared, and I felt my jaw snap shut.

'Please,' Casey said, stepping forward. 'We could be of help. Just tell us what you may require amongst the human world and we can assist you.'

'I don't need anything from you. Now back off.'

'I will not,' Casey replied, defiantly. 'I don't care who you are, I –'

Before he could finish his sentence, the sorcerer flicked his hand and a large steel pole smashed through the roof and impaled Casey right through his head. Jodie shrieked, as did several of the others. Outside, dark clouds began to appear, and thunder could be heard rumbling close by. I couldn't quite believe what I was witnessing.

'I can always do with an extra supply of human blood,' the sorcerer quipped. A flash of lightning hit Casey's body and it disappeared. 'I suppose he was useful for something.'

'How dare you!' Jodie suddenly shouted, lunging forward.

Anybody could have seen that this was probably the stupidest thing she could have done, but she was either spurred on by grief or had a death wish. She was barely anywhere near her target when she was flung into the air and repeatedly slammed into the wall. Blood splattered everywhere and then she too was gone in a flash of lightning.

'Anybody else want to take me on?' The sorcerer growled. There was a deathly silence. 'I thought not. Now, I'm going to leave... and everybody is going to get on with their lives. I could wipe your memories, of course, but it's more fun for me if I don't – because if anything happens, then I have reason to find you and... well, you saw what happened to the others who were reckless enough to take me on.'

Everybody looked at one another and it was clear that they were in no way going to say anything about what had just happened. However, Alice stepped forward and looked the sorcerer right in the eye, her own were swimming with tears.

'Can you bring her back?' she asked, signalling towards Val.

'I'm afraid not.'

'But –'

'She died a human death. I'm sorry, but she doesn't belong in this world anymore. There's nothing I can do. Some things just can't be done.'

Alice dropped to floor, crying. Sam squatted down to comfort her.

'Come along,' the sorcerer said, holding out his hand to Osiris. 'I'm sure the sooner you leave, the sooner these people can go back to some normality.'

She gave me an apologetic look, and then steadily took his hand. They walked over to the window and he raised his hands ready to click his fingers. I thought about what Madame Malina had told me – that my decisions would affect the outcome of my future. I couldn't just allow Osiris to be taken away from me without a fight.

'Don't!' I yelled.

They both turned.

I walked over and dropped to my knees. 'Please don't take her away from me!' I pleaded. 'Please! You don't know how much she means to me!'

I looked directly into his soulless black eyes, willing him to demonstrate some compassion.

He looked at me and then back to Osiris. 'Remarkably, this young man sees purely through the eyes of love. It's foolish, perhaps – but nonetheless admirable. Maybe I'm being a little hasty in taking you away from the human world. After all, you've made quite an impact on his life; almost as though the two of you were destined to cross paths.'

I tentatively waited, not daring to believe that he might grant me my request, when he suddenly let go of Osiris's hand. She looked as shocked as I felt and then suddenly ran over to me.

I looked back at the sorcerer. 'Thank you,' I whispered.

He gave me a sly wink and disappeared with a bang. The clouds suddenly evaporated, and the thunder died away.

'What happens now?' Osiris asked, timidly, as I pulled her into a hug.

Her question hung in the air without anyone able to answer it. A dead body was lying on the floor and everybody was unable to grasp what had just went down. All I cared about at that moment was keeping Osiris close to me and getting out of there. Then, without any notice, Alice picked up her rifle and angled it towards the four cult members.

'Right, I want all of you to get on the floor with your hands behind your heads!' she commanded. 'We're going to call the police, but first we need to know where any camera footage is kept in this place.'

Chapter 30

The direct aftermath of the ordeal was a blur to me. Sitting beside Osiris on the floor, I watched the others making movements, taking in what they were doing with the small amount of concentration I had left.

I could see Alice bending down next to Val and it looked as though she was closing her eyelids. Matt and Emmie were very shaken up and left the room in each other's arms. Things continued to be hazy, my concentration mainly focused on the fact that Osiris had her head leant against my shoulder and was gently caressing my hand with the tips of her fingers. I was able to make out Alice marching the four cult members out of the room. Even in my restless state, I could see that they looked frightened – no matter how much they'd believed what Casey had fed them about magic, I bet they'd never fully believed it was a reality and had gotten a real wake-up call by what just happened. Sam lifted Val's limp body and took it away.

This left Osiris and I in the room alone for what seemed like hours. We didn't say a word to each other; the fact that we were both there and were safe was enough. My attention was eventually brought back to reality when Alice returned to the room and sat down next to us. She still looked very much traumatised by the events.

'The police are on their way.' Her face was ashen. 'They shouldn't be too long.'

I didn't reply.

'They'll probably want to speak to us all separately,' she continued. 'There's obviously no evidence of their mermaid claims, so we can just say that Jodie and Casey were a couple of mad psychopaths who wanted you dead for not giving into their delusions. We're just going to have to make up they ran off because that... that man, he seems to have wiped away any trace of them.' I looked to see that the splatters of their blood had indeed vanished when he'd caused them to disappear. 'There's no security tape in this room, but there are ones in all of the hallways of the building that'll show their associates manhandling you lot. Both me and Harris's fingerprints are on the rifle, so we'll let them know the truth about what happened there.'

'What happens if they are told about me being a mermaid?' Osiris asked.

Alice wiped her nose with the sleeve of her jacket. 'Nobody will believe them. They'll look crazy and it will add to the fact that they were helping Jodie and Casey the whole time.'

We sat in silence for a while as I let everything mull over in my head. It was nice to have time for quiet contemplation given the investigation that was no doubt about to unfold. Having this brief golden moment of relaxation before it was all going to happen was something we all sorely needed and I intended to get the most out of it. Yet I still felt like I needed to talk more with Alice. We'd barely conversed before outside of snide remarks and arguments and it felt soothing to talk as if we were friends.

'I didn't expect anyone to come and help us,' I admitted to her. 'As soon as they had us captured, I thought we were all doomed. And if there was a hope of someone finding us, you'd have been the last person I'd have expected to show up.'

She patted me on the leg. 'This must have all come as a bit of a shock. I know I haven't been the friendliest of people towards you. Or anybody for that matter.'

'I don't know,' I said. 'That punch you gave my sister brought you up in my estimations.'

'Glad it amused you,' she replied, almost emitting a chuckle which turned into a snivel.

'Is there any particular reason you gave me a hard time?' I asked. 'Sorry, it's just I've never had a chance to really talk to you before... but after what just happened, I think I want to get to know you better.'

'I think I was just angry at people in general. I haven't spoken to my dad for years – we were never really close, but it got worse when I brought Valerie home for him to meet.'

I recalled Val telling me that the first time she met Alice's parents it hadn't been a success, but she'd never specified it in any detail.

'It didn't help that my mam was ill at the time,' Alice went on. 'My dad had a lot on his mind, what with her and his job. I think me being with someone like Valerie was just a bit too much for him to handle. I guess I took my frustration out on others.'

I lifted my spare hand and rested it on her shoulder. It was a situation I wouldn't have thought possible before that moment: Alice had opened up to me and I was comforting her. That day had shown me for the first time that she was indeed capable of actual human emotions and was more layered than I'd given her credit for.

She then asked a question directed at Osiris. 'That mermaid they mentioned – Telanthera, I think – did you know her?'

'I remember someone by that name,' she said, 'but I didn't know that she'd been to the surface.'

'Maybe it's for the best that way, though,' I said. 'It sounds like she knew that she was betrayed, and it probably soured her view on humans. She might have convinced you not to go to the land if you'd asked her about it.'

The idea of not having met Osiris was almost unthinkable. As far as I was concerned, no matter what, we were always destined to find one another. There had been too many coincidences binding us together for that not to be the case. Not only had I been the only one on the beach that day that she'd been on shore, but I'd also managed to come across her at the hospital simply by chance as my dad was at the same place. Factoring in the fact that Madame Malina had sensed a connection between me and someone associated with the sea, nothing could take the belief away from me that it was destiny.

After a short silence, Alice said, with a quiver in her voice, 'I should go see if they've arrived. They'll want to take Valerie away and...' her bottom lip began to tremble, 'I... I want to be there when they do.'

'Okay,' I answered, quietly.

She steadily got to her feet and walked out of the room, her footsteps echoing loudly against the stillness. I felt immense compassion towards her as I watched a broken woman exit, knowing that she was unlikely to ever be the same again. I also experienced a certain level of shame in that I did not make much of an effort to get to know her properly before all of this happened, though I had to remind myself that Alice had always been a rather closed off individual, so this may not necessarily be for me to blame myself for.

Osiris let out a long sigh.

'How are you feeling?' I asked her.

She shrugged. 'I'm not sure. It's weird because I'm happy that we don't have to worry about those awful people anymore, but I'm still in shock over everything that's happened. I just can't believe it about Val.'

'Which part – her being a backstabber or her dying?'

'All of it, I suppose.' She rubbed her eyes, which were bloodshot. 'I mean, her working against us came as a shock, but for her to just die like that...' she ended with a shudder.

'I know what you mean,' I said. 'I wish I could've heard from Val a bit more, for her to explain what she did. I didn't want to believe it could be true when Casey first brought her out. Though when I think back to the night you were taken, Val had visited and made me a drink – I fell asleep almost straight away afterwards, so I'm guessing she drugged me. What exactly happened to you that night?'

Although it was obvious that Osiris was exhausted from what had happened, I didn't want to wait until after the inevitable police investigation to find out the exact details of the events and betrayals that had occurred. Also, if I pressed her about it then it would be easier for me to inform her on what to recite when the investigators questioned her.

'I remember waking up because I heard footsteps, but I just assumed it was you. Before I knew what was happening, a group of people dressed completely in black were in the room. I went to scream, but they covered my mouth with some sort of cloth and I felt myself go back to sleep. When I woke up, I was in the back of a van. They pulled up outside of here and carried me inside. That's when I was brought in this room.'

I squeezed her knee for reassurance. 'You must have been scared.'

'I was more confused than anything really,' she said. 'Those people – Jodie and Casey – they kept asking questions, but I refused to answer. That's when they got mad.'

I felt a sudden pang of unease when I realised that Osiris was about to explain about what happened that resulted her being chained up. I had to hear her story, but it didn't feel right when I flashed back to the image of her tied up in fear.

She took a deep breath and resumed. 'I tried to make a run for it, but they were too strong. I remember getting punched and everything going black. When I woke up, there were chains over my hands and feet and Jodie was watching me, telling me that I was going to make her a very rich lady. They kept giving me water, but no food, and telling me what they had planned for the night of the full moon. I was terrified.'

Tears began to roll down her cheeks and I brushed them away with my hand before kissing her gently. She blushed and put her arm around my waist.

'There's no need to be frightened anymore,' I whispered. 'It's over now, for good.'

'What should I tell the police if they ask me about my involvement?'

I thought over her question for a moment, and then replied, 'Tell them the truth. You were snatched from the house and taken to London. Tell them what these people were accusing you of – it will make them look crazy and we can back this up by showing them Jodie's website and all of Casey's notes. There's no way they'll actually believe you were once a mermaid, so we'll be fine.'

'Are they going to do anything to Alice for bringing the rifle that killed Val?'

'She should be okay,' I answered, though I wasn't sure if this was the truth or not. They'd hopefully believe our story that Val's shooting had been an accident and that Alice only brought a weapon for self-defence purposes, but we'd just have to see what happened and take things one step at a time.

'It's lucky Alice was able to find out where Casey would be at and that Sam was able to team up with her to save us,' Osiris noted.

'I don't know about luck. I'm starting to think that maybe the universe likes to give a gentle nudge to help us out every now and again.'

'You know, maybe we should have just let Alice in on everything the same time that we did with Matt and Emmie. We did sort of leave her out of the loop.'

'Well, in our defence, she's never been particularly approachable.'

Osiris managed a smile as we heard footsteps and voices becoming louder outside. She began to breathe heavier and I grasped her hand. I wasn't looking forward to the oncoming enquiry either, but I knew I'd have to remain strong and hoped she'd be able to pull through as well. Once it was all over, we'd never have to look back again.

Epilogue

It didn't take long for the days that followed that fateful night to turn into weeks and eventually months. Before I knew it, a year had passed and everything that happened in London was finally starting to feel like a distant dream. Admittedly, sometimes it became more of a nightmare, but that's why I was going regularly to see a therapist.

Dr. Blake Madden (who insisted that I call him by his first name) turned out to be a real asset to my gradual recovery. To say that I was reluctant to open up during our first session would be an understatement; I'd basically sat and mumbled some vague responses in reply to his constant questions. By my third time seeing him, though, I was a lot more expressive and was soon pouring out all my feelings. I was surprised to find how honest and frank I became with sharing personal thoughts with him, but I guess it showed how much I truly needed to unload and that it was best to have a qualified expert listen to me.

I had already felt significant relief when I had told Osiris about my prom night, but nothing compared to how much better it got when I finally told my family and friends. The ordeal wasn't over by any means and that's why I still needed to talk to a professional, but I finally felt as though I was going to make real progress in my recovery. The fact that I was over a year sober was something I reminded myself of nearly every day.

I did feel some guilt when it came to the fact that I could never truly tell Blake the truth about how Osiris and I met, or the significance our romance has played in structuring my life. Even though I knew that there was doctor-patient confidentiality in place and that they'd revoke his license if they found out he was so much as whispering anything to do with what we've discussed in his room, I still didn't want to risk the possible consequences it could bring if he were to be told about magic and mermaids. After all, there was a chance he'd deem me insane and haul me into a psychiatric hospital.

'Dr. Madden won't be long,' his receptionist told me. She had just gotten back from getting a coffee, which she was now holding. 'He had to quickly go sort out some paperwork, but he assured me he'd be back in time to make your appointment.'

'Great, thanks,' I said. There was still five minutes to go until my session was due to start and waiting wasn't a bother since the reception area was reasonably comfortable.

I still looked back on the day that I first met Osiris and wondered how things would've been different if it had never happened. On the one hand, Val would almost certainly still be alive. That was the main part that still haunted me. She was my best friend and even though I'd never be able to understand her actions – not even able to ask her what was going through her mind – I still visited her grave regularly and left flowers: black roses, which were her favourite. Then I thought about Osiris. Meeting me had been a contributing factor in her decision to seek out becoming human, but it was possible that she could still have done that at some point without our encounter to spur her on. Then there was the chance that someone other than me could have seen her that day – maybe by someone like Jodie or Casey, who might've caused her harm. The thought didn't bear thinking about and I was just sincerely glad that it didn't happen that way.

So, whilst there had been negatives along the way, they were far outweighed by the positives we'd experiences on this incredible journey. I guess death is inevitable no matter what happens and it's better to not focus on the various scenarios of what could have been because that would do nothing but eat a person up from the inside.

If life had proven hard for me since that fateful night, it was nothing compared to what Alice had been through. Since her fingerprints were found on the weapon that was used to murder Val, she had been taken in for questioning and had faced months of torment trying to clear her name. Sam, Matt, Emmie, Osiris and I had come forward to testify that it had been Harris who'd been the one to fire the trigger and that Alice had only brought the weapon as a defence against the possible threat that the cult provided. The jury decided that this was seemed likely given the documents that were found in the headquarters, as well as Jodie's website and electronic correspondences between her and Casey. Alice was let go, but given a hefty fine for purchasing the rifle through illegal means. I'd kept in touch with her, though our communication had rarely included contact in person.

'Here's Dr. Madden now,' his receptionist suddenly announced.

I looked up to see that Blake had indeed just appeared. He gave me a wide smile as he approached. I wondered if he gave all his patients such enthusiastic greetings or whether this was reserved for people he genuinely liked.

'Hi Luke, would you like to step inside?' he said, before handing a file over to his receptionist and saying, 'Karen, could you please sort this out for Fiona, please?'

'No problem, Dr. Madden,' she replied, brightly.

I got up and walked over. He stepped aside to let me in first and then he followed, closing the door firmly behind him.

His room was a very comforting one. It had a beige carpet and cream walls, with brown furniture – a chair for him and a sofa for the patient. The blinds on his window were always closed so you could feel total privacy, which I appreciated. In terms of decorations, there were a few potted plants and statues, but nothing relating to his personal life.

'Please, take a seat,' he said, offering a hand towards the sofa.

My first opinion on Blake had been one of scepticism because of how young he was. I'd never actually asked his exact age, but would estimate him to be in his early thirties at least. He was clean-shaven and had short sandy hair, which made him appear younger, though the way he spoke and conducted himself gave away that he was a bit older than the initial twentysomething I'd put him as. What had won me over with him was that he had a sweet nature to his voice and was the type of person you just knew had a kind heart.

I took my place and waited whilst he messed with some papers on his desk and then sat down with a notepad and pen. During my first session, he'd told me that a lot of his patients felt better when they were laid on the sofa, but I preferred to be sat upright.

'So, Luke, what's been happening since we last spoke?'

In all honestly, not a lot. In terms of my everyday life, I was doing everything I normally did.

'Luke?' he said, pointedly.

I smirked and said, 'Well, I bought an engagement ring. I haven't given her it yet, but I'm going to propose... soon, I'm thinking.' I pulled out the box from inside my jacket pocket and opened it to show him. It wasn't much, but it had a blue diamond that reminded me of the ocean. It seemed appropriate enough – not that many people would understand the significance, of course. 'What do you think?'

He wrote something down on his notepad. 'That's quite a big step, Luke. I know you live together and everything, but marriage is a commitment. Do you think you're ready for that?'

'Yeah, I do.' I had given it a lot of thought over the past few weeks. 'I'm more than ready.'

'And what about Osiris? Do you think she is?'

'I hope so,' I laughed, closing the ring and pocketing the box.

He jotted something else down and then continued, 'So, you haven't given her it yet? Why not? I'm guessing you've had it for a few days.'

I shrugged. 'There just hasn't been a good time. I keep thinking of the perfect way in which to do it, but I just draw a blank. I thought about having a small party – you know, with a few friends and some family members – and doing it there in front of everyone. I don't know, though, it just didn't feel right.'

'It'll come to you,' Blake assured me. 'When the time is right, you'll know.'

'All I know is that it will be soon,' I said, with confidence. 'I've never been surer of anything in my life. When I first met Osiris, I knew that I was starting a whole new chapter in my life, but it wasn't until I told everyone the truth about... about what happened on my prom night, that I've finally felt like I've truly turned the page on the last one. And that makes me want to say something that I never thought I would ever say again after that night.'

Blake looked intrigued. 'Oh yeah, and what's that?'

'I'm happy.'

And I was. Sure, there would no doubt be struggles in the future, as there always is, but that's normal and I would face them when they came. But in that moment, none of that mattered because I was content with life and very much looking forward to seeing what the future would bring.

*

Later that afternoon, after I'd finished my session with Blake, I drove home with the intent of meeting Osiris at the beach as we had agreed on that morning. With the move into relatively warm weather, we had been spending more time by the sea – perhaps a sign that, even though she had never truly enjoyed her life there, it would always be a part of her.

There was a crisp breeze in the air as I left my car, though there was still a pleasant sun shining down that dispelled it to an extent. As soon as I arrived on the beach, I spotted Osiris immediately. There weren't a lot of people there and she was stood right at the shore, her hair blowing in the wind. She turned and waved to me; I jogged over and lifted her into a mock dramatic twirl, which she seemed to appreciate.

'You're so corny sometimes,' she laughed, kissing me on the cheek as I put her down.

I smiled and took her hand, as we gently strolled along the sand, looking out at where the water met the sky.

'How's your day been?' I asked.

'Not bad,' she said. 'How was your session?'

'It was good. I think I can finally say I'm making progress, so that's something to celebrate, I guess. I don't think I'm ready to stop them just yet, though.'

'You continue them for as long as you feel necessary. And if that's the rest of your life, then that's perfectly fine by me.'

'I'm sorry if it's causing you any hassle,' I muttered. 'I know it can't be easy to know that I'm seeing a professional every week. I don't want you to feel like I'm... I don't know, pawning my problems off on someone else.'

'Don't be silly,' she said. 'We're a team. And that means supporting each other, no matter what. I'm happy that you're getting the help you need.'

'I just don't want you to have any worries. I want you to be content in your life as a human.'

'The whole idea of being human is to face the problems that come with it. I'm sure it was you who said that battling through all the obstacles we have makes us stronger people. I'm more than happy with my life right now. I've dreamed about living out of the sea my entire life, but I could never have imagined it being as wonderful as this. I wish with all my heart that my family could see how happy I am now, here with you.'

This last comment caught me off guard and I asked, 'Do you think about your family often?'

She didn't respond straight away. It wasn't a topic we ever broached, though I did wonder about it from time to time. Osiris had never been happy as a mermaid and wanted more than anything to be a human, but she had made an extremely brave decision in making this a reality because it meant that she had to sacrifice ever seeing her family again.

'Sometimes,' she said, at last. 'When I think about what they must be going through, it makes me feel guilty. I just disappeared and they'll never know what happened to me – they probably think I've been killed. I just want them to know that I'm safe and that I'm where I've always longed to be. And I want them to meet you, Luke. I'd love for them to see that I met my soulmate.'

I digested what she said, and my hand instinctively reached inside my jacket, where I began to grasp the small box inside. 'I don't know if that will ever happen,' I admitted. 'There's nothing I'd want more than to reunite you with your family, Osiris, but that's out of my control. I... I do know what I *can* do, though.'

We stopped and she looked at quizzically at me. 'What?'

I noticed that we'd arrived at the very place where we'd first met – it all seemed to have aligned so perfectly. 'I want us to start our own family. Whether that means just the two of us, or if we'll expand that at some point – I don't care. All I know is that I want to spend the rest of my life with you.'

She smiled and looked as though she was going to lean in for a kiss, but I was already bending down on one knee.

'What are you doing?' she asked.

'Osiris, I want you to make me the happiest man on the face of this earth.' I opened the box and beamed as she gasped in awe. 'Will you marry me?'

'*Yes*,' she answered, without hesitation. 'Of course I will!'

I stood back up and slid the ring onto her finger, which was no easy task as I found myself shaking uncontrollably. She admired it on her hand for a moment and then we kissed passionately, before we broke apart and hugged – tighter than ever before.

There was bound to be turbulent times ahead of us, as there are for everyone. However, as I held her close to me, I knew that everything would be fine. No matter what may come our way, we would deal with it together.

'I love you,' Osiris whispered.

'I love you, too,' I replied. 'More than you'll ever know.'

About the Author

Dan Farrell grew up in County Durham, England. He is a graduate from the University of Sunderland, with both a Bachelor's and Master's Degree in English. Outside of writing, he has an avid passion for film and television.

For more, please visit him online at:

Twitter: **@danfaz94**
Instagram: **danfaz94**
Goodreads: **www.goodreads.com/user/show/99197621-dan-farrell**

43550738R00134

Printed in Poland
by Amazon Fulfillment
Poland Sp. z o.o., Wrocław